DEAREST ENEMY

DEAREST ENEMY
Sara Woods

But wherefore do I tell these news to thee?
Why, Harry, do I tell thee of my foes,
Which art my near'st and dearest enemy?
King Henry IV, Part I
Act III, scene ii

ST. MARTIN'S PRESS
NEW YORK

Copyright © 1981 by Probandi Books Ltd.
For information, write: St. Martin's Press,
175 Fifth Avenue, New York, N.Y. 10010
Manufactured in the United States of America

Library of Congress Cataloging in Publication Data

Woods, Sara, pseud.
    Dearest enemy.

    I. Title.
PR6073.063D4   1981   823'.914   81-8721
ISBN 0-312-18546-4   AACR2

PART ONE

Hilary Term, 1973

I

'You can't say, darling,' said Meg Farrell, settling herself more comfortably in a chair in the Maitlands' living room, 'that I ever ask for favours. At least, not often,' she added hastily, seeing a distinctly sardonic look in her host's eye.

It was, however, her husband who answered her. 'I don't know how you can say a thing like that, Meg,' said Roger Farrell bluntly. 'Have you forgotten how you first introduced me to Jenny and Antony nearly ten years ago now? And then two years later –'

'Well, I know that had horrible effects at the time,' said Meg, who perhaps thought that the earlier occasion was best forgotten by all concerned, 'but I'm sure that Antony would agree it was worth it. Jon Kellaway would still be in prison if Antony had let him be convicted, and now he's one of the most respected figures in the theatre in this country.'

'All the same –' Roger persisted, but this time Antony Maitland interrupted ruthlessly.

'What is it now, Meg?' he demanded.

Meg, whose many admirers among the theatre-going public knew her as Margaret Hamilton, eyed him in silence for a moment, as though weighing up how he would take what she was about to say. She was a small woman, and Antony sometimes thought that she had changed very little, in appearance at least, since the day her path first crossed his and Jenny's. She had acquired a surface sophistication, but her dark hair was still braided round her head, and her eyes had lost nothing of their sparkle, nor of a directness that was sometimes disconcerting. 'It's something quite simple really, darling,' she said.

'Yes, Meg, I know all about that. The thing is, whose fortunes – or misfortunes – are you trying to embroil me in this time?'

'Two people I've always admired,' she said. 'The Buckleys.'

Jenny Maitland, who on the whole was a better listener than a talker (some people would have said that was a good thing, in view of her choice of a marriage partner), looked up at that. 'Do you mean the ones the papers always call the Perfect Couple?' she

7

asked. 'We saw them in a play only a few months ago, and they seemed quite all right then.'

'Seemed,' said Meg, dropping her voice to its lowest register to emphasise the word. 'The thing is, Antony –'

'You'd better start from the beginning, Meg,' said Roger, apparently resigned.

'That might be a good idea,' said Jenny seriously. It was Sunday evening, dinner was over, and the four of them were gathered round the fire with the curtains close drawn against the cold January night.

'You see, darlings, there's this play I want to do,' said Meg, glancing round at her companions with a look of dewy-eyed innocence that Antony, who had known her for a long time now, immediately suspected. He wasn't surprised, however, because ever since the Farrells arrived he had been conscious of an air of suppressed excitement about Meg. Now she added with a touch of defiance in her tone, 'Roger doesn't want me to take the part, of course.'

'But, Meg, that other thing only came off in November,' Roger protested. 'And it was such a lemon –'

'It ran for a full year,' said Meg, jutting her chin.

'Yes, but that was only because you were in it. With anyone else in the role it would have been off in a week,' Roger insisted. 'I'm only afraid of your getting two such – such poor vehicles in succession.'

Antony who knew well enough his friend's desire to get his wife to himself occasionally, but who was equally sure Meg wasn't going to give up a part that had caught her fancy, thought it was time to intervene. 'This is the first we've heard of a new play, Meg,' he said. 'What's so special about it?'

'It's by Jeremy Skelton.'

'Oh!' Jeremy Skelton's affairs were another thing of which Maitland did not wish to be reminded.

'But he doesn't write plays,' Jenny objected.

'This is his first,' said Meg. 'I suppose that's why Roger thinks it may not be much good. But it's the adaptation of one of his books – do you remember *Done in by Daggers*? – and you know he's always been good at dialogue. Besides, I think I'm a good judge by now, all the climaxes come in the right place.'

'But Meg, that doesn't sound like your kind of thing.'

'It's not just a mystery or a thriller, or whatever you like to call it. You know Jeremy has always had a sardonic way with words, and there's lots of humour in it. And I've never done anything like

8

that,' Meg added a little wistfully. Her first success had been as a very young, very venomous Lady Macbeth, and though she had by no means stuck to Shakespeare in the intervening years it was true that her reputation was based on the fact that she was, as even the most bad tempered critics admitted unoriginally, one of the foremost dramatic actresses of the day.

'That's no reason for starting now,' said Roger flatly. And then coming more honestly to the heart of his objection, 'You said you were going to take a rest this time.'

'Darling, I've been resting for nearly two months. The public will forget all about me.'

'No, Meg, I don't think that will happen,' said Jenny. 'And perhaps if the play is no good, Roger, it won't run for very long after all.'

Funnily enough, Jenny's gentle persuasion could sometimes succeed with Roger where all Meg's blandishments failed. 'I didn't mean to be abrupt,' he said. 'Of course Meg must do as she likes.' He grinned suddenly. 'She will anyway,' he confided. 'And I believe – though she hasn't confirmed this to me yet – that she's given Skelton her word already.'

'I didn't exactly,' said Meg, but, perhaps wisely, left the subject there. 'You really don't mind, do you darling? It's a chance to do something completely different, and you know how hard it would be to turn that down.'

'I know,' said Roger, who had faced the fact of Meg's commitment to her profession before they were married, though sometimes – being very much in love with her – he wondered ruefully if he had realised how difficult it would be to accept. 'When do rehearsals start?'

'On Wednesday,' said Meg, with a sidelong look in Antony's direction as though she expected him to pounce on the admission that she had made up her mind already and that her air of indecision was only a formality. 'We've got the Alhambra Theatre, and the rest of the cast are lined up already,' she added.

'People you've acted with before?' Antony asked her. He had by no means forgotten that she had a request to make of him, but he wasn't at all sure he wanted to hear it. Every minute's delay was pure gain from his point of view.

'I've played with Andy Murray, but not for quite some time. He'll be my husband,' said Meg. 'My unfaithful husband,' she added.

'Do I also gather that he will be the *corpus delicti*?' said Antony.

9

'As a matter of fact he will, though it seems a pity to waste someone of his calibre on a part that only lasts for one act. Then there's Ellie Dorman, who plays his lover. I think I've seen her at a party somewhere, but we've never been introduced. I know Gordon Hewitt and Dominic Eldred, but I haven't acted with them. There's also a young man called Claude Aubin, but I don't know him at all. And I don't know the understudies either.'

'And is that all the cast?' Antony hesitated, knowing well enough that once Meg had formulated her problem he would be committed to trying to solve it. She had always had a special place in his and Jenny's affections, and in all the years since they first met he had never discovered the trick of saying no to her. But as well now as later, obviously he was going to hear what was on her mind. 'You talked about the Buckleys,' he said. 'Leonard and Victoria, aren't those their names?'

'Yes, and Jenny put her finger on it when she called them the Perfect Couple. I've known of them for years, though not known them personally, and admired them both as actors and as examples of an ideal marriage. They play Andy's – well, his name is Douglas Carteret in the play – uncle and aunt.'

'And does that cause a problem?'

'Don't laugh at me, Antony, it's serious.' Meg's voice had deepened again. Conveying sincerity, as Maitland thought rather cynically. 'They'll really be marvellous in the parts, and Jeremy was mad keen to get them, he told me.'

'What's the trouble then? Did they refuse?'

'No. The contracts are signed and everything's in order. In any case, darling, I wouldn't be silly enough to think you could do anything about that.'

'I hope not,' said Antony rather sceptically. 'What *is* the matter then?'

'They're not the perfect couple at all,' said Meg, 'I don't think they even like each other. And Leonard is absolutely convinced that Victoria is trying to poison him.'

'Oh, good Lord!' Antony's tone was rather disgusted. He was a tall man, dark-haired, with a thin, intelligent face, and a look of amusement would have come more naturally to him. 'I do sympathise, Meg, you've set your heart on this play going on and I suppose any friction among the cast can only harm the production. But even if what Mr Buckley believes is true, what on earth can I do about it?'

'It was really Jeremy's idea,' said Meg, but did not immediately amplify the statement.

10

'I suppose he's in town for the rehearsals.'

'Yes, of course, and Anne is with him. They really are happy together, Antony, you ought to congratulate yourself about that.'

'Never mind their happiness,' said Antony firmly; he didn't fancy himself in the role of match-maker. 'What does Jeremy expect me to do about this problem of yours?'

'Well, you see,' said Meg, 'none of us quite believe what Leonard is saying. But Jeremy thought if you talked to them both – separately, you know – you might be able to find out definitely.'

'My dear girl, I can't go up to Mrs Buckley and ask her if she's poisoning her husband.'

'No, of course not. Not *quite* like that,' said Meg, conceding a point. 'But if you just talk to her, you might find out if there's anything in it. And if there is ... well, darling, I hate to remind you, but don't you think your reputation might scare her off?'

That was a reminder that Maitland hated, as Meg knew well enough. She must indeed be feeling pretty desperate to have brought the matter up at all. Jenny cast an anxious look in her husband's direction, but she knew as well as he did that he was hooked already. Meg was a very old friend and circumstances had thrown Antony and Roger into an intimacy that both of them found congenial.

Antony was frowning but he quoted quite promptly, '"None of us believe what Leonard Buckley is saying." Do you mean the whole cast knows about this?'

'No, of course not. It's lucky they don't. I meant Jeremy and Anne and me. I happened to be there when Leonard talked to Jeremy about it.'

'That didn't make Skelton reconsider the matter of their contract?'

'I don't think he would have done anyway, but as I said it was signed already. Anyway, they're perfect for the two parts.'

'Couldn't one of them have played, and somebody else have taken the second part?'

'Oh no, that's out of the question. They've always played together, their whole reputation is based on forty-three years of happy marriage,' said Meg earnestly. 'Apart from their ability, that reputation is valuable in itself.'

'How old are these two paragons?'

'Leonard is seventy and Victoria is sixty-three. Really, Antony,

I know you'd like them, so if you'd just take an opportunity of talking to them –'

'And how is this opportunity to arise?'

'I could give a dinner party,' said Meg. 'Next Saturday perhaps, the rehearsals won't have reached the stage where we have to go on right through the weekend. It will be quite natural to ask you and Jenny to meet Jeremy and Anne, in view of your past association with them.'

'Jenny has never met them,' said Antony, as if this was an insuperable difficulty.

'Well, never mind, she'll like them both. And you can't deny *your* association with them Antony, whatever you say. Then I can invite Leonard and Victoria, and unless I'm very much mistaken Leonard at least will ask you for another meeting.'

'Prompted by you in the meantime no doubt.'

'Yes, of course. And if I can manage it I'll make the same suggestion to Victoria too.'

'Does she know what her husband is saying about her.'

'I'm afraid she does. She has her own bitterness about her husband, as far as I can make out, but it hasn't run to an accusation of attempted murder yet.'

'It might work,' said Roger surprisingly.

Antony looked at him reproachfully. '*Et tu Brute?*' he said.

'Well, I do agree with Meg,' said Roger. 'It can't do any harm and it might clear the air.'

'Then I leave it up to Jenny. Do you mind sitting through a whole evening, love, where two members of the party hate each other like poison? Literally like poison, according to one of them.'

'I can think of worse things,' said Jenny. 'Like letting Meg be worried, for instance.'

'Well, if that was all ... but I don't see what I can do about it with the best will in the world.'

'You can try,' said Jenny. She was sitting curled up in her favourite place on the sofa, and her grey eyes met his with their usual serenity. 'Even Uncle Nick couldn't mind you just talking to them,' she added. 'It won't get you into trouble with the police, and it won't result in anyone trying to murder you.'

'Unless Victoria Buckley –'

'No, I don't think so,' said Jenny in a considering way, treating what was meant as a light-hearted comment as though it were a serious suggestion. 'I've seen her quite often on the stage, and I don't believe for a moment that she's capable of killing anyone.'

12

'I'll take your word for it, love.' He smiled at her and turned back to Meg. 'Count us in then,' he told her. 'What time do you want us to present ourselves next Saturday?'

'Well, what do you think about that?' said Antony when he came back into the living room later, after seeing the visitors out. The Maitlands had their own quarters at the top of Sir Nicholas Harding's house in Kempenfeldt Square. Sir Nicholas was Antony's uncle as well as the head of the chambers in the Inner Temple to which he belonged, and Antony himself had been a member of the household since he was thirteen years old. The division had been made as a temporary matter, but it was a long time now since anyone had questioned it, except for a brief period following Sir Nicholas's marriage some eighteen months before to Miss Vera Langhorne, barrister-at-law. That had caused Antony to consider his position, but fortunately he got over that before it could wreck the new arrangements. Sir Nicholas's household ran much more smoothly since the new Lady Harding had taken control, but apart from that Vera was an acquisition in herself.

'Meg's problem? I think it is summat and nowt, as our friends in Yorkshire would say.'

'I thought you did,' said Antony, coming across the room and kicking the fire into a blaze. It entered his mind to suggest to her that seeing a person on the stage gave you no idea of his or her real character, but he decided against voicing the thought aloud. For one thing he had no wish to alarm her, and for another he quite agreed that no harm could come of the proposed interviews, except a little temporary inconvenience to himself. 'There's something on your mind though. What is it, Jenny love?'

'I'm just a bit worried about Roger,' said Jenny. 'He really doesn't want Meg taking this part.'

'He's never wanted her to take a single part since they were married,' Antony pointed out. 'He spends his evenings here mostly, and she spends hers at the theatre. It's not an ideal arrangement.'

'The trouble is,' Jenny confided, 'I can see both of their points of view.'

'Oh, so can I. And I did warn Roger before ever they were married. The theatre is in Meg's blood, or something like that.'

'Yes, I think so too. I just get the feeling it's more serious this time. As if her taking the part or not was a test of some kind.'

13

'A test of whether she really loves him, you mean? That's nonsense Jenny, if ever I saw a couple who were made for each other—'

'That isn't always enough,' said Jenny sadly. 'Has it ever occurred to you, Antony, Roger is a very sensitive person?'

This was very true. Roger might have posed any day for a picture of a pirate, in fact a young friend of theirs had once done a portrait of him in that guise, but there was never any question about his responsiveness to other people's moods. 'Of course it has,' said Antony. 'For one thing, he bears with me, doesn't he? That should be enough proof for anybody.'

Jenny held out her hand and after a moment's hesitation he went to sit beside her on the sofa. 'That may be because you're more honest with him than you are with anyone else,' she said. 'Even with yourself.'

'I've never told you a lie, Jenny love.'

'No, I know you haven't. You don't tell lies,' she added, obviously thinking of the words carefully. 'Not to anybody. But you don't always tell the whole truth either.'

This being a fair enough comment, Antony considered it and was silent. After a while he got up and went across to the writing table where the tray of drinks was standing, and poured them both a nightcap. There was no more talk that night.

SATURDAY, 20th January

I

The following Saturday, as was their custom, the Maitlands took luncheon with Sir Nicholas and Lady Harding, a meal which Gibbs, Sir Nicholas's ancient butler, insisted on serving himself, making of it a more ceremonious occasion than was necessary. Gibbs was a bad tempered old man, and even Vera, who had more influence over him than anyone else in living memory, had not been able to persuade him to retire; though he was accustomed to choose – apparently quite arbitrarily – what duties he would perform, and woe betide anybody who needed his services after ten p.m. He had disapproved of Antony as a schoolboy, and had never apparently had any cause to change his opinion. One of his favourite tricks was to hover at the back of the hall, ostensibly in case there should be any visitors, but really – or so Maitland always said – to express, as he well knew how, his disapproval of what was going on. In other words, if you were late you lacked all consideration, setting the whole household by the ears; if you were early, on the other hand, it was quite obvious you were neglecting your duties in chambers.

So it was not until they had moved into the study with their coffee that there was an opportunity for any but the most general conversation. The study was Sir Nicholas's favourite room, and even since his marriage it was the one he and Vera most generally used. In fact, it would be difficult to do otherwise, as Vera, with Antony's help and her husband's encouragement, had converted the big drawing room into a music room, where her expensive stereo equipment and the collection of records that had been her one extravagance before her marriage could be suitably housed. Once a year the *status quo* was restored and they gave – as had been Sir Nicholas's custom when he was a bachelor – a fairly large formal party; but this year that occasion was safely over well before the beginning of the Hilary Term.

Sir Nicholas was making his leisurely preparations for the enjoyment of a cigar. He was a man as tall as his nephew, though rather more heavily built, with hair that had always been fair so that now the streaks of white were hardly visible. He had an

15

authoritative manner which was mostly unconscious, and was known to have turned down on at least three occasions the offer of a High Court judgeship, ostensibly because the possibility of having to hear his nephew plead a case before him made him nervous. Neither of the Maitlands believed that for a moment, but Antony for one had always been sure that such an appointment would change everything, and consequently had been glad when the offers had been refused. Now his uncle, having selected a cigar with as much care as if his life depended on the choice, looked up and said casually, 'Hasn't Meg been resting for rather longer than usual?'

'It's funny you should say that,' said Jenny. 'She started rehearsing a new play this week.'

'Poor Roger,' said Vera, well enough aware of the state of affairs.

'Poor Roger nothing!' said Sir Nicholas vigorously. 'Meg is a charming creature.' Antony and Jenny exchanged a glance at this, they knew well enough that their uncle considered the Farrells as family, and therefore felt quite free to criticise them as much as he liked and whenever he liked.

'She is also on occasion,' said Antony with feeling, 'a damn nuisance, if you'll forgive the expression, Vera.'

'What's she up to now?' said Sir Nicholas, still indulgently.

'She's taking a part in a play by Jeremy Skelton,' Antony told him. 'You remember Jeremy, Vera?'

'Couldn't help it,' said Vera. She was a tall woman, with hair that had been dark but was now liberally streaked with grey, and that had a habit of escaping from its confining pins, rather like the White Queen's, when she was at all agitated, and even sometimes when she wasn't. She had a habit of dressing in sack-like garments, but at least since her marriage she seemed to have acquired a sense of colour and the sacks were well-cut ones. Jenny denied all responsibility for this, and speculated with her husband sometimes as to whether Sir Nicholas took his wife shopping. The idea was a pleasant one, but on the whole unlikely. 'Largely my doing you came down to Chedcombe when he was accused of killing his first wife,' Vera was recalling.

'And I led the defence,' said Sir Nicholas reminiscently. Somehow he managed to convey in these few words both a compliment to Vera and a reproof to his nephew, whose methods of obtaining his effects he frequently deplored. 'But Skelton isn't a playwright,' he objected.

16

'No, this is an adaptation of one of his books, one called *Done in by Daggers*. Do you remember it?'

Sir Nicholas ignored the query. 'Nor is that the kind of play with which Meg's name is usually associated,' he went on.

'No, according to her it has got a strong comic element. That's why she wants to do it, something quite different. We're going to dine with them this evening as a matter of fact, and with the Skeltons and another couple,' he added, his voice trailing off rather uncertainly.

That was quite enough for his uncle. 'There's something going on,' he declared, looking from one to the other of the two Maitlands. And when Antony made no immediate reply he turned directly to Jenny.

'Who is this other couple?' he demanded.

'The Buckleys,' said Jenny. 'Another stage couple,' she added, when she saw Vera's enquiring look.

'Never heard of them,' said Vera at her most elliptical.

'I think perhaps you have, my dear,' Sir Nicholas corrected her. 'An elderly couple who have been married for many years, and who have always acted together.'

'The Perfect Couple,' said Vera, enlightened.

'So the press are accustomed to refer to them. Now why, I wonder, should the mention of their names cause you any uneasiness, Antony?'

Antony had had no intention of allowing the conversation to reach this point, only it seemed to have got away from him. Now he hesitated for a moment before he replied. 'It's just a small chore that Meg wants me to do for her,' he said evasively.

'Yes?' queried Sir Nicholas.

'Well, you see, Uncle Nick, it seems they aren't a perfect couple at all.'

'I have no doubt that the remark is in some way relevant, but you must forgive me if I fail immediately to see how.'

'It's just that ... well, Meg wanted me to talk to them.'

'You are thinking of deserting the bar and setting up as a marriage counsellor?' enquired his uncle courteously.

'You know perfectly well, Uncle Nick – ' Jenny began indignantly.

'If that isn't the case I fail to see how Antony comes into it at all. Unless, of course,' he added hopefully, 'there's some question of one of them suing the other.'

'Nothing like that, Uncle Nick,' said Antony hastily. Sir

Nicholas was silent waiting for him to continue. 'Mr Buckley says Mrs Buckley is trying to poison him.'

'If he wants a divorce he needs a solicitor, not a barrister,' said Sir Nicholas austerely. 'It isn't exactly Geoffrey Horton's line, but he might be willing to take it on to oblige Meg.'

'There's no question of that. As far as I can gather their whole professional life depends on the public looking on them as an ideal example of wedded bliss.'

'Then what does Meg think you can do about it?'

'Got something of a reputation,' said Vera gruffly.

'I'm only too sadly aware of it.' For once his wife's intervention had no mollifying effect on Sir Nicholas. 'If this Mr Buckley is right, and if you're right too that he doesn't want a divorce, it seems to me to be a matter for the police.'

'That's just what they don't want,' said Antony. 'The publicity could be fatal to them.'

'If Mr Buckley prefers a literal fatality to a metaphorical one –' Sir Nicholas began.

'It's quite simple, Uncle Nick,' said Jenny. 'First Meg wants to know whether Leonard Buckley is right in what he says, and if he is right perhaps Antony can persuade Victoria Buckley not to proceed any further in the matter. On the other hand, if he isn't –'

'For you, Jenny, that is an extremely lucid explanation,' Sir Nicholas congratulated her when she broke off. 'Perhaps you can also tell us what Antony is to do if Mr Buckley is *not* right in his contention.'

'Well ... I suppose ... Vera mentioned his reputation. I know you're pretending she meant for unorthodox behaviour, Uncle Nick, but he has a reputation for being perceptive about people too. He might very well be able to persuade Leonard Buckley that he was wrong.'

'Thank you, my dear.' Sir Nicholas smiled with one of his sudden changes of mood, but there was still a little sarcasm left in his tone. 'And all this is to be accomplished in the course of a dinner party this evening?'

'No, of course not.' Jenny glanced at her husband and he took over the explanation.

'Meg promised to talk to both of them, to persuade them to ask me for a private interview,' he said. 'I don't know how she's going to do it, but we shall just have to wait and see.'

'This is something quite outside your own sphere,' said Sir

18

Nicholas didactically. 'We all know where meddling in Meg's affairs may lead, and as for Jeremy Skelton –'

'He has nothing to do with this except that he wrote the play,' said Antony a little desperately. 'I agree with you, Uncle Nick, I've let myself in for a couple of very uncomfortable hours. But I don't see why anybody should complain about that except me.'

His uncle surveyed him in silence for a moment. 'As to that, we shall see,' he said, and turned to address his wife. 'It seems to me,' he remarked, 'to have the makings of an extremely unpleasant situation.'

II

Meg and Roger Farrell lived in Chelsea, and Antony and Jenny accomplished the journey that evening by taxi, to save the need of finding anywhere to park. Meg, enjoying her unaccustomed role as hostess – the life she led left little time for entertaining, and such as they did was generally in a restaurant – met them at the door, giving a hand to each and drawing them into the narrow hall. 'Darlings, you don't know how glad I am to see you,' she said. 'I thought you might have second thoughts, Antony, and fail to turn up.'

'You know me better than that, Meg,' said Antony lightly. 'My word is my bond and all that sort of thing. Are your other friends here yet?' he asked cautiously.

'Only the Skeltons. Come and meet them. Oh, there you are, Roger darling, get Antony and Jenny something to drink.'

Roger, who had appeared in the door of the drawing room, made welcoming noises and then disappeared to do her bidding. Antony and Jenny followed Meg, who was still talking rather frenziedly. For once, in fact, Antony was pretty sure it wasn't just her natural vivaciousness, but a fit of nerves.

Jeremy and Anne Skelton were an old married couple now. As Jeremy rose to greet them Antony thought for the first time that perhaps the other man was finding this meeting as difficult as he was himself, with its reminder of things past and best forgotten. If so there was no sign of it in his manner. Jeremy was a big man who must be in his early forties now, but whom to Antony's eye looked exactly the same as the last time they had met. He had wide shoulders, even having regard to his height, a shock of darkish hair, and there was about him an air of restless energy which was perhaps the most noticeable thing about him. He greeted Antony like an old friend, which was fair enough in the circumstances, and eyed Jenny with open admiration. 'Come and sit down here next to Anne,' he invited. 'She's been longing to meet you.'

Anne Skelton, who had been Anne Fabian when Antony had known her before, was sitting quietly waiting for her husband's exuberance to allow her the chance of making her own greetings. As soon as he saw her Antony was put in mind of their first meeting, when her brown gold hair had immediately reminded him of Jenny, though it was smooth and straight while Jenny's was curly. She too seemed to have changed hardly at all, her figure was as trim as ever, and her eyes, more violet than blue, looked up at them with warm friendliness.

'Yes, Jenny, do come and talk to me,' she said. 'Isn't this a nice house? But of course you know it well, I expect.'

'Meg and Roger are very old friends of ours,' said Jenny, seating herself. 'Where are you staying while you're in London?'

'Jeremy found a flat. Actually it's not very far from you, so Meg tells me, in Avery Street, only at the other end from Kempenfeldt Square.'

'That's very convenient.'

'Yes of course it is.' Anne sounded a little doubtful. 'To tell you the truth,' she added in a burst of confidence, 'I don't really like being in London at all. We have a place in the country now,' she glanced up at Antony for a moment and then back at Jenny again, 'nowhere near Chedcombe. And I absolutely love that, only then Jeremy got this idea he must write a play, so here we are.'

'Meg is very keen on it.'

'Yes, I think so. I wonder though whether her husband ... whether Roger is quite so keen.'

'That's nothing to do with the play,' Jenny assured her. 'It's just that he's always hoping Meg will take a little time off, only she never does, not for very long.'

'I can understand that, about both of them I mean.' Roger appeared then with Jenny's sherry and pulled up a chair to join them. Meg had disappeared about some housewifely duty.

Antony and Jeremy had strolled over to the window, but the curtains had been drawn and there was nothing to be seen. Maitland, when anything disturbed him, had always had an instinct towards movement, and from what he remembered of Jeremy Skelton he would be happier on his feet than sitting decorously in a chair. It occurred to him for the first time that he didn't know yet whether Jeremy knew he had agreed to Meg's request which might have created a certain awkwardness if

20

Skelton hadn't started the ball rolling by saying emphatically, 'It's very good of you to concern yourself with our problem.'

Antony, who until that moment had been conscious only of the difficulties of the situation, suddenly saw the humour of it too. 'My uncle asked me if I was giving up the law and setting up as a marriage counsellor,' he said, and smiled as he spoke.

'That sounds like Sir Nicholas,' said Jeremy appreciatively. 'But you know,' he added seriously, 'the qualities required by each of those occupations are not too dissimilar.'

Antony thought about that for a moment, a little startled by this view of his professional activities. 'The trouble is,' he confided, 'it's awfully difficult to say no to Meg. But I can't imagine that my meeting or even talking to the Buckleys can do any good at all.'

'At least it can't do any harm,' said Jeremy, and turned a little so that the group near the fire came more easily within his range of vision. 'Your Jenny is something of a beauty, isn't she?'

Antony too turned his head, trying to see his wife through the other man's eyes. 'I think she's perfection,' he said with unaccustomed honesty. 'But beautiful? I think that's an exaggeration.'

'A darling anyway,' said Jeremy sincerely, and then grinned. 'But I expect you hear altogether too much of that word from Meg.'

'Yes, that's true. As for you and Anne ... marriage obviously agrees with her. I don't think either of you has changed at all.'

'You certainly haven't.' He hesitated, but it was not in his nature to balk at an awkward question. 'Meg's husband,' he said. 'Is there a little strain there?'

'No more than there always is when she takes on a new part,' said Antony. 'Roger would like to have her to himself for a while, and could well afford to do so as a matter of fact,' he added with perhaps a little envy in his tone. 'But I warned him before they married that he'd have to give her her head.'

'Well, I'm thankful she took the part. This play means a good deal to me you know, Antony, that's why I'm hoping so much you can do something about the Buckleys. They're the ... I suppose you could say the turning point of the whole plot, besides having a name that is almost as much a draw as Margaret Hamilton's, though I dare say she could pack them in quite well by herself. But if you can straighten them out –'

'I told you, Jeremy, I don't think there's any chance of that. But I'll do what I can, of course.' And as he made this rash promise the bell rang.

21

This time it was Roger who went to open the door, and came back a few moments later ushering Leonard and Victoria Buckley before him. Antony had expected it to be very different meeting them in person from seeing them on the stage, but he found them comfortably familiar, two small, well-rounded people with the odd likeness between them that sometimes comes with years of marriage, so that they might well have been taken for brother and sister. And Leonard had just the right proprietorial air about him, as though he were indeed proud of such a treasure; and Victoria as the evening wore on showed a pretty deference to his opinion, and an affection that was obvious though not overplayed. In watching them Antony would have sworn that Meg was in the wrong of it, that the story she'd told them had been pure nonsense. But Jenny, for once seeing more clearly than he did, said to him later, 'It's become a habit to play up to an audience. After all these years I don't suppose they can help themselves.'

Chairs were moved, more drinks were served, the party coalesced in one group round the fire. And now the conversation became general, though with Meg and Jeremy doing most of the talking, and not unnaturally mostly about the play. Roger, who might have been out of his element, was also playing his role to perfection, thought Antony, amused. But every now and then he would find one of the Buckleys eyeing him in a considering sort of way, so that he wasn't at all surprised when Leonard cornered him after dinner and said gruffly, 'Something I should like to talk over with you, Mr Maitland.'

And that was another thing, was he supposed to know that Meg was in the background of this suggestion? He seemed to have come to this meeting very ill-equipped. 'A professional matter?' said Antony cautiously.

'Quite frankly I don't know whether you'll consider it so or not. But Meg says you'd be glad to listen to me, and perhaps you may be able to help.'

Well, that was one mystery cleared up at any rate. 'If I can,' said Antony, still cautious.

'A situation has arisen,' said Leonard, but Maitland didn't allow him to continue.

'Yes, but I think that can wait, can't it? Till we're on our own.'

'Quite right, quite right. It's a little difficult for me now we're rehearsing. Is there any chance that you could see me tomorrow?'

'Do you want me to come to your place?'

'No, certainly not. That wouldn't do at all. Some neutral ground perhaps,' Leonard suggested.

Antony cast his mind quickly over their engagements for the following day. There would be a crowd of them at tea time, but he thought Vera had said something about a concert in the evening, which seemed to have become a habit, so that he would be able to use the study if he wanted. 'In the morning,' he said, 'I could see you at home. Or in the evening if you prefer that.'

'That's very kind of you,' said Leonard again. 'Meg gave me your address as a matter of fact. Could I come in the morning?'

'If that suits you, certainly. About eleven o'clock?' Maitland suggested.

'Very well.' Buckley seemed to become conscious suddenly of their isolation. 'We'd better get back to the others,' he said.

It wasn't until later in the evening that Victoria Buckley made her approach, following Antony into the kitchen, where he had gone to replenish one of the decanters. 'Leonard has been talking to you, hasn't he?' she said accusingly. And suddenly it was quite easy to believe, not in murder of course, but in the fact that there was some animosity between the two.

'I think I've had some talk with all of Meg and Roger's guests,' Antony told her, bending down to rummage in the cupboard for a fresh bottle.

'That's not what I meant.'

'What did you mean, Mrs Buckley?'

'Well, if he's going to talk to you I'm going to talk to you too. Meg said you would,' she added belligerently. The contrast with her former manner was very marked.

'Certainly, if that's what you wish. May I ask if it's a professional matter?'

'It could be slander,' she said, 'but don't worry, I'll get even with him without that. All the same I've heard of you, Mr Maitland.' (She didn't know how much he hated that remark.) 'And I think you might be able to help.'

As her husband had already pre-empted the morning, Antony suggested that she should call at Kempenfeldt Square after dinner. 'We can be quite alone there,' he assured her, 'and you can tell me whatever you like.'

It wasn't until much later, talking the evening over with Jenny, that he wondered again how Meg had got her effects.

'Just by being Meg,' said Jenny wisely. 'I don't think there's anything at all to be surprised about in that.'

23

'That's all very well, but what am I going to say to them?' asked Antony helplessly.

She might have reminded him that it had been in his power to refuse. 'You'll think of something,' said Jenny with perfect confidence. But then she knew him very well indeed.

I

Leonard Buckley was prompt the next morning, and it was precisely eleven o'clock when Gibbs used the house phone to announce his arrival. (Before Vera joined the household the old man would have toiled upstairs with the news, enjoying his martyrdom.) 'Please send him up,' said Antony, and turned and added in a hollow tone to Jenny, 'He's here!'

'It will soon be over,' said Jenny comfortingly, gathering up her book and preparing to depart for the bedroom, where she proposed to turn on the electric fire and make herself comfortable. 'And after all it was his suggestion, so you can leave him to make the running.'

'So I can,' said Antony, uncomforted. 'And then there's Victoria this evening.' But he went out into the hall to open the door to their guest with a fairly good grace.

Leonard Buckley seemed to have taken the two flights of stairs easily enough, and showed no shortness of breath. Also he had had no change of heart since the previous evening, which Maitland had rather hoped would have been the case. He shook Antony's hand warmly and said, following him into the living room, 'This is very kind of you.' He stood a moment looking around him with interest and then said appreciatively, 'A nice room, it would make a good stage set. That sofa looks comfortable. Do you mind if I sit down?'

'Of course not,' said Antony, who so far had hardly had a chance of getting a word in. The thought came to him that there might be amusement as well as embarrassment in this interview, but as to that he'd know soon enough. Meanwhile he followed the actor across to the hearth, watched him subside in Jenny's favourite corner, and kicked the fire a little so that it blazed. He turned then and smiled down encouragingly at his visitor. Obviously Buckley was going to take the initiative, but when he spoke his words came as a complete surprise.

'Are you in love with your wife?' he asked abruptly.

That was an easy enough question to answer, and for some reason Antony didn't find it offensive. Perhaps it was merely

Buckley's way of leading into his subject. 'As a matter of fact, I am,' he said.

'Have you been long married?'

'Quite a while, but not so long as you and Mrs Buckley I believe.'

'Well I'm glad to hear it, I'm sure. That you're happy with your wife. I'm not,' said Leonard flatly. 'Surprised you, didn't I?' he added in rather a pleased tone, his eyes on his host's face.

Antony was still on his feet, and had taken up his usual position, a little to one side of the fire and with one shoulder leaning against the high mantel. 'I'm very sorry to hear it,' he said, thinking that the last part of the statement was perhaps better ignored. 'That doesn't quite equate with your public image, as I'm sure you know.'

'I know all about that. Have you seen us on the stage?'

'Oh, yes, many times. Do you think there's anybody in England who hasn't?'

'Not everybody likes the theatre,' said Buckley. 'But if you have seen us you know how it is. Producers have got into the habit of regarding us almost as one person, you take one you take them both. If we were to split up now –'

'Do you know, Mr Buckley, I wonder if you're right about that. As far as acting ability goes I'm sure you'd both be very much in demand.'

'No, no, I don't think so at all. After forty-three years ... Victoria was twenty when we met and married and I was twenty-seven. We were playing at the Prince's Theatre in Bradford, a try-out before we went to the West End. You know they always say if you can make a Yorkshire audience laugh you'll be a success anywhere. Anyway there was Victoria, the prettiest little thing and just the right size. By which I mean not tall enough to loom over me, you've noticed yourself I'm not a big man.'

'Did you know each other long before you married?'

'Marry in haste, they say, don't they? We knew each other for about a month, and were married before we moved to London with the play. Well you know, Mr Maitland, we were young and very much in love, it seemed natural that we should try to make our next engagement a joint one. And it worked out. There are a lot of sentimental people about you know, and I expect they liked the thought that we were married in real life. Acting out our own romance before their eyes, you might say. And then we were offered another joint appearance, and after that it all just seemed

26

to fall into place. Everybody wanted the pair of us, even as we grew older and were playing character parts.'

He paused so long there that Antony thought it best to prompt him. 'And now you're telling me that the idyllic happiness you represent on the stage isn't repeated in your own lives,' he said, choosing his words as carefully as he could.

'No, it isn't!'

'How long –'

'Ten years, fifteen years. These things come on gradually, I can't give you an exact answer. Little things began to irritate me, she *would* use teabags instead of making a proper pot of tea, she'd never give me a direct answer to a question, and she was always rushing off to the doctor and talking endlessly about her ailments when I knew perfectly well there was nothing wrong with her. And I'll admit to you, Mr Maitland, I'm not perfect myself. I dare say she could give you a list of things that annoyed *her* about *me*. But there it was, we generally spent pretty well every penny we made, there was no question of breaking up. But I didn't think – not for a moment – that it would ever come to this.'

'What are you trying to tell me, Mr Buckley?'

'It seems to me you might be the very man to help me,' said Leonard, 'so when Meg mentioned you were a friend of hers I rather jumped at the chance of confiding in you. Victoria knows you by reputation of course, as I do. If you were to talk to her you might well be able to scare her into leaving things as they are.'

'I've never really fancied myself in the role of the big, bad wolf,' said Maitland. He was trying to speak lightly, but there was a certain stiffness in his tone. He was never happy at being reminded that the press was very interested indeed in his doings. 'Besides, Mr Buckley, you haven't exactly confided in me yet.'

'No, I haven't. I supposed Meg might have done that.' He paused a moment, obviously to give the full dramatic effect to his words. 'You see, Mr Maitland, things have got to such a pitch I'm quite sure Victoria is trying to poison me.'

Having been forewarned, Antony took this calmly. 'That's a very serious allegation,' he said.

'It will be still more serious if she succeeds,' Leonard retorted. 'I may be a septuagenarian, but I have no desire to fold my hands and die just yet.'

'No, of course it's serious from that point of view as well. But what I should like to know, Mr Buckley, is what kind of proof you have of this?'

'I've always had a stomach like an ox,' said Leonard, patting that part of his anatomy in an approving way. 'Whatever I ate I've never had any indigestion or a bilious attack, or anything of that kind. Not until a month ago.'

Maitland too let the silence lengthen for a moment. Then, 'Tell me about it,' he said.

'I remember it very well. We'd just been offered the part in Jeremy Skelton's play – I should say two parts, of course, but I know that's how other people look at it – and were discussing it over tea on Sunday afternoon. Victoria was a little doubtful. Meg stands so high in the profession she was afraid we'd be overshadowed. But I pointed out that the part might have been made for us, and I thought we should accept. She looked absolute daggers at me – you'll find this hard to believe, Mr Maitland – and said in quite a vicious tone, "Of course you *would* say that. And if I was playing against anybody else I'd accept without hesitation. But if you only knew how tired I am of playing opposite you."'

'Excuse me, Mr Buckley, don't you think there's a point there? Your public image as the ideal couple must be as much to Mrs Buckley's advantage as it is to yours.'

'It is, of course, but perhaps she has more self-confidence than I have,' said Leonard a little hesitantly. 'To tell you the truth I don't think she's the slightest doubt that she could get on without me. And perhaps she may be right,' he added thoughtfully. 'I don't think she is, but she may be.'

'You were telling me what happened.'

'Yes, I was. We enjoy our tea on Sunday, it's usually the only day of the week we have free. Unless we're resting of course. And there were bloater paste sandwiches; Victoria always refers to them as pâté, but I think that's rather affected. I'm particularly fond of them, and I've never known her to refuse them either, but I did notice that that day she didn't eat even one. Not more than about an hour later I was taken ill, with considerable vomiting, which I suppose is what saved my life, and a cold perspiration, and difficulty in getting my breath. The doctor just said a slight touch of food poisoning – I should like to know what he thinks a heavy dose would be – and said it was probably the fish paste. There were some of the sandwiches left, I know, but when I insisted they ought to be analysed there wasn't a single one to be found. They'd gone down the chute – we live in a block of flats in Kensington – and been hauled away with the rest of the refuse the following morning. Don't you think that was rather odd?'

'No, to tell you the truth I don't. If Mrs Buckley had some cause to think there was something wrong with them –'

'*I* think she got rid of them deliberately, so that nobody should ever know what she put in them. You must admit that a thing like bloater paste would hide any taste the stuff might have.'

'And even at that early date you suspected Mrs Buckley of trying to get rid of you?'

'It was the first thing that came into my mind when I began to feel more myself. I searched the flat, I don't mind admitting that, but I couldn't find anything she could be using. But with the ladies there's always their handbags, naturally I couldn't search that. If she went out, of course, she took it with her, and I began to notice that when she was at home she always kept it near at hand.'

'Was that contrary to her usual habit?'

'I'd never noticed it before,' said Leonard.

'So for all you know it may have been her custom.'

'Yes, perhaps, but I think it was very suspicious. And that wasn't all that happened, you know.'

'You're going to tell me, aren't you?' said Antony smiling. Leonard returned the smile without embarrassment.

'I know you think I'm imagining things,' he said, 'a silly old fuddyduddy with nothing better to do than imagine that someone is out to get him. But you must remember that attack came as a complete surprise to me, I'd never suffered anything like it in my life before. And if the doctor had been right I shouldn't ever have done so again.'

'To go on to the next episode, then.'

'Well, I was keeping my eyes open, as you can imagine. I thought if I stuck to things that Victoria herself was eating I'd be safe enough. And then one evening, it was the following Thursday as far as I remember, I wanted a glass of water. I always keep some bottled spring water in the fridge, so that it's nice and cold. The kind I use has a screw top, and some had been taken already, but I thought it would be safe enough ... nothing to disguise the taste of anything that shouldn't be there. But then I had another attack, much the same symptoms, and again as you see I got over it, though it took a little longer that time.'

'Mr Buckley, what do you suspect had been used?'

'Well, after the water episode – and I do assure you it's the only thing I'd had that Victoria hadn't shared – I came to the conclusion it must be arsenic. And I thought perhaps the individual attempts weren't meant to be fatal immediately, but to have a cumulative effect.'

'Did you confide this idea in your doctor?'

'Yes, I did.' Leonard's tone had taken on a little defiance.

'What had he to say to that?'

'He wouldn't take me seriously. He said it was all very well to talk about having a strong stomach all my life, that might all have changed. I'd better go in for some tests, there are a hundred and one things that could be causing what had happened. But I knew what I knew and I refused point blank.'

'Was there any of the water left? You could have had it tested yourself.'

'No, that's what made it absolutely certain. The bottle was empty, Victoria said she drank it herself, but I think it went down the sink.'

'When did the last attack occur?'

'A week ago last Wednesday. But that was after eating fishcakes with cauliflower and cheese.'

'Fish again. Are you sure you and Mrs Buckley hadn't shared a fish dish the day you drank the spring water?'

'The doctor asked me that too,' said Leonard rather sulkily. 'I couldn't remember then and I can't now.'

'Did Mrs Buckley share the fishcakes?'

'Yes, she did. I told you I wouldn't eat anything that she didn't partake of too.'

'Then if there was something wrong with them why wasn't she ill as well?'

'I've been reading it up in the meantime. People can take small doses of arsenic, increasing them gradually over the years, and finally be able to ingest quite a large quantity with no effect at all. So since that occasion I've been preparing my own meals, and that's why I haven't been ill again.'

'And you still haven't taken those tests the doctor suggested?'

'No, I told you what I thought of that idea.'

'Well, there is one test I might have suggested if the last attack hadn't been so long ago. Arsenic might be secreted in the urine. It can also be found in nail parings, and hair, but I'm not quite sure how long after the start of a course of it that symptom appears.'

'I don't need any proof,' said Leonard flatly.

'No, I can see you've quite made up your mind. How many attacks did you have in all?'

'Five.'

'Then why aren't you dead?' asked Maitland reasonably.

'Victoria may have been working up gradually to a grand finale, so that poisoning wouldn't be suspected. Or it may be that I have a resistance to the stuff, on each occasion I vomited very freely, and I can't help thinking that may have had something to do with my getting over it.'

'I see. And until just over a week ago Mrs Buckley prepared all your meals?'

'She always did when we were resting. I think that was pure vanity myself, because there was once an article in the paper about us, and it stressed her domestic qualities.'

'What did she say when you told her you didn't want her to do that any longer?'

'She protested, of course.'

'Did you tell her why?'

'Yes, I did. I thought it might scare her off if she thought somebody knew.'

'I can't help feeling,' said Maitland reflectively, 'that you must have been living a very uncomfortable sort of life together these last few weeks. That can't have been calculated to make the situation between the two of you any easier.'

'It didn't, of course. Not that it could have been much worse. Victoria denied everything, which was no more than I expected, said everyone had bilious attacks at times and I should go to the doctor if I was really worried. Only she didn't think it was necessary at all. So then I told her she was a fine one to talk, always rushing off to the doctor herself when nothing whatever was the matter, and then talking endlessly about her aches and pains. I'd been *really* ill, she must have seen that.'

'So even after this rather frank discussion you were no further ahead?'

'No further at all. What do you think I ought to do, Mr Maitland?'

'Well, first of all,' said Antony slowly, 'I think you should take your wife's advice and the doctor's. It might set your mind at rest.'

'I think I told you I've never had a day's illness in my life,' said Leonard. 'Why should I start now?'

'I'm not a medical man, but I do know that our bodies change as we get older,' said Antony carefully. 'There are one or two things that occur to me, and perhaps if you consider them you may decide to take my advice.'

'What are they?'

'You say the attacks have stopped?'

'Since I've been preparing my own meals.'

'Yes, but don't you think subconsciously you may have been

31

making sure you didn't take anything indigestible? I think that's a distinct possibility.'

'I've been eating as I've always done. No, no, the attacks stopped because she's had no opportunity to try again.'

'People who feel as you two do about each other generally separate.'

'I've told you why that's out of the question, particularly since we've signed a contract for this play of Skelton's.'

'But supposing these attempts on your life had been successful, what would Mrs Buckley have done then?'

'*I* couldn't manage without her,' said Leonard, 'professionally I mean. We've always been together, you see, I can't imagine anyone wanting me without her. But Victoria, that's a different matter. She has all the self-confidence in the world, and would be quite sure she could get on perfectly well alone.'

'Have you made a will in her favour?'

'We both made our wills years ago, when things were still all right between us. I suppose they still stand, as I haven't done anything to alter mine. But there's very little to leave, I told you we'd always lived right up to our income.'

'Well, is there anyone else who would gain from your death? Some trust perhaps which would be the beneficiary and which would pass to someone else?'

'Nothing like that. Nothing like that at all. If I had any independent income I'd leave Victoria like a shot.'

'You do realise, don't you, Mr Buckley, that all you've told me about these attacks of yours is nothing like proof that your wife tried to kill you?'

'It's proof enough for me.'

'Yes, but I have to consider the legal angle. And let's think of the points one by one. You've never been ill before in your life, and on each occasion, after the attack, the food or drink that you thought had caused it had been disposed of. You and Mrs Buckley don't get on, but there are many other couples in a similar situation. I'm afraid it doesn't add up to anything a court would accept.'

'That's the last thing I want anyway,' Leonard assured him. 'The scandal would ruin us.'

'What do you want me to do, then?'

'Couldn't you see Victoria, perhaps scare her a little? If you could, and if we could go on just as we have been doing all these years, that would satisfy me very well.'

'Even living with someone you've ceased to love?'

32

'That's putting it rather mildly. I've sometimes wondered if I hate her, only that's a horrible word,' Leonard told him. 'But I've always thought,' he added confidingly, 'that a successful barrister must have something of the actor in him, so perhaps you'll understand what I'm going to say. To be on the stage, playing a part – perhaps a very difficult part – to the best of one's ability ... that's just about the best feeling there is in the world.'

'Yes, I can understand that,' said Antony. In spite of what he considered the other man's totally unreasonable attitude he was beginning to like him. 'Well, I'm going to see Mrs Buckley, this evening in fact. She approached me at Meg's party, just as you did.'

'Then–'

'I can't follow your wishes exactly, Mr Buckley, you must understand that. I'm by no means convinced that you're right in what you believe. But speaking of Mrs Buckley has put me in mind of something I must say to you. In the absence of the legal proof I spoke of I think you should be very careful to whom you mention this matter. It's all right to a lawyer like myself, and Meg certainly isn't a gossip, but I shouldn't breathe a word about it to your other associates.'

'No, of course I shan't, it would be all over town in no time, though I did mention it to Skelton, I thought it was only fair. I've known Meg for years, she's perfectly safe, and I admit I hoped to reach you through her. And now you don't believe me,' he added wistfully, 'so I suppose it's all been a waste of time.'

'Perhaps not. Perhaps after I've talked to Mrs Buckley I shall be able to convince you that you're wrong.'

'Don't you think I've tried to convince myself? Well, I'm grateful for your time, Mr Maitland, I won't waste any more of it. I'll just have to go on taking my precautions.'

II

After all it was as well he had been – however unwillingly – frank with Sir Nicholas and Vera about what was going on. The first thing Meg said when the Farrells arrived at tea time – the others were already gathered together as was their custom – was, 'What did you make of Leonard, Antony?'

'I liked him.'

'Yes, darling, but you like everybody.'

'Do I?' Antony wondered. 'I don't think you're right about that.

33

In any case, I was about to add that he's also a wrong-headed old bastard. If you'll forgive the plain language, Vera.'

'You might apologise to Jenny and me too,' Meg grumbled. 'You don't believe Victoria is really trying to poison him, then?'

'Do you?'

'It seems very unlikely,' Meg admitted. 'But he's awfully sure about it, and those attacks he's had really do sound a bit queer.'

'He ought to see a doctor,' said Jenny.

'He did.'

'Yes, but I meant for a really thorough check-up.'

'Well, he won't,' said Antony. 'That was one thing he was quite sure about. I pointed out this and that to him – the dangers of spreading a story like this for instance – but I don't think I had the slightest effect on the very firm belief he has in Mrs Buckley's guilt. One thing he said, Meg, was that he didn't think he could get on without her, but he was quite sure she thought she could get on without him. Do you think that's right?'

'I've thought of them almost as one person for so many years,' said Meg, 'that it's really rather hard to answer. But I've got the impression lately that Leonard isn't too sure of himself, he may dislike Victoria now but he leans on her as well. She's a much more decided person. You may change your mind about Leonard's story when you've talked to her.'

'And for my sins I'm doing that this evening.' He glanced at his uncle. 'I think I heard Vera say you're going to a concert as usual,' he said. 'Have you any objections to my using the study?'

'No objection in the world,' said Sir Nicholas lazily. 'But I shall expect a full report of your conclusions after you've seen both these people.'

'But it's probably only a nonsense,' Antony protested.

'Vera is interested,' said Sir Nicholas placidly, neatly laying the blame for his own curiosity on his wife's shoulders. 'Besides, Meg takes it seriously enough to have enlisted your help. That being so, even I find the situation intriguing.'

'One thing,' said Vera. 'How are your rehearsals going, Meg?'

'Smooth as silk,' said Meg with satisfaction. She paused there to lay one hand over Roger's. He was sitting between her and Jenny on the sofa, and the gesture surprised Antony because Margaret Hamilton, who could run through a whole gamut of emotion on the stage, was in private life rather reserved. 'None of this is common knowledge, and as for the Buckleys, butter wouldn't melt in their mouths when they talk to each other.'

'I went to a rehearsal myself,' said Roger suddenly. 'It isn't a bad sort of play at all.'

'Of course it isn't, darling, I wouldn't have taken the part if I hadn't liked it,' Meg pointed out. 'I think Kevin Elliott – that's the director – has got together quite a perfect cast.'

'Especially that fellow Murray,' said Roger. Antony thought he could detect some strain in his friend's voice, as if it was an effort to speak lightly. 'He's too good-looking by half.'

'But, darling, that's the whole point of the play,' Meg protested. 'He's an actor ... I mean he's acting the part of an actor ... the English language is terribly difficult, isn't it?' she appealed to Sir Nicholas. 'And one of the main points of the play is that he's irresistible to women, so he has to be at least reasonably good-looking. Anyway,' she added, as though this might be some consolation to her husband, 'he gets himself murdered at the end of the first act.'

'We shall all come to the first night,' Vera decided. Sometimes she had a rather grim way of speaking, and this made the words sound almost like a threat. 'Can you get us five seats together, Meg, so that we can all come and cheer you on?'

'Yes, of course, I've arranged that already.'

'When are you opening?'

'On the fourteenth of next month.'

'Isn't that rather quick?'

'Not really, not with such an experienced cast.'

'I thought there was always a lot of rewriting to be done, particularly as Jeremy has never written a play before.'

'Oh, but it was done in the provinces. He got a local repertory company to put it on, and I think everything got ironed out then. Anyway, there should be no difficulties on that score.'

'I think,' said Roger rather gloomily, 'they want to get well settled in before the tourist season starts.'

'Well, you must admit that's a good idea, darling.' She paused a moment and then returned to her first question again. 'So you don't think you had any success with Leonard, in convincing him he might be wrong, I mean?'

'Not a bit of success. But I did think perhaps, if Mrs Buckley shows the slightest sign of being reasonable, we might get them together to talk things out. In which case, Uncle Nick,' he added hesitantly, 'I thought perhaps you might be willing to act as a sort of moderator.'

'Heaven forbid!' said Sir Nicholas piously.

'You said you were interested.'

'So I am, in a rather incredulous way. But I don't think much of that for an idea, Antony, unless you want to bring on the very thing Meg's afraid of, and see one of them murder the other before your eyes.'

'You could soothe them, Uncle Nick,' said Jenny insinuatingly.

'Leave me out of your schemes,' said Sir Nicholas flatly. 'I shall enjoy seeing the play, and all the more for knowing some of the background, but I do think, Meg, you ought to know better than to try to embroil Antony in an affair of this kind. No possible good can come of it.'

'No harm either,' said Meg with spirit. 'In fact, I think he may very well have a really good effect on them in the long run. But if you're going to be disagreeable, darling, I think we'd better talk of something else.' She looked across at Vera. 'What is the concert tonight?' she enquired.

III

The fact that Sir Nicholas Harding regarded Meg and Roger Farrell as honorary members of his family worked both ways. On the one hand, as has already been mentioned, it meant that he considered himself free to criticise their actions as he chose; on the other hand he could on occasion treat Meg at least with some indulgence. Antony had been expecting some blistering comment, and was surprised when his uncle accepted this drastic change of subject without comment. After that they avoided the subject of the play and the marital problems of the Buckleys, and Roger cheered up after a while and became quite his usual self. Sir Nicholas and Vera left before dinner – they preferred to eat after the concert – and the evening had become quite lively by the time Antony was reminded via the house phone that Mrs Buckley had called by arrangement. He glanced at his watch. 'Not quite as punctual as her husband was,' he commented. 'Anyway, here goes. Let's get it over.'

Victoria Buckley was much more composed than her husband had been, though, sitting in the chair in the study that was now regarded as Vera's, she looked as if she'd be more comfortable with a footstool. 'You've been talking to Leonard,' she said accusingly, as Antony went in, and not giving him time for any formal greeting.

'Yes, we had a word this morning,' said Antony, pleased enough to let her take the initiative.

'He says he told you all about this ridiculous idea of his that I'm poisoning him,' said Victoria. 'And he said now you knew it wouldn't be safe for me to continue. Tell me, Mr Maitland, what did you make of him?'

'I'm afraid, Mrs Buckley, I have to say I think he believes what he says.'

'He's growing senile, that's what it is. You didn't agree with him?' she added belligerently.

'I told him,' said Antony, doing his best to be accurate, 'that there was nothing like legal proof. I also pointed out to him several things which I thought militated against his idea.'

'What were they?'

'For one thing, he says you don't wish to separate – either of you – because the professional image the public have of you is beneficial financially. In that case, would you be likely to wish to get rid of him?'

'The present arrangement suits me very well,' said Victoria thoughtfully. 'Otherwise I wouldn't consent to live with a man I've come to detest. But if it came to the point I could manage very well on my own.' She paused for a moment. 'And so for that matter could Leonard,' she said, with what appeared to be a rather unwilling generosity. 'He has no self-confidence at all, but he's a much better actor than he thinks.'

'Then why don't you just insist on a separation and get it over with?'

'Not until the run of this play is over,' said Victoria decidedly. 'And you know it's likely to run for quite a long time, particularly with Meg in the lead. What are these other points of yours against Leonard's idea?'

'Oh, I suppose just the general unlikelihood of such a thing,' said Maitland vaguely. He smiled at Victoria, hoping for some response, for some relaxation of her rather severe attitude. 'I'd be glad though if you'd give me your side of the story.'

'So that you can make up your mind whether I'm a murderess or not,' she said spitefully. She waited a moment, but Antony didn't reply; that was, in fact, very much what had been in his mind. 'Well, there isn't any my side of the story,' she protested. 'Leonard had a series of bilious attacks, rather severe ones, and that's all there is to it. I think he should have a check up but he won't agree to that.'

'The doctor who attended him the first time seems to have made too light of the matter for his liking. He did, however, think of sending the remains of his meals for analysis himself, but tells me that in each case they'd been disposed of. Even the bottled water out of the fridge.'

'I don't leave things lying about in my kitchen,' said Victoria. 'And I finished the bottled water myself. And that's another thing, Mr Maitland – your wife would understand this – it's really too much of a nuisance having him always underfoot when I'm trying to prepare my own meals.'

'Well, I'd still recommend separation. You needn't publicise it.'

'Not until the play's run is over,' she insisted again. And then added grudgingly, 'At least you've more sense than to suggest a marriage counsellor.'

If Maitland had been honest he would have said at that point, I don't believe in them. Instead, 'Why do you dislike your husband so much?' he asked curiously.

'He's grown into a thoroughly tiresome old man. For one thing he smokes a pipe, the kind that have a cartridge in them to collect all the nicotine. Then he leaves the dirty ones around, they smell perfectly filthy, and I have to clear them away. And if that weren't enough he suffers from insomnia sometimes, and insists on reading in bed.'

'That could be solved very simply by having separate rooms. The pipe, I admit, is more difficult.'

'We haven't a second bedroom, and Leonard flatly refuses to sleep on the sofa,' said Victoria. It had obviously never occurred to her that she might make this move herself. 'And he absolutely refuses to have one of those angled lamps. I even went out and bought him one, but he put it in the store room, so I just have to lie awake too.'

'That's all very dreadful,' said Antony.

'You don't think so at all,' she told him shrewdly. 'But after forty-three years –'

'You didn't dislike each other all that time,' he protested. 'According to Mr Buckley you were both very much in love when you married.'

'I was a pretty girl,' she said, preening herself. Maitland had never seen this done before, and had thought it just an expression that some novelists used. 'So I can quite imagine how he felt, even if we hadn't been thrown together right from the beginning. And, of course, I didn't know then what marriage would entail.'

'How long – ?' Antony broke off there, finding the question too embarrassing.

'Oh, years and years now, but my profession has always come

38

first with me,' she told him. 'I suppose going our separate ways came upon us gradually, but we haven't been truly close for a very long time.'

'By going your separate ways what exactly do you mean, Mrs Buckley?'

'Not infidelity, if that's what you're getting at.' She spoke stiffly, and the conviction came over him that the statement was too slick, too positive, to be completely true. Then she relented a little and leaned forward confidentially, perhaps aware of the impression she had made and trying to correct it. 'I can't say I wouldn't have embarked on an affaire if I'd ever felt like it,' she said. 'But it just hasn't happened that way. As for Leonard ... he was never a particularly passionate man, except when he was younger on the stage. I think he used up all his energies there.'

'I see.' And for once in his life, when he used this phrase, Antony thought he did. Quite frankly the picture he was getting of a marriage without passion, and – even worse – without affection, appalled him. 'Why did you want to see me, Mrs Buckley?'

'Meg says you're perceptive,' said Victoria. 'I take it she means you're a good judge of character. I thought perhaps I might be able to persuade you that I haven't any designs on Leonard's life, and that you in turn could persuade him.'

'If you care so little for him does it matter so much?'

'It's a matter of convenience. The present situation is intolerable, I should have thought you could imagine that. For that matter, Mr Maitland, since we've been frank with each other, why did Leonard want to see you?'

Antony smiled. Again it didn't seem to have the disarming effect he hoped for. 'I think he hoped I might scare you into desisting from your efforts to kill him,' he said precisely.

'Are you endorsing his opinion?' she asked suspiciously.

'Far from it. And even if I did – you'll forgive me, Mrs Buckley, you did say we were being frank with each other – I don't think you're a woman to scare easily.'

'To go back to your question,' she said, not acknowledging this comment at all, 'I hoped that a talk with a lawyer might persuade Leonard not to go on spreading these scandalous stories of his.'

'I've already warned him that it's injudicious,' Maitland told her. 'But in fairness, Mrs Buckley, I think I should say that he has as little desire to make your differences public as you have.'

'He told Meg, didn't he?'

'Yes, but Meg's dislike of gossip is notorious.' No need to mention that he had also spoken to Jeremy Skelton. 'And I think

– don't you? – that perhaps it was a way of getting a message to me.'

Again she ignored the question. 'Well, I wouldn't dream of taking any action,' she said, 'not until the play's run is over at any rate. But I do think he ought to realise that he's laying himself open to being sued for slander.'

'As I said, Mrs Buckley, I did my best to warn him.' At the beginning of their talk he had seated himself in Sir Nicholas's chair, but now he got up and stood looking down at her. 'I don't think there's any more that can usefully be said, Mrs Buckley. I wish I could persuade you both to a separation. Who knows, after a few weeks apart you might find that marriage wasn't so intolerable after all.'

She wriggled herself forward in her chair until her feet touched the ground and then stood up facing him. 'I suppose I shouldn't complain that you don't believe a word I've said to you about how annoying Leonard can be,' she said, 'because quite obviously you don't believe him either about these murder attempts I'm supposed to have made.' She turned away from him abruptly then and marched to the door. 'I suppose you're thinking it's been a wasted evening,' she said. 'Well, so do I! And now you'd better get back to that pretty little wife of yours. Who knows what she may be up to in your absence?'

IV

Maitland went upstairs rather slowly after he had shut the front door behind his visitor. He heard the murmur of voices as he went into his own hall and would have been glad enough to slip quietly into the living room and join the conversation without having to face any questions as to the interview that had just passed. His shoulder was aching a little more insistently than usual, as it often did when he was tired, and he thought a little ruefully that if he felt like this before the term had fairly started goodness knew how he would feel by the time the Easter recess was reached. He loved Meg like a brother, and what was perhaps more important he knew that Jenny had a very special feeling for her, but this problem she had set him he found particularly distasteful and the only consolation was that tonight should have seen the end of it. Except, of course, for the cross-examination he might expect as soon as he opened the living room door.

And sure enough they all fell silent for a moment when he went in, though every eye was turned in his direction. Jenny looked anxious, trust her to know the kind of thing he found upsetting; Roger too – there was that odd streak of sensitivity in Roger that probably made him equally aware of how his friend felt; as for Meg she was unashamedly curious, but sympathetic as well. 'Darling, you look absolutely worn out,' she said. 'Do come and sit down and tell us about it.'

'There isn't much to tell.' Instead of obeying her Maitland went across to the hearth rug, and found his almost untouched glass of brandy waiting for him beside the clock. Paradoxically, he felt too tired to take his usual chair with his back to the window. Roger had moved himself into Sir Nicholas's place, and Meg and Jenny shared the sofa. 'At one point, Meg, your Mrs Buckley stated that she was glad I had enough sense not to suggest a marriage counsellor, and it struck me very forcefully when she said that, that it was exactly the role you'd cast me for.'

Meg thought about that. 'Every lawyer has to be something of a psychiatrist,' she said at last.

'Did you invent that or read it somewhere?' asked Antony nastily. 'Anyway, Meg, I don't think my intervention has done the slightest good. And I don't think Victoria Buckley is a very nice woman, whatever image you, along with the rest of the world, may have formed of her,' he added, thinking of that last crack about Jenny. Not that it had disturbed him in the slightest, but it all went to show . . .

'And I don't think, in spite of what I said the other evening, that anything you did or said could have helped matters,' said Roger, with more vigour than the remark seemed to warrant. 'If this tiresome old couple of yours can't manage their own affairs at their age, Meg, it's high time they learned.'

'Darling!' Meg protested. 'Supposing Leonard is right?'

'Now you're just trying to make our flesh creep,' Antony accused her, and sipped at his cognac. 'It's quite obvious they hate the sight of each other –'

'I told you that,' said Meg complacently.

' – and each has a list of complaints about the other, silly little things. I was going to say trivial, but perhaps they don't seem so trivial after so many years.' He stopped there and smiled down at Jenny, and the humour that was never very far beneath the surface of his thoughts reasserted itself. 'What habits have I got that drive you to distraction, love?' he asked.

Jenny returned his smile, a little reassured by the lightness of his tone. 'None that I can't cope with,' she told him. 'But I can promise you I won't resort to poison.'

'So I can breathe again. Anyway, having heard them both out – Mr Buckley might be telling the truth though there's no proof of that – there was nothing I could do except suggest a separation. It seems the only thing in a situation like this, and it needn't be publicised, of course.'

'You don't know the press, darling,' Meg put in.

'Oh, don't I!' Maitland's tone was rather bitter, his own dealings with the media had not been uniformly pleasant. 'Anyway, I should think anything would be better than the sort of cat and dog life they're leading, and I think Victoria might agree, but only after the play is over. Leonard treated the whole idea with extreme horror.'

'He wouldn't have any choice if Victoria left him,' Roger pointed out.

'No, of course not. But I don't think he'd like it, I don't think he feels safe professionally any more.'

'Nonsense,' said Meg, 'he's quite capable of standing on his own feet.'

'Don't say nonsense, it reminds me of Mrs Buckley,' Antony pleaded. 'I didn't really enjoy my talk with her, I don't think we're altogether twin souls.'

'But she always seems so nice on the stage,' said Jenny. 'You know I said when you first told us about all this, Meg, that she couldn't possibly do anything so horrible as trying to poison her husband. And even last night at your place –'

'You must remember they've been practising for years presenting a united front in public,' said Meg.

'Yes, that's what I thought, but –'

'And the whole point about that is that they're the ideal couple, and that's the sort of character they represent on stage,' Meg went on, intent on making her point.

'Well, I've shot my bolt,' said Antony looking critically at his glass and finding that he had disposed of the contents. 'Victoria's long term views may incline towards separation when she sorts things out, but at least she's quite determined to let nothing interfere with this play of yours, Meg. So I think you can stop worrying about the effects of their relationship on the production.'

'It was good of you to try,' said Meg, rather belatedly remembering that some gratitude was due to him. 'And I'm sorry, darling, really I am, if it was a terrible bore.' But Jenny had got up quietly and gone over the tray where the decanter stood, and in the ensuing small flurry of activity the subject was lost, Antony hoped forever.

WEDNESDAY, 14th February

I

After that, for Antony and Sir Nicholas, the Hilary term continued its usual litigious course. Sir Nicholas, who would have told you that so far as work was concerned he was completely in the hands of his clerk, old Mr Mallory, was now in fact in the habit of picking and choosing his cases pretty carefully, but his nephew still had to give some consideration to the financial side of his profession. In addition, he had never learned the trick of managing Mallory, and was consequently quite frequently encumbered with cases which he considered either dull or unpleasant. John Willett, now second in seniority in the clerk's office, had his own ways of circumventing his superior, and a great deal of good will towards Maitland into the bargain, Antony having got him the job in the first place, but even he wasn't quite infallible.

As a consequence, Antony found himself almost uncomfortably busy during the next few weeks, even to the extent of on one occasion being on his feet in front of Mr Justice Carruthers, while at the same time he should have been attending to a case that Mr Justice Conway was hearing. Fortunately his friend Derek Stringer, also in Sir Nicholas's chambers, filled in for him in the latter case until he could get into court, but he certainly had no time to think of the new production of *Done in by Daggers* by Jeremy Skelton, in which Miss Margaret Hamilton was starring.

But one evening, about a week before the opening, when Roger came round to Kempenfeldt Square as he so often did, he reported that there had been a small paragraph in the newspaper – which both of the Maitlands had missed – reporting a rumour that Leonard and Victoria Buckley were departing from their usual custom and playing a couple not altogether in harmony. Meg, Roger said, had thrown up her hands to heaven on reading it, and exclaimed dramatically, 'There you see, I knew something would leak out.'

'But it doesn't talk about their relationship with each other,' Jenny protested, 'only about that of the characters they're supposed to be playing.'

'Yes, but don't you see in the play they just have their usual sort

44

of parts? Meg thinks it must mean that something of the real life situation has become known.'

'I don't think that follows at all,' said Jenny consolingly. 'And I think you ought to add that the characters they represent are just as usual, except that –'

'Don't tell me,' Antony implored. 'It would spoil the whole thing. Jenny's been to several rehearsals,' he told Roger.

'Has she though? I never knew you to do that before, Jenny. You've always said, like Antony, that you like it to come as a surprise to you.'

'It was a bit different this time,' said Jenny. 'Anne Skelton took me. I like her so much.'

'You're two of a kind,' said Maitland, smiling at her.

Jenny thought that over. 'Because our hair is much the same colour?' she asked.

'No, I didn't mean that. You both belong to the minority of people who're capable of listening to what's said to them, but now I come to think of it there's only one Jenny. Anne hasn't your serenity, love.'

'You always say that, but I don't always feel that way,' said Jenny.

'And when you lose it,' said Antony, intent on his own train of thought, 'it's usually my doing.' If anybody but Roger had been present he would rather have died than have said such a thing, but somehow in his friend's case he didn't mind giving himself away. And for the same reason Jenny answered with perfect simplicity.

'I wouldn't have it any other way.' Then she turned to Roger, perhaps just to prove to him that she hadn't altogether forgotten he was there. 'Antony doesn't really know Anne as well as I do,' she said, 'in spite of having met her before she was married to Jeremy. She does worry about things more than I do' – Roger and Antony exchanged a smile there – 'but she's really a very restful person, which is a good thing because Jeremy must be rather exhausting to live with.'

'An energetic type,' Roger agreed. From his tone one would have thought he deplored this, but as a matter of fact, though a stockbroker by profession, he was, when circumstances permitted, a man of action himself. 'But that doesn't explain why you found it necessary to go to rehearsals this time, Jenny.'

'Anne seemed a little shy about going by herself and Jeremy wanted her there,' said Jenny. 'It was a new experience for me, I never realised how much the actors had to go through – and the author too – before they started to play before an audience.'

45

'Educational, I suppose,' Roger nodded.

'Yes, I think so. It really is a good play, Roger, I'm sure Meg was quite right in insisting on taking the part.'

'Yes, I dare say she was.' But it couldn't be denied that his tone had its reservations. 'Anyway the die's cast now, and if the public likes the play I wouldn't be surprised if it runs forever,' he added gloomily.

'Look on the bright side,' said Antony. 'It may flop.'

Roger grinned at that. 'Then I'd have Meg's reactions to live with,' he confided. 'She isn't used to failures. And this being her first attempt at a lighter role –'

'I shouldn't worry,' Antony told him. 'Meg may not have had many reverses in her career, but in ordinary life she's had all the usual ups and downs.'

'Yes, I know. She's told me about some of them,' said Roger in a rather thoughtful tone. 'Anyway she's taken the part and there's nothing to be done about it now. No snags have developed, I hope, about the opening night. You won't be too bored to come, Jenny? And Sir Nicholas and Vera will be in town?'

'Of course I shan't,' said Jenny. 'Seeing a rehearsal isn't at all the same thing as seeing an actual performance. And if Uncle Nick shows any signs of backing out, which I don't think he wants to do anyway, Vera is certainly quite capable of getting him to the theatre. She has actually, – Jenny smiled round at her audience – 'ordered a new sack for the occasion.' (Vera's taste in clothes had become rather a joke between the Maitlands, though only to be shared with someone as close as Roger, and not at all unkindly in intention.)

'What colour?' asked her husband in rather a hollow tone.

'It will be in a flowered material,' said Jenny. 'Small flowers, I don't think Vera could get away with big ones, but it's the first time she's departed from plain colours and it's in Meg's honour, so I think she should be gratified, Roger.'

'I'm sure she will be,' said Roger. Suddenly his mood seemed to have mellowed. 'I can't wait to see it,' he added, but Antony had the impression that it was the dress he meant, not the first night.

II

So at last the evening of the opening arrived. The party from Kempenfeldt Square got to the theatre in good time, and in unusual comfort, Sir Nicholas having arranged for a limousine to be at their disposal all the evening. That had caused some amusement in the upstairs quarters, Antony and Jenny being fully aware that this extravagance was entirely for Vera's pleasure, nothing but the best being good enough for her. Roger had taken Meg to the theatre as usual, but departed from custom by staying in her dressing room until almost curtain time. He slipped into his place about five minutes before the house darkened.

In the meantime Jenny, familiar to a certain extent with what was to come, had been looking round, watching the arrivals, and waving to the Skeltons who were occupying one of the boxes. Anne, she knew, would have preferred a less conspicuous place, but Jeremy, on this occasion uncharacteristically unsure of himself, preferred to be where he could slip out into the corridor without attracting notice if he couldn't bear what he was seeing any longer.

Antony had been too busy studying the programme to have much time for looking about him. The play was in two acts, he saw, and the action took place throughout in Mary Carteret's drawing room. Below was a list of characters, some familiar, some he had never heard of before:

MARY CARTERET	*Margaret Hamilton*
DOUGLAS CARTERET	*Andrew Murray*
LARRY VAUGHAN	*Gordon Hewitt*
DONALD TURNSTALL	*Leonard Buckley*
GLADYS TURNSTALL	*Victoria Buckley*
PAULA NASH	*Ellie Dorman*
INSPECTOR MURCHISON	*Dominic Eldred*
SERGEANT DRAPER	*Claude Aubin*

He had just reached UNDERSTUDY TO MISS HAMILTON, *Frances Cathers*, when Vera dug him violently in the ribs and asked for his confirmation – 'Your eyes are better than mine, Antony' – that that was Bruce Halloran she could see sitting at the far side of the auditorium. As soon as he had confirmed her impression Roger joined them, and there was some general conversation, mainly about how Meg felt about her opening night.

'She always has the jitters, and then she is always perfectly magnificent,' said Roger firmly, and very shortly after that the house darkened and the curtain went up.

There had been a very orthodox piece of staging; no tubular steel erections, no ladders leading nowhere. However Jeremy Skelton's play might turn out it was obvious that his idea of his story's venue was strictly traditional. Mrs Carteret's drawing room was

47

obviously that of a fairly conventional upper middle class lady, whose tastes were neither old fashioned nor startingly modern. Only a picture over the mantel – under which a very convincing fire was lighted – hinted, with a bright splash of incomprehensible colour, that there might be more to its owner than met the eye.

Meg was discovered with her feet up on the sofa reading a newspaper, but she folded it carefully and put it under the cushions when Andrew Murray, who played her husband, entered. This was so uncharacteristic on her part – Meg Farrell would have thrown it down on the floor, letting the pages fall where they would – that Antony sat up and took notice immediately. But it soon became evident from the dialogue that it wasn't characteristic of Mary Carteret either; they were expecting her husband's aunt and uncle to visit them, an elderly couple who would like to see everything just so.

These two – Donald and Gladys Turnstall – arrived presently in the persons of the Buckleys, and some amusing dialogue ensued. It was immediately obvious that Jeremy Skelton, by transferring his talents from the written word to the spoken, had lost nothing of his wit, and the actors were playing up magnificently.

It was also clear, whatever had been said in the paper, that the characters of the two Turnstalls were every bit as sentimentally attached to each other as any that Leonard and Victoria Buckley had ever played. There were certainly no signs of strain, of underlying tension; but the tensions of the plot itself were very soon evident. Douglas Carteret was keeping a mistress, and his wife was dallying, gracefully and very amusingly, with a young friend of theirs, Larry Vaughan. Roger was right, Meg was magnificent in the part, and certainly kept the audience completely in the dark as to whether her actions were merely prompted by pique at her husband's neglect, or whether perhaps the flirtation with Mr Vaughan was not quite so innocent as it seemed.

Through all this the Buckleys moved with gentle placidity, part of the action and yet not involved in it. But for all that a master hand was playing upon the audience, and by the time the end of the first act was neared there was throughout the theatre a strained sense of excitement. There came a moment where Douglas Carteret and his aunt Gladys were alone on the stage, she gently reproving him for what she had discovered that day about his lifestyle, he sitting on the edge of his chair some distance away from her and obviously itching to be gone. But in the middle of one of her sentences the lights on the stage went out, so that the whole theatre was in complete blackness.

48

Gladys Turnstall said, rather quaveringly, 'You'd better see if a fuse has blown, Douglas,' and Carteret's voice was heard replying, 'No use, it must be a general blackout, we'll just have to wait.' After which a silence fell between them, during which, without hearing any footsteps, for the stage was carpeted, the audience was conscious of some movement, and then of a long drawn out sound that was more a sigh than anything else. Another pause, seemingly interminable, and then the stage lights went on again, for a moment blinding in their intensity, to show Andrew Murray in the character of Douglas Carteret, lying flat on the stage with a dagger in his back, and Victoria Buckley, in the character of his aunt, stretched out not quite so gracefully, also having apparently been stabbed. And her husband Leonard, standing almost centre stage, with a look of complete bewilderment on his face. After a few moments he took the few paces that would lead him to his wife's side. 'Victoria,' he said, almost tentatively. And then, more urgently, 'Victoria!'

'But that's not – ' began Jenny, for a moment forgetting herself. And as she spoke Andrew Murray raised his head.

Antony started to say, 'That's not how the act is meant to end?' but the answer was only too obvious. Roger was already on his feet. 'Something's wrong. Come on, Antony!' he said, and the two of them plunged towards the aisle, with less consideration than they would normally have shown for the feelings of their neighbours. As Antony followed his friend through the door that led backstage he was aware that the curtain was coming down.

III

Not surprisingly, it was late when Maitland got home, long past Gibbs's bedtime in fact, so he didn't have to undergo the small annoyance of having to run the gauntlet of the old man's disapproval. There was a light in the study and the door invitingly open, and when he went in he found Jenny with Sir Nicholas and Vera. 'You see us here,' said Sir Nicholas placidly, 'all agog to hear your adventures.' But when Antony approached nearer and he got a good look at his nephew's face he got up purposefully. 'Whisky, I think,' he said in a business-like way, 'and don't talk till you're ready.'

Contrary to his usual custom Antony's tiredness that evening didn't prompt him to restlessness and a desire to wander up and down the room. Instead he sank back wearily on the sofa, stretched out a hand to Jenny, and smiled at Vera. He took his uncle's advice and didn't attempt to speak until he had had a good swig of the scotch Sir Nicholas brought him. Then he said, 'You want to know what happened, of course. Well, to begin with, Victoria Buckley is dead.'

'All seems very strange,' said Vera. 'Jenny's told us about the plot, she said it was the man, Douglas Carteret, who was supposed to be murdered.'

'The idea is,' said Jenny, 'though this isn't brought out until the second act, that somebody turned the lights off at the main, having marked where he was sitting, and then came in and stabbed him in the back. The movement we heard, and that sort of sigh he gave, was all part of what was intended. When the lights went on again Victoria Buckley, of course, should still have been alive and would rush across to see what she could do for her nephew.' She paused there. 'I say, we're going to get awfully muddled if we keep on referring to them by their stage names and their real names indiscriminately.'

'Yes, I agree, there's enough to muddle us without that,' said Antony with feeling. 'And you've missed out part of the story, Jenny. Leonard Buckley wasn't supposed to be on stage at all until a little later.'

'No, I can't understand that.'

'He's been arrested for his wife's murder,' said Antony, and tasted his scotch again.

'But ... you like him Antony,' Jenny protested. 'We both did.'

'That isn't a guarantee of his innocence,' her husband pointed out. 'However, there are one or two points—'

'You'd better tell us exactly what happened when you and Roger got backstage,' said Sir Nicholas. 'Vera and Jenny will probably die of frustrated curiosity if you don't.'

'Nonsense, Uncle Nick,' said Antony with more energy, 'you're as curious as either of them yourself.'

'Well, I must admit it was an odd ending to what promised to be a very pleasant evening,' said his uncle thoughtfully. 'You were going to tell us—'

'Yes, of course. I think I ought to begin by saying that the first few minutes when we got backstage are more or less a blur to me. Everything was in a state of complete confusion. I just followed in Roger's wake, over the years he's learned to find his way about pretty well in the various theatres where Meg has played. He was looking for her, as no doubt you've guessed, and it wasn't long before he found her.'

'I trust he had no genuine cause for alarm on her behalf.'

'No, none at all. She was quite calm, as you might expect, and dealing pretty efficiently with a woman whose name I later discovered to be Ellie Dorman who was having a fine old fit of hysterics.'

'Well, let's see, the door you went through is to the left of the stage as we looked at it from the stalls. Does that mean that Meg and this other woman were in the wings on that side?'

'Yes, they were. So was Gordon Hewitt. Andrew Murray, of course, was playing dead on stage, Victoria Buckley actually was dead, and her husband was standing somewhere between them. But that last bit you saw for yourself.'

'Leonard Buckley had no business to be there,' said Jenny, 'and Victoria should have been sitting exactly where she was when the lights went out.'

'Yes, I gathered as much. Also in the wings at that side were Dominic Eldred and Claude Aubin, ready to impersonate two detectives, but not due to come on until the second act. Also Meg's understudy, Frances Cathers. The lights, of course, were put out on cue by someone or other – would it have been the stage manager? – who was nowhere near the stage. All those people can vouch for each other's position when darkness fell, and when the lights went on again. The interval, I understand, was precisely one and a half minutes, which is a surprisingly long time when you come to measure it out. Anything might have happened in the meantime.'

'I have always wondered,' said Sir Nicholas idly, 'how actors and actresses manage when the entire theatre is in pitch darkness. There can't even be a light in the wings in case it spills over on to the stage.'

'Meg says it's all done with phosphorescent paint,' said Antony. 'The furniture is marked so that they can find their way around when necessary, and in this case there was also a dab of the stuff on Andrew Murray's back, where Leonard Buckley – the murderer in the play – was supposed to fix the property dagger. I'm guessing that somebody had daubed the dress Mrs Buckley was wearing too, you remember it was a sort of oatmeal colour, she might never have noticed it, and there were other marks on the furniture.'

'And in her case a real weapon was used?'

'It certainly was. It had been struck home with great force, and though there's no question of my knowing the doctor's opinion yet, I'd be very much surprised to learn she didn't die instantly.'

'Did you have any conversation with all these bystanders?'

51

'No, not really. You see the police arrived in record time.'

'Somebody had the presence of mind to call them, then?'

'Somebody may well have done, though I'm not sure about that. Anyway, all the usual experts with their paraphernalia turned up a little later. But I'm talking about two much more important people. Detective Chief Superintendent Briggs, and Detective Chief Inspector Sykes,' said Antony, giving both gentlemen their full titles.

Even Sir Nicholas was moved to surprise by this statement. 'Good God,' he said blankly. 'For one thing, how did they get there so quickly? And for another, Chief Superintendents don't go out on investigations unless the matter is extremely important. Like someone murdering the Prime Minister, for instance.'

'They were both in the audience,' Antony explained.

'I didn't see either of them.'

'No, neither did I. Superintendent Briggs, not having friends at court as we have, was much further back in the stalls; while Sykes and his wife were in the circle.'

'Isn't that a bit of a coincidence?' asked Sir Nicholas, his eyes narrowing as he thought it out.

'That's what I thought at first, but Sykes took a moment later on to explain it to me,' said Antony. 'It was Jeremy Skelton's name that caught Briggs's attention, he knew that when Jeremy was arrested for murder down in Chedcombe you and Vera were going to defend him, and that I was mixed up in the affair somehow. That piqued Sykes's curiosity, too, and Mrs Sykes apparently likes nothing better than a good crime story, so there they both were.'

His uncle gave him a long, hard look. 'What it is to have a reputation as a troublemaker,' he said. 'Don't tell me Sykes had looked in his crystal ball and foreseen what was going to happen.'

'Nothing like that, of course. They were just as flabbergasted as we were. But it meant there was no opportunity for gossiping with the cast, which I admit I should very much like to have done. We were all herded into what was called the Green Room, and Sykes himself stood guard over us until a constable relieved him. After that everyone was interviewed in turn, and must have gone straight home from their interviews because we never saw them again. Except for Meg, who was allowed to come back and wait for Roger. Roger dropped me off here just now on their way home, but it didn't leave us much time for talk, and I'm not sure how much Meg knew anyway.'

'What about your own interview with Briggs?'

'It was just about as amicable as usual,' his nephew replied. 'But I hadn't seen anything that he hadn't also seen for himself, so it didn't last very long. Besides, Sykes was doing the questioning, being officially in charge. As you said yourself, Chief Superintendents don't go out on just any old murder.'

'I may have meant that, but I hope I phrased it a little better. Did Sykes know about Leonard Buckley's suspicions of his wife?'

'I think by the time he got to me, which was last, he knew everything there was to know about their relationship. He asked me if I knew them, and I told them, Jenny, that we'd met them at the Farrells, but didn't know them well. I think that was near enough to the truth. It was only when I was leaving that Briggs informed me that Leonard Buckley had been arrested.'

Sir Nicholas smiled suddenly. 'Had *you* no questions for *him* after that bit of information?' he asked.

'Well, naturally.' Maitland's answering smile was a little rueful. 'But I came up against a blank wall. Sykes just sat there looking like a sphinx, and Briggs did the We-are-here-to-ask-questions-not-to-answer-them bit. I had the pleasant job of breaking it to Meg, I think she's rather fond of the old boy. And of course I couldn't answer any of her questions.'

'But, Antony, I can tell you what made the police suspicious,' said Jenny. 'I've seen that scene half a dozen times, and Mr Buckley wasn't supposed to be on stage at all when the lights came on again.'

'Any explanation for that?' asked Vera. 'Seems a bit odd to me.'

'Unfortunately, as I told you, I'd no chance of conversing with any of them. I wonder ... you know it's an intriguing situation, Uncle Nick. He really thought, rightly or wrongly, that his wife was trying to kill him—'

'Heaven forgive you!' said Sir Nicholas. 'You're thinking up a line of defence already.'

'I'll bet you anything your own mind is running on those lines too,' said Antony undutifully. 'Not to mention Vera's. Anyway there's no harm in being a little ahead of the game.'

Sir Nicholas closed his eyes for a moment as though in pain. It was his habit to affect an extreme aversion to slang, though somehow he managed to tolerate it well enough from his wife. 'Are you trying to tell me,' he said, opening his eyes again, 'that you have some reason to suppose that you may be offered a brief in this matter?'

53

'Well – ' said Antony.

'I see what it is, Meg's been talking to you,' said his uncle accusingly. Antony looked deprecating.

'If you've ever discovered a way of resisting her blandishments, Uncle Nick, I wish you'd tell me,' he said. 'I know of absolutely no way of doing so.'

'Nonsense!' said Sir Nicholas dampingly. 'May I remind you, Antony, that Buckley's solicitors, whoever they are, may not have the faintest intention of calling on your services?'

'I realise that all right, but Meg didn't seem to think he had a solicitor. And if that's the case, I shouldn't be at all surprised at her putting forward Geoffrey Horton's name, and if she does that you know as well as I do–'

'Yes, I know perfectly well,' Sir Nicholas interrupted him. 'I also know that in a case where Chief Superintendent Briggs is involved it would be extremely unwise to let yourself be embroiled.'

'He was leaving it pretty much to Sykes, as I told you, just sitting in on the interviews out of interest, I think.'

'That makes not the slightest difference. Briggs is Sykes's superior. And after what happened last March–'

'But, Uncle Nick, even Briggs must have realised I hadn't really been tampering with the evidence.'

'That makes not the slightest difference. I find myself quite unable to fathom the superintendent's thought processes, but the fact remains that he doesn't trust you and probably never will.'

'It's very unjust,' said Jenny indignantly, and Vera added, 'Stupid,' in her grimmest tone.

Maitland may have been gratified by their backing but for the moment he didn't show it. 'But Uncle Nick,' he protested, 'I couldn't do Buckley any harm by appearing for him in court, the harm has been done already by them arresting him.'

'That's true enough,' Sir Nicholas admitted, and again he went through one of his sudden reversals of mood. 'I quite see, my dear boy,' he said, 'that if Meg has set her heart on your acting there's nothing more to be said. Would you favour a plea of self defence, or do you think diminished responsibility might be better? Or perhaps even,' he added thoughtfully, 'straight insanity?'

What Maitland wasn't prepared for, in spite of what he had said to his uncle, was a full scale assault on his defences the very next day. Meg was on the telephone before he had been half an hour in chambers. 'I want you to come to lunch with us, darling,' she cooed.

'Us?' queried Antony, rather brusquely.

'With the Skeltons and myself. Roger doesn't think he can get away.'

'Well, I don't know that I can either.'

'Don't be difficult, darling. You know you can do anything you set your mind to,' said Meg, which when he thought it over seemed rather a doubtful compliment. 'We'll go to Astroff's since that's so convenient for you,' she added, as though that ought to clinch the matter.

'All right then.' Antony looked a little sadly at the papers piled on his desk, he had meant to send out for a sandwich and work straight through that day. 'What time will suit you?'

'There's a rehearsal called for two o'clock, so if you can make it at twelve-thirty or even a quarter past – ' Meg began.

'Rehearsal?' The one word came out almost as a yelp of surprise. 'You don't mean to say you're going on with that damn play?'

'It's an extremely good play,' said Meg, 'and I'll thank you not to say anything like that in front of Jeremy or Anne. Well of course we're going on with it, darling, what did you expect?'

'A little proper feeling I suppose,' said Antony in a very good – though quite unconscious – imitation of his uncle's manner. 'However, we can talk about that when I see you. In the dining room at Astroff's at twelve-fifteen.'

He had been afraid that Meg would go on chattering, but for once in her life she took her dismissal quietly. Antony put down the receiver and picked up instead the proof of one of the defence witnesses in a case of affray, scowling at it in a way that might well have intimidated the solicitor who prepared the statement. It might be possible to plead guilty to a lesser charge, unlawful assembly perhaps ... at that point in his cogitations the telephone rang again, sounding to his unwilling ear to be doing so with unusual persistence.

'Yes, Hill, what is it?' he asked, tempering his tone, however, because the clerk who answered the telephone in chambers was of a mild disposition and generally believed to have been born apologising.

'Mr Horton, Mr Maitland. I thought perhaps you'd want—'

'Yes, I do, Hill, thank you. Put him on.' There was a pause, and then Geoffrey Horton's more decisive tones in his ear.

'What's all this about your attending a murder, Antony?' he asked.

Geoffrey Horton was another old friend, a solicitor with whom Maitland had worked many times over the years, and who had done his best to keep Antony himself out of trouble on several occasions. The informality of his greeting therefore was not unexpected, the only surprising thing was the speed with which Meg seemed to have worked. 'I take it you're talking about the murder last night at the Alhambra theatre,' he said. 'Nobody saw what happened, the place was in pitch darkness.'

'I read the morning papers,' said Geoffrey, not at all grateful for this gratuitous piece of information. 'And I had a call late last evening from the Lennox Street police station, saying they had a man in custody who wanted my help.'

'Leonard Buckley?'

'Who do you think? Of course it was.'

'You know who you have to thank for this, don't you?'

'I rather thought ... you.'

'Not on your life. I wouldn't mind betting it was Meg Farrell's idea, she was already hinting to me that I should take a hand last night, and getting at you was the obvious first step in the game. The only thing I don't quite understand, though I expect she'll tell me, is how she managed to get at Mr Buckley. The police didn't give any of us a chance of talking to the others.'

'I thought you said—'

'I said I was in the auditorium when the murder took place, but I went backstage with Roger immediately. He was worried about Meg, and I don't wonder. So I can tell you exactly what happened from the audience's point of view, but—'

'That's not what I want and you know it,' said Geoffrey bracingly. 'I went round to see Buckley last night, and he had some rigmarole about your having tried to help him in some trouble he was having with his wife. Didn't sound quite your cup of tea, but you seemed to have impressed him with your aptitude. Quite a simple soul really,' said Geoffrey, 'takes everyone at their face value.'

'Thank you,' said Antony meekly.

'Anyway, if I talk to Mallory will you take the brief?'

'I knew this was coming,' said Antony, 'and I said to Uncle Nick last night that if he knew a way of resisting Meg I didn't.'

'That means you'll do it?' asked Geoffrey eagerly.

'I don't see why not. Only if it's a matter of going to the magistrate's court –'

'I'll take care of that, I know you're busy. And from what I hear the only thing to do is reserve our defence.'

'Did Buckley tell you how he came to be still on stage when the lights went on again?'

'He told me a lot of things, some useful, some not. I think we'd better go into all that when I see you. The trouble is – I said he was an old innocent – he'd made a statement to the police before I got there. I could well have done without that.'

'Yes, I can imagine. When are you proposing we should meet, Geoffrey?'

'As soon as possible I should say.'

'I have a conference at four. Rather a complicated affair, but I'll try and get through it as quickly as I can. If you don't mind being late home, come round here when you leave the office and wait till I've finished.'

'All right then, I'll do that. I'm obliged to you,' said Geoffrey, with sudden and unexpected formality. But then a thought seemed to strike him. 'I say, you don't think your having been at the theatre makes it improper for you to act?'

'My dear Geoffrey, the investigating officer was in the theatre too, not to mention Chief Superintendent Briggs,' Antony pointed out. 'I'd like to see the prosecution trying to make anything of it in view of that. I'm meeting Meg for lunch,' he added, 'along with the Skeltons. She'll be surprised to know she's preaching to the converted.'

'Don't let her talk you into anything beyond the scope of your brief,' Geoffrey advised. He knew Meg's wiles of old.

'I shan't,' Maitland assured him. And when he spoke he really thought he was telling the truth.

II

Maitland was in good time for his luncheon engagement but the

57

others were there before him. 'You could have gone to our table, Meg,' he said, as he seated himself after greeting them.

'But, darling, Uncle Nick might have wanted it,' Meg protested. 'And we wanted to talk to you.'

'Uncle Nick wouldn't have minded sitting somewhere else for once, if he does come in, which I doubt. He's in court, and Bruce Halloran is prosecuting, so I expect they'll go to lunch together. And Halloran has his own favourite watering-hole.' He paused and looked from one to the other of his companions. 'Does that mean you're going to tell me something that Uncle Nick shouldn't hear?' he enquired mildly.

'Nothing of the sort,' said Meg hastily.

'But we're to talk about Mrs Buckley's murder?'

'Yes, of course,' said Meg, as though that was the most natural thing in the world.

'Then before we start you can satisfy my curiosity.' He paused while the waiter took their orders for drinks and then went on as though there had been no interruption. 'How did you manage to tip Leonard Buckley off to ask for Geoffrey Horton to represent him?' he asked.

'I think I was rather clever about that,' said Meg complacently. 'You know we all had to sit in silence, not daring to speak a word.'

'I know that must have been very difficult for you,' said Antony.

'Don't be horrid, darling. They called Leonard first, as you know, but before that there was quite a long interval while they pursued their enquiries or whatever it is detectives do. I sat down beside him on the sofa and slipped a note into his pocket.'

'You're telling me, Meg, that you knew he was going to be arrested.'

'Well, it seemed so much the most obvious thing,' Meg explained. 'Everybody in the cast knew about this vendetta between him and Victoria, even though we tried very hard to keep it quiet. They were bound to hear about it some time.'

'By "they" you mean the detectives?'

'Yes, of course I do. Don't be so stupid, Antony. There was also the fact that he was on stage when he shouldn't have been. I thought he might find it difficult to explain that away.'

'I see.'

'I take it from what you say, darling, that Geoffrey Horton has already approached you.'

'Indeed he has, just after you phoned this morning. And I think you knew, Meg, that I'd take the case after what you said last night, so what's all this about?'

'And Uncle Nick doesn't want you to because Briggs is involved,' said Meg shrewdly.

'I can manage Uncle Nick,' said Antony rashly, an exaggeration for which he may be forgiven. He paused, considering the accuracy of the statement. 'Or at least Vera can,' he added, grinning.

'I should like to see Miss Langhorne – Lady Harding – again,' said Jeremy Skelton. Now that he came to think of it Antony was surprised that the writer had been content to sit quietly for so long. 'She was part and parcel of Chedcombe for so long that it seems odd to think of her settled here in London.'

'I'd like to have been a fly on the wall during their courtship,' said Antony. 'I hadn't an idea of what was going on, though Jenny swears it was obvious. From something Vera once said I got the idea that Uncle Nick tried to lure her up here by telling her about all the concerts she'd be able to attend, but she retorted flatly that if she came to live in London it wouldn't be for that reason.'

'That sounds very like Miss Langhorne,' said Jeremy reminiscently.

'We owe her a great debt of gratitude,' said Anne Skelton in her gentle way, 'for taking Jeremy's case at all and then for introducing Sir Nicholas into the affair.'

'Quite enough on that subject has been said already,' said Antony, smiling at her.

'Well, one thing I wanted to ask you,' said Jeremy, 'is whether the presence of very senior detectives from Scotland Yard in the audience last night was quite fortuitous.'

'Even detectives have to relax sometimes. What was on your mind, Jeremy?'

'I thought perhaps they wanted to have a look at me,' said Jeremy bluntly.

'That was acute of you.'

'But you proved quite conclusively that I didn't murder Lydia,' Jeremy protested.

'I was going to add that it was more likely your previous association with me that interested them,' Antony explained.

'I don't get that,' said Jeremy, frowning.

'As far as Chief Inspector Sykes is concerned it will be just that, a quite straightforward interest in you and all your works, heightened a little by your brush with the law a few years ago. But with Briggs it's quite different.'

'I think he hates you,' said Meg, shuddering.

'Don't be melodramatic, Meg.'

'Well if it isn't that, what *did* you mean?' asked Jeremy.

'Nothing much,' said Antony trying to strike a lighter note. 'Merely that he's a chap who interprets the words Criminal Lawyer rather more literally than is customary . . . at least in my case.'

Jeremy took a moment to think that out, and while he was doing so Anne voiced the question that was in both their minds. 'We don't know quite what you mean, Antony,' she said.

'Merely that he's been trying for years to hang some charge or other round my neck, and after something that happened last year we were forced to the reluctant conclusion that he's never believed the proof to the contrary that we've been able to provide. In that case it was subornation of perjury . . . tampering with witnesses,' he added to Anne.

'But there hadn't been a crime last night until Victoria was killed,' said Jeremy.

'No, I said it was just curiosity.'

'He wanted to see the wicked murderer who'd been saved from justice by your almost as wicked wiles?' said Jeremy.

'Something like that, I think. I should add,' he went on, seeing Anne's expression, 'that Briggs is one of a kind. You'd have to go a long way to find anyone who shared his opinion.'

'That's just as well,' said Jeremy, letting out a deep breath. He picked up his glass, drank deeply, and set it down empty. 'Where's that waiter?' he said. 'We'll have another round and order lunch at the same time.'

Nothing but small talk passed between them while this was being done. Meg was crumbling a roll, and glancing from time to time at Antony almost as though – but this seemed very unlikely – she was nervous. When the new round of drinks arrived he turned to her and asked bluntly, 'You still haven't answered my question, Meg. If you knew I'd take the case what is there to talk about?'

'It's always a pleasure to see you, darling,' said Meg dulcetly.

'Come off it,' said Antony crudely. 'You needn't have gone to such lengths to do that.'

'Jenny and I have told you time after time you ought to have a proper lunch, instead of eating at your desk while you're working,' said Meg severely. 'You ought to be grateful to me instead of growling like that.'

'I'm sorry if I was growling. I'm glad to see you all, of course,' said Antony, though the remark seemed to be addressed more to Anne than to anybody else. 'But–'

'The question is,' said Meg, 'how do you intend to treat the defence?'

'That's up to Geoffrey.'

'Now you know perfectly well, darling, that he'll do whatever you say,' said Meg.

'You're exaggerating a little, but in any case that's something I couldn't possibly discuss with any of you. Certainly not before I've talked to Geoffrey, and after that only under very special circumstances, if Mr Buckley gave his consent for instance.'

'Now you're being stuffy,' Meg complained. 'I've spoken to you about that before. You're growing very like Uncle Nick,' she added thoughtfully.

'So we may as well relax and enjoy ourselves,' said Antony hopefully, ignoring the criticism, which he had heard before.

'Not just yet.' That was Jeremy Skelton, his natural vigour reasserting itself. 'What we really want to know is what assumption you will be making in preparing his defence. Will you presume him guilty?'

'How on earth can I answer that until I've talked to him?'

'You're going to do that at least,' Anne put in eagerly.

'Yes, of course. Geoffrey would tell you I've a weakness for hearing everything at first hand, though he'd also say that's because I'm too lazy to read my brief properly. But – as you know, Jeremy, though the others don't – there are always a number of alternatives to be put before a client and we should be failing in our duty if we didn't do that.'

'Such as guilty but insane, or that he was acting in self defence,' said Jeremy. 'No you needn't bother to answer that,' – Maitland was thinking of his talk with his uncle the evening before – 'all we're asking is that you keep an open mind for the present.'

'He didn't do it,' said Meg flatly.

Antony turned back to her. 'What reason have you for saying that, *darling*?' he asked.

'I think I'm a pretty good judge of character,' said Meg with dignity.

'Is that all?'

'Isn't it enough? You make judgments on that basis yourself,' Meg pointed out. 'Uncle Nick's always complaining about it.'

'Yes, I have to plead guilty to that,' Antony admitted. 'All the same, character evidence is all very well, but nobody would believe

61

a flat statement like that, particularly if it proves to go against all the evidence.'

'But I'm not talking about everybody,' said Meg, 'only you, Antony. After all you've known me a long time and ought to realise I'm not in the habit of making wild guesses.'

'No, Meg, but I think you have a very nice nature and are almost as unwilling as Jenny is to think ill of anybody.' He turned again, looking from one to the other of the Skeltons. 'Do you agree with her?' he asked.

'We know so well,' said Anne quietly, 'how easy it is for the police to be wrong.'

'Yes, I know how that must seem to you, but we have to remember that they aren't always wrong,' said Antony, and remembered as he spoke that something very like that had been said to him on occasion.

'He's a very nice man,' Anne persisted.

'Yes, I liked him too. Unfortunately that doesn't mean he's innocent.'

'Well, put it like this.' Jeremy came forcefully into the conversation again. 'The fact that it happened as it did makes me feel responsible somehow –'

'That's nonsense.'

' – and I'd like to see Leonard get the very best defence possible. In my book that's you, and I may tell you I'm quite willing to foot the bill.'

'You mustn't talk to Antony about money,' said Meg, giving Maitland a dagger-like glance. 'All barristers' souls are above that sort of thing.'

'No, I know I mustn't. Anyway, Leonard has been very kind to me during the rehearsals. Meg will tell you there were lots of changes to be made, even though I thought we'd got everything ironed out in Bradford. It's my first play, remember, and I didn't exactly hit it off with the director, Kevin Elliott –'

'You're too much alike, Jeremy,' said Anne.

' – but Leonard, who after all is by far the most experienced of the cast, was always ready to help me out. So, guilty or not, as I said, I'd like him to have the best defence. But I'd also like to be assured that you'll go into it with an open mind, and try to find out the real truth if you come to the conclusion that he's innocent.'

'I have to see Geoffrey,' said Antony, 'and then he'll take me to see Mr Buckley. Until then I don't know how we'll treat the matter, we'll just have to wait and see. But in any event, I shall do the best I can in court.'

'That's all right then,' said Meg.

'What do you mean? I haven't agreed to an investigation.'

'No, darling, but you'll find that I'm right,' she told him. 'And when you do I know you quite well enough to realise that you'll embark on what Geoffrey always calls one of your damned crusades. And Uncle Nick will fume a bit, and Chief Superintendent Briggs will bristle with suspicion I dare say, but you'll find out the truth and get Leonard off one way or another.'

'That raises the question of who else could have done it?'

'I think almost anybody who was in the vicinity,' said Jeremy. 'We haven't time to go into it now,' he added, as the waiter approached with a laden tray. 'Perhaps we can talk later.'

'Yes, of course.'

'I was in front when it happened, as you were,' said Jeremy, 'but I'll do a bit of detective work myself after rehearsal and see what I can find out from the others.'

'That will be splendid. The ones who are being called by the prosecution I shan't be able to see myself. I think our talk had better be after I've seen Mr Buckley.'

'Yes, that's a good idea.'

'And you're rehearsing again this afternoon?' said Antony, sitting back to allow his order of plaice to be laid before him.

'Yes, of course, with the understudies.'

'Won't you find it rather gruesome going through that scene again?'

'I'm not going near the theatre,' said Anne, shuddering almost as dramatically as Meg herself had done.

'Nonsense, darling, you know you will. The thing is, everybody is assuring me it's what Victoria would have wished. Not that I believe it for a moment, but the publicity won't do us any harm, and with things as they are today I think most of the cast are hoping for a long run.'

'As you are, darling,' said Anne with gentle malice.

'I admit it. I admit it freely,' said Jeremy.

'What about the understudies? Will they do as well as the Buckleys did?'

'They're both absolutely terrified,' said Meg frankly. 'Monica was on the phone to me this morning and I did my best to reassure her. Of course, there'll be the question of makeup, they're both quite young things, but I dare say we'll get by.'

'I'm surprised the police have released the theatre so quickly.'

63

'For that I think we must thank the fact that they got on the job so quickly,' said Jeremy. 'All the measurements had been made and the photographs taken ... you know better than I do, Antony, what's involved. Anyway, Chief Inspector Sykes, who's rather a nice fellow, said we could have possession again at two o'clock. It's a short enough time to rehearse for tonight, but thank heaven both David and Monica know the parts quite well. And tonight,' he concluded with some satisfaction, 'I expect it will be standing room only.'

III

Geoffrey Horton, bearing his inevitable bulging briefcase, arrived in chambers just after Maitland's clients, lay and solicitor, had left. 'I don't know why you always lug that thing with you when you come here,' said Antony, as Geoffrey came into his room, which was narrow and rather dark. 'You can't possibly have many papers for me in this matter yet, and even if you had you know I'd rather hear the story from you.'

'The brief is being prepared,' said Geoffrey, seating himself and putting down the offending briefcase close to his right leg. It was his habit to pat it from time to time while he was talking, and Maitland had never been able to decide whether this was to reassure himself as to its continued presence, or whether he was a frustrated dog owner. 'Meanwhile Mr Buckley's been committed for trial, on the minimum of evidence presented by the prosecution but it sounds bad. We reserved our defence, but so far I don't think we've got one.'

'Come now, Geoffrey, don't be despondent at this stage,' Antony exhorted him. They were old friends these two. Time, and the generous application of hair oil, had done something to dim the vivid red of Geoffrey's hair, otherwise he was very much the same as he had been when they first met, off duty a cheerful companion, but with a streak of seriousness where his profession was concerned that Antony found amusing, at least on those occasions when he was not himself absorbed in a case. 'You've seen your client, of course, he must have had something to say for himself.'

'Nothing that can be construed as proof of his innocence by the wildest stretch of the imagination,' Geoffrey grumbled. 'He was the murderer in the play, you know –'

'A nice twist of dramatic irony.'

' – and even though no one could see him he was supposed to

64

go on stage at that point so that the audience would get the sensation of some stealthy movement. There was also the property dagger to fix on Andrew Murray's back.'

'That's all very well, but Jenny says he shouldn't have been still there when the lights went on.'

'No, what he says is that someone else was moving around the stage and bumped into him. That was after he'd planted the dagger and he was so startled that he more or less froze in his tracks.'

'Andrew Murray gave quite a convincing moan as he died,' said Antony helpfully. 'Victoria Buckley apparently died quite silently.'

'Yes, but of course it was a shock to Mr Buckley to find the two of them stretched out when the lights came on. Then he went across to Victoria, because she was the one who shouldn't have been there. His first thought was that somebody with a distorted sense of humour was playing a joke, and it even went through his mind that Jeremy Skelton himself might be behind it, but then he saw that it wasn't a property dagger at all that had been used, but a silver handled thing. Rather ornate, but definitely lethal.'

'Did the police have anything to say about its provenance?'

'Nothing at all in court. Nothing yet. And Mr Buckley says he never saw it before.'

'What about the medical evidence?'

'Death instantaneous, or almost so, and definitely due to stabbing. Incidentally, traces of phosphorescent paint were found on Mrs Buckley's dress, which accounts for the murderer knowing exactly where to strike.'

'And you say Mr Buckley had made a statement to the police before you were called in?'

'Yes, he had,' said Geoffrey disgustedly. 'Of course I told him he ought to have clammed up, but he just said, what was the use, they'd already been told that he and his wife hated each other? And that's the very essence of the case against him. We could try to deny it in court, but if the judge admits his statement –'

'I will not get up and say it was beaten out of him,' said Antony firmly.

'And I wouldn't ask you to, there's far too much of that sort of thing nowadays,' said Geoffrey. 'But you must admit it doesn't help us.'

'There's one thing ... was anything said about fingerprints? Would this silver handled dagger of yours have taken them?'

'Perfectly, I should think. The nude figure of a woman, rather like that book we all read when we were very young.'

'I don't think there were any nude women in the books I read,' said Maitland pensively.

'You've just forgotten, and I only said that was what the handle of the dagger was formed of,' Geoffrey retorted. 'The police said the handle was perfectly clean.'

'Leonard Buckley wasn't wearing gloves,' said Antony positively. 'There was no reason why he should, after all. Nobody was going to worry about whether his fingerprints were on the dagger used to stab Andrew Murray or not.'

'No, but there's a nasty little twist here,' said Geoffrey. 'He had a pair of black cotton gloves in his pocket.'

'Something to do with the play?' Maitland hazarded.

'Yes, I gather they were going to be discovered dramatically there later, as part of the proof of his guilt.'

'A perfectly reasonable explanation.'

'Maybe. But the fact remains that he could have slipped them on, stabbed his wife, and then peeled them off again. Perhaps he hadn't time to get off the stage and so invented this story of bumping into somebody else.'

'Are you telling me you think our client is guilty?' said Antony in a shocked tone.

'I haven't made up my mind. He's a nice old boy, there's something rather ... rather innocent about him,' said Geoffrey, surprising his friend who hadn't believed him capable of such an imaginative description. 'But that doesn't necessarily include his being innocent of this crime. In any case my instructions are to plead Not Guilty.'

'Then until I see him ... will you arrange that, Geoffrey?'

'I've already done so, subject to your approval. Ten o'clock tomorrow morning at the prison.'

'Thank you,' said Maitland, grimacing a little as he spoke because of all things he detested prison visiting. 'Then there's just one question I still want to ask you. Mr Buckley said the police already knew the terms he was on with his wife. Who told them?'

'I don't know if he'd learned it from more than one source, but the fellow who was going to be stabbed in the play, Andrew Murray, had certainly spilled the beans,' said Geoffrey. 'He was one of their witnesses, but only questioned very briefly, and as I told you I wasn't doing anything to interfere at that stage.'

'No, I'm sure that was the wisest course. Well, Geoffrey, that didn't take so long after all,' he added, and began piling together the papers on his desk. 'Joan won't be sending out a search party for you. And I'll hear Leonard Buckley's story in detail tomorrow. Will you pick me up in Kempenfeldt Square?'

'Yes, of course I will.' Geoffrey, who had been expecting something in the nature of a close cross-examination, gave his friend a doubtful, or perhaps it would be more accurate to say, a suspicious look. 'You've got some idea in your head,' he declared. 'Don't tell me we're going to go haring off one of your wild goose chases.'

'No idea in the world,' Antony told him. 'In fact, my mind's as near a blank as it's possible for anyone's to be. I had lunch with Meg and the Skeltons,' he added with apparent inconsequence. 'Meg thinks Mr Buckley's innocent.'

'So that's it!' said Geoffrey, enlightened.

'It has nothing at all to do with it, whatever you mean by that. Skelton isn't so sure—'

'He wants to do his best for the old boy because he feels responsible,' Geoffrey concluded for him. 'He's already been in touch with me on the subject of fees. I must say I thought it was rather a nice gesture.'

'He's a good chap,' Antony agreed. 'Did you know, by the way, that Briggs was in the theatre last night?'

'Was he though? No, I didn't know that. It was Detective Chief Inspector Sykes who appeared in court as the investigating officer, and though Mr Buckley did mention another man had been present at his questioning, a big man going bald, I didn't connect the description with Briggs.'

'Well, he was there as large as life,' said Antony resignedly. 'And I'm only telling you because Uncle Nick's sure to ask me if I've done so. He thinks we should be prepared for squalls.'

'No harm in that,' said Geoffrey soberly, giving the briefcase a last pat and picking it up. 'I'll see you in the morning then, but don't come down and wait in the cold, I'll ring the bell when I arrive. If the traffic's heavy I can't say to a minute when what will be.'

IV

Roger Farrell arrived that evening just as Antony and Jenny were clearing the table after dinner. He was such a regular visitor that even Gibbs didn't insist on announcing him, and as the door of the upstairs flat was open in anticipation of his visit he came straight

67

in, possessed himself of the tray, and preceded them into the kitchen. 'Have you eaten, Roger?' asked Jenny anxiously. 'I can easily warm something up for you if you'd like.'

'Not this evening, Jenny, thank you. I ate early with Meg. She's in a bit of a tizzy about tonight's performance, more so than usual, though I expect you'll think that's natural. So I took her to the theatre and waited while she got her makeup on, and then left her to it. That fellow Murray had come in to talk to her, so she wasn't without company.'

'I expect she'd have preferred yours,' said Jenny, setting the coffee pot on a low flame to drip. 'Leave the tray on the table, Roger, it's Mrs Clean's morning tomorrow so I'm not going to wash up. We can use this little one for the coffee cups.'

'The thing is,' Roger confided, obeying her, 'I can't stand the chap.'

'Never mind. He's an interesting corpse by the end of the first act,' said Antony. 'You didn't feel you wanted to see the last half of the play?'

'Frankly, no. I don't know what it is,' he added disconsolately as they all went through into the living room, 'Meg doing this particular one seems to have got under my skin somehow.'

'More than usual?' asked Jenny sympathetically, but Antony was following his own train of thought.

'I warned you before you married her,' he said, 'that the theatre was in her blood.'

'So you did, and I've tried to live up to what I said then, that I'd never interfere. Are Uncle Nick and Vera coming up later?' he added.

'I should think it very likely,' said Antony with a little dryness in his tone.

'Then I'll sit here by you, Jenny. And Antony, I expect, will hover over us,' said Roger, knowing his friend's habits well enough. Maitland grinned at him, settled himself on the hearth rug as Roger had predicted, and returned without hesitation to the point that interested him.

'But this time you're finding it even more difficult than usual, aren't you?' he said.

'Yes, I am.' It was obvious that Roger, here with his most intimate friends, was in a mood for confidences. 'You see,' he said, 'I'm not at all sure why she wanted to take this part.'

'It's a good play,' Antony pointed out. 'You saw part of it for yourself last night, and Jenny says the second act is just as exciting.'

68

'That isn't the point. In any case, I attended one rehearsal so that isn't a surprise to me. She's played with this fellow Murray – Andy she calls him – before,' said Roger, returning to his grievance, 'and I'm not at all sure that isn't the reason –'

'Don't be so silly, Roger,' said Jenny, exasperated. 'You know perfectly well Meg hasn't looked at another man since you were married. And anyway,' she added, hoping this might be of some consolation to him, 'they're at daggers drawn in the play, so they don't have any love scenes together.'

'That isn't the point either,' said Roger a little ruefully. 'I've got used to seeing her in another man's arms on stage. No, I just have this feeling, she knew I didn't want her to take the part ... and don't say again that you warned me, Antony, or I'll probably do something violent.'

'I won't,' said Antony pacifically. 'Like Jenny, I think you're just about as wrong as you can be, but as for that, who lives may learn. The only members of the cast I've heard her comment on are the Buckleys; she's violently pro-Leonard, did you know that?'

'Yes, I did,' said Roger. 'But even I couldn't be jealous of Leonard,' he added with an attempt at humour that was more usual with him than all this gloom. 'She told me all about your meeting at lunch time.'

'Did you know Jeremy Skelton's paying for the defence?'

'Yes, I did. I think it's pretty decent of him. Nice chap,' said Roger approvingly.

'He's reserving judgement about Mr Buckley's guilt or innocence, just wants to make sure that everything is done that can be. And Meg can't offer me any proof of her theory, just a feeling.'

'Well, she ought to know more about it than the rest of us do,' said Roger. 'I've always found her a pretty reliable judge. She also told me your theory as to why Superintendent Briggs was in the audience last night.'

'I only propounded it because Jeremy asked me.'

'Yes, but I dare say it's right. And I suppose it was stupid of me never to have thought before that the kind of interest he's shown in Jeremy might apply equally to me.'

'Do you think it occurred to Meg?' Antony asked, and almost in the same breath, 'I don't know what you're talking about,' said Jenny.

'If you think about it, love, you'll know the answer as well as I do.' Rather belatedly he had learned that Jenny could face up to anything so long as he was frank with her. 'You know we discovered over the Selden affair that in spite of everything that's happened Briggs still doesn't trust me?'

'Yes, of course I remember that.'

'Well, I think it follows – I didn't spell this out for you, Jenny, there didn't seem to be any need to – that he thinks some of the acquittals I've obtained in the past have been obtained unfairly.'

'Yes, you said that last night, but–'

'What Antony means, Jenny,' Roger intervened, 'is that Superintendent Briggs may well still think that I was hand in glove with Uncle Hubert when he was involved in all those bullion robberies, and was probably his accomplice later when he came out of prison and was trying to recover the gold.'

'That's just silly,' said Jenny. 'Isn't it, Antony?'

'No, love, I don't think so. I wish I did. If I thought any other members of the force agreed with him I'd seriously consider retiring altogether, but so long as it's only Briggs I don't suppose there's much harm done.'

'Well, I know how I'd feel if I was a client of yours,' said Jenny with her chin in the air, a gesture she'd caught from Meg. 'If I was really innocent, I mean. I'd rather go free because you found out the truth, even if it meant the superintendent had a bee in his bonnet about me for the rest of his life.'

Roger put his arm round her shoulders and gave her a quick hug. 'Hear, hear!' he said. 'There's nothing to worry about Jenny, really.'

'I'm not,' said Jenny. Which was probably the literal truth. Antony had realised long since that it was physical danger to him that appalled her, rather than the more subtle difficulties which he himself found equally alarming. Even so he wasn't altogether sorry when he heard the outer door open, and went out into the hall to greet his uncle and Vera.

He'd been expecting them, knowing perfectly well that Sir Nicholas didn't really approve of his taking on Leonard Buckley's defence and wanted to be kept completely up to date with everything that was happening. Consequently, the day's activities had to be gone over once again. 'So it's your wife who's encouraging Antony to embroil himself in this affair,' said Sir Nicholas accusingly to Roger when Antony had finished speaking.

'I thought that was Geoffrey Horton's doing,' said Roger, straight-faced.

'There's nothing decided yet,' said Maitland in a hurry. 'When I've talked to my client I may decide he's as guilty as hell, in which case it will just be a matter of a court appearance. I'll study my brief, of course,' he added, probably thinking as he spoke that if Geoffrey Horton had been present he wouldn't have believed a word of this last statement.

'It isn't that that I'm afraid of,' said Sir Nicholas. 'If you once get it into your head that this is a case where that infernal meddling of yours is justified –'

'I'll have Superintendent Briggs thinking all over again that I'm rigging the evidence,' Antony interrupted him. His uncle appeared to go into a swoon, but opened his eyes after a moment to say, 'I agree that was in my mind.'

'We were just talking about that. He thinks I'm paranoid,' said Antony shrugging, 'and that I can't bear to lose a case.'

'I have often said much the same thing about you to your aunt, my dear boy,' said Sir Nicholas annoyingly. And added, whether to soften the blow or make doubly sure it was on target, 'You don't approach your briefs with the proper cynicism.'

'That isn't true, Uncle Nick.' But he left the subject rather abruptly. 'Anyway, what harm can Briggs do? He can't get up in court and say I've been tampering with the witnesses. An unsupported statement like that would be the end of his credibility and he knows it.'

'That may be so, but ... would you say you are becoming an obsession with him, Antony?'

'I'd say exactly that.'

'Then what is there to prevent him from doing a little – what was that foul phrase you used – rigging the evidence against you himself?'

'He wouldn't go as far as that,' said Antony positively.

'Don't be too sure, my boy. And he may have some justification,' said Sir Nicholas thoughtfully. 'Roger will agree with me, even if Vera and Jenny don't, that on occasion you'd madden a saint.'

'Are you suggesting that I give up criminal practice, Uncle Nick?'

'Far from it, only that you do what you can to avoid any contacts with Briggs that may tend to exacerbate his feelings towards you.'

'Our meeting last night was purely fortuitous.'

'Yes, of course it was. And as for giving up your criminal practice, Antony,' said Sir Nicholas, reverting to a point that seemed to be causing him some anxiety, 'that's the last thing I should suggest. After all, there has to be someone besides Kevin O'Brien to take on all the hopeless cases that come before the courts.'

'I see what you mean,' said Antony, and smiled perfectly spontaneously for the first time that evening.

'However,' his uncle went on, 'I should like to take issue with you on one statement you made just now. Vera will agree with me – won't you, my dear? – that while we were discussing the matter last night some thought came into your mind that predisposed you to believe this contention of Meg's as to Leonard Buckley's innocence.'

'Think it was obvious,' said Vera at her most elliptical.

'It was quite a small point,' said Antony, 'nothing conclusive about it either way. But it did occur to me that when Mr Buckley saw his wife lying there, and particularly when he went over to her and must have suspected she was dead, he was genuinely distressed about it; either because he had some affection left for her in spite of all he had said on the subject, or because he really felt he couldn't get on without her.'

'I knew it! Far from going into this with an open mind you're convinced already – ' Sir Nicholas broke off there and threw up his hands in a despairing gesture. Jenny got up quietly and went to rummage in the cupboard for the cognac bottle while Antony endeavoured, without too much success, to persuade his uncle that he was quite wrong in his conclusion.

I

Perhaps the traffic the next morning wasn't as heavy as Geoffrey had expected. In any event he arrived in good time in Kempenfeldt Square, and Antony came downstairs and out into the car, grumbling as he got in about the weather, which was still very cold, though Horton knew him well enough to be aware of the real cause of his ill humour. There was nothing unfamiliar about the routine of visiting their client at Brixton, where he had been taken after the magistrate's court hearing . . . the heavy doors swinging open, clanging shut, and then the grating sound of a key in the lock. To Maitland it was a recurrent nightmare, and he was glad that once they had reached the waiting room they weren't kept waiting long. Leonard Buckley was ushered in by a warder, who then closed the door firmly, leaving himself in the corridor outside; though as Antony knew well enough he was still on guard.

Even the two nights he had spent in confinement had changed the actor. He no longer looked a spry seventy year old but a much older man. Geoffrey, seeing him hesitating, went quickly to take his arm and guide him to a chair at the end of the table, and Leonard followed his guidance docilely enough, but rather as though he really couldn't see. He sank into the chair and looked up at Antony standing at the other end of the table. 'Mr Maitland,' he said rather hesitantly. 'Mr Horton told me you'd come, but I thought perhaps you wouldn't want to have anything more to do with me.'

'Now why should you think that?' asked Antony as bracingly as he could. It occurred to him that he was probably not helping matters by looming over the prisoner so he sat down himself, though as so often happened he would have much preferred to remain standing. 'I'm sorry we have to meet again like this, and I think I should start by expressing my sympathy at the loss of your wife.'

'My poor girl! You know, Mr Maitland, I don't expect you to believe this but when I realised what had happened all I could think of was how she looked the first time I saw her, in a blue dress and wearing a fair wig. You can't think how pretty she looked. And

73

I was just sorry it had ended like this, and more sorry than ever that there had been no reconciliation. She was seven years younger than I am, you know.'

Geoffrey also had seated himself. 'And now I'm afraid we're going to have to ask you to put aside your grief, Mr Buckley, and tell us again exactly what happened. I've given Mr Maitland the gist of your statement, but I think he'd like to hear it from you again, and I'm sure that in addition he'll have some questions for you.'

'Yes, of course, I'm at your service gentlemen,' said Buckley looking from one of them to the other. 'Where do you want me to start?'

'I think we'll begin with your first interview with the police,' said Antony. 'You were the first person backstage to be interviewed, weren't you?'

'The first one called out of the Green Room to be interviewed,' Buckley corrected him. 'You know there was quite a crowd of us gathered there, all the members of the cast, some of the understudies, yourself and Mr Farrell from the front of the house, and Mr Skelton, who had also come backstage. But when I went in – there were three policemen present, a man whom I took to be very senior and who didn't speak much, Chief Inspector Sykes who gave evidence yesterday when I appeared in court, and a constable who was taking notes – it was quite obvious that they'd had an account of what had happened from somebody, at least they knew that I'd been alone on the stage with Andy and poor Victoria when the lights went on again.'

'Did they also know that you should have made your exit again by that time?'

'They certainly did. If you want my impressions, Mr Maitland, the inspector was very open-minded, at least he didn't display any hostility towards me, but I sensed something in the other man, the one who didn't speak much, as if he had already judged me and found me guilty.'

'There was no question of their warning you? You know what I mean by that?'

'Not at that stage. They asked me to explain the action on the stage immediately before the – the fatality. Was the darkness expected?'

'Perhaps then you'll explain it to us as you explained it to them.'

'Certainly, certainly. We had reached the stage where Andy and his aunt were sitting together, arguing over his conduct, of which

74

she didn't approve. On cue the lights were to go out and both would have fallen silent very soon. I know Bill Kemp, the stage manager, said he was going to attend to that himself on the first night, to make sure nothing went wrong. I was in the wings waiting with the property dagger, with which Andy was supposed to be killed. The idea was that the audience should be conscious of the movement on the stage even though they couldn't see a thing, and in addition, in view of the fact that the dagger was supposed to be driven up to the hilt in his back, it would be rather difficult for him to fix it himself. We found our way about the stage in those circumstances by the use of a small amount of phosphorescent paint – '

'Yes, Meg explained that to me.'

' – and there was also a mark on the back of Andy's jacket, so that I knew where to fix the weapon. You know that they say now that that had been done to Victoria too, but I didn't notice it even though I passed behind her chair on my way to Andy's. I was concentrating on the marks on the furniture that would lead me to him.'

'And then?'

'I got right across, fixed the dagger in place, and heard him fall forward, giving that long sigh which I thought myself was extremely effective dramatically. Then I started back across the stage, and it was then that someone brushed past me.'

'Wait a bit! If I remember the setting of that scene correctly, and the person that touched you had just stabbed your wife, he must have entered from the left of the stage as we looked at it from the audience, and be making his way back into the wings by the same route.'

'Yes, when I think about it that is how it must have been.'

'And such a man, too, could have found his way about the stage by these paint marks that you mentioned?'

'Oh yes, certainly. But I don't think I can convey to you,' Leonard went on, 'what a shock he gave me. You see there shouldn't have been anybody wandering round the stage except myself. Victoria was supposed to have stayed in her chair, until the lights went on again and she saw Andy lying dead when she would have screamed and the rest of the cast – as far as they had appeared so far that is – would have rushed in.'

'You were so startled that you stood quite still for a moment?'

'That's right. For long enough for the lights to go on again. I think the fact that I was the only one there, except for Andy lying where he had fallen, made them immediately suspicious. In any

75

case, they asked me to turn out my pockets, and that's when the gloves came to light – of course I knew they were there all the time – of which they made such a point at the hearing.'

'Did they ask you who was at that side of the stage, the side from which the murderer must have come, if it was indeed he you bumped into.'

Leonard considered that question, his head a little on one side. 'I'm not sure I like the way you put that, Mr Maitland,' he said. 'Do you believe me or don't you when I say I didn't kill Victoria?'

'It isn't what I think, Mr Buckley, it's what the jury comes to believe.'

'I see,' Leonard sighed. 'Well, I can't expect anything else, I suppose.'

'You didn't answer my question.'

'Yes, they did ask me that and I couldn't help them. Except that I supposed most of the cast would be gathered there, ready to rush on when Victoria screamed. So after that they let me go, but they asked me to wait in my dressing room and I think there was a policeman in the corridor.'

'And then later on –'

'They asked me to accompany them to the police station to make a statement.'

'Still no warning?'

'Oh yes, this time they went through that formality.'

'Just exactly what did you admit to the police, Mr Buckley?'

'I've always found it the best policy to be truthful, Mr Maitland.' This was said with some dignity, but then he relaxed a little. 'In any case they seemed to know about what had been happening between Victoria and me, so there didn't seem to be any harm –'

'Had it been suggested to you that you should have a solicitor present before you made this statement?'

'Oh yes, but I didn't know who to send for. It was only later that I found Meg's note.'

'It didn't come to light when you turned out your pockets and the gloves were discovered?'

'No, they were in the right hand pocket of my jacket, the first place I looked. And after that the police seemed to lose interest and I didn't look any further. Only later I put my hands in my pockets, which is a bad habit of mine when I'm nervous, and found the note then.'

'You say that all you know about other people's whereabouts

is that some of the actors at least must have been on the opposite side from that from which you entered.'

'Yes, that's right.'

'Is that all you can tell me in that direction?'

'Only that there was nobody on my side of the stage when the lights went out except the prompter.'

'Could he have followed you on in the darkness?'

'If his intention had been to stab Victoria, he wouldn't have needed to be as far across as the man was whom I bumped into.'

'I see. That brings us to Andy Murray, then.'

'He was certainly in his chair when I reached it, and I'm quite sure he fell on the floor as arranged. Are you thinking about him, Mr Maitland, because he gave some evidence at the hearing which was not exactly beneficial to me?'

'No, at this stage I'm thinking of anybody and everybody.'

'It's difficult to say, but as a matter of timing my impression is that he could have done it. In which case he would have been returning to his own place when I bumped into him. But you know I simply can't believe —'

Maitland smiled ruefully. 'People never can believe anything really bad about people they know,' he said. 'It's one of the banes of our lives, isn't it, Geoffrey? All the same it leads to another question, you told me once that nobody had a motive for wanting you dead, but of course at the time I didn't think to ask you if the same applied to Mrs Buckley. What do you think about it now?'

'I don't think Victoria had an enemy in the world,' said Leonard Buckley very positively indeed.

'Think about it a little.'

'Mr Maitland, you know I told you there couldn't be any financial motive for disposing of me, and the same applies to her of course.'

'There are other motives.'

'To my cost, I know there are. The police think I have one,' said Leonard, 'but I do assure you, however difficult the situation had become between us, I wouldn't have dreamed —'

'It isn't Mr Horton and me you have to convince, Mr Buckley, but the jury,' said Maitland rather sharply.

'Well, there isn't anybody who could possibly have wanted her dead,' Buckley protested. 'I can't help you there.'

Geoffrey Horton rather expected his colleague to point out that it was the prisoner himself who needed help, far more than his

77

lawyers did. However, Antony only said mildly, 'Then let's talk about the dagger.'

'I'd never seen it before.'

'Nor seen it in the possession of any of your fellow actors?'

'Certainly not.'

'Have you a more detailed description of it, Geoffrey?'

'Not yet.'

'Still, from what we've been told it must be a fairly distinctive piece. It shouldn't be too hard to trace.'

'I don't really agree with you there,' Leonard Buckley broke in eagerly. 'It's the sort of thing I should have thought someone might have had in the family for centuries.'

'Well, unless they kept it hidden in the attic that shouldn't prove too insuperable a difficulty.' Maitland turned to the solicitor. 'Have you any other questions you want to put to Mr Buckley, Geoffrey?'

'I think you've covered everything for the moment.'

'Exactly ... for the moment. We may need to see you again, Mr Buckley, and have some more questions for you.' Leonard started to get to his feet, but was halted by a gesture. 'Before we leave you however, there's something we should tell you. In spite of the fact that we have been instructed that you will plead Not Guilty, we should be failing in our duty if we didn't put certain possibilities before you. I don't, frankly, think that a plea of Not Guilty by reason of insanity would be either justifiable or acceptable to the court.'

'I'm not mad,' said Leonard Buckley rather huffily.

'That's just what I meant. My uncle, Sir Nicholas Harding, when I talked the matter over with him, suggested self defence, but of course he didn't intend me to take that idea seriously. I only mention it because it may be something that has occurred to you. But it would presuppose reasonable grounds for your belief that your wife was trying to poison you, which I don't think could be established, and also that no more force than necessary was used ... again, not altogether consistent with the facts.'

'I had wondered,' Buckley agreed, but rather doubtfully as though all this confused him.

'There remains diminished responsibility,' Maitland went on, 'which we might have some hope of establishing if the jury could be persuaded that you were genuinely, but mistakenly, of the opinion that Mrs Buckley's continued existence posed a threat to you. Success with that plea might result in a conviction for manslaughter rather than murder.'

'But I didn't kill her!'

'So you have told us. It is, however, necessary to put the alternatives to you, before you reach a final decision.'

'You're trying to tell me that if I admitted to killing Victoria I might get away with a lighter sentence.'

'If we could establish our claim,' said Maitland precisely. 'The question is, could you?'

'In the circumstances I think so, but of course I can't guarantee it.'

'I don't know why I'm discussing it at all,' said Buckley, giving himself a kind of shake as though to remove a load that was resting on his shoulders. 'I'm not guilty, and that's all there is to it.'

This time it was Maitland who got to his feet and the other two men followed suit. 'Very well, Mr Buckley, your position is noted,' he said formally. 'If I don't see you again myself before the trial Mr Horton will be in touch. But it may be necessary – '

'I should of course be delighted to see you,' said Buckley, and Antony smiled sympathetically.

'One way of passing the time,' he suggested.

'As you say yourself ... exactly.' But by now Geoffrey had succeeded in attracting the warder's attention, and the door was unlocked, and the man departed with his prisoner in one direction while the two lawyers took the opposite way.

II

Geoffrey waited until they were back into the car again before he spoke. He was well enough aware of his friend's emotions, and of Antony's relief – illogical though it might be – when the outer gate finally clanged to behind them. 'What did you make of that?' he said, his hand on the ignition key.

'I was just about to ask you the same thing,' said Antony, stretching himself out comfortably. 'What do you make of our client?'

'He says he's not guilty,' said Geoffrey.

'That wasn't what I asked you.'

The car moved smoothly forward and there was a moment's silence until Geoffrey had safely insinuated it into the main stream of traffic. 'I think,' he said then slowly, 'that your plea of diminished responsibility would be just about right. He definitely had a bee in his bonnet about his wife, and living together as they did the atmosphere must have been enough to drive anyone to violence. And that brings me back to *my* question.'

'I like the old boy,' said Antony, 'but I wish he'd told us all the truth.'

'You think he was lying, then?'

'In places, yes.'

If Geoffrey was tempted to take his eyes off the road and to glance at his companion, he resisted the idea. 'And yet you believe him when he says he didn't kill his wife,' he said positively.

'What? Oh I know, I spoke to him once a little abruptly.' Maitland had his moments of regretting Geoffrey's percipience where his reactions were concerned. 'You must allow me to digress from my normal pattern of behaviour from time to time,' he added.

'Yes, of course, but I don't think you were doing that just now. What exactly didn't you believe?'

'He'd certainly seen the dagger before,' said Antony, 'he denied it much too quickly. And I think – though I'm not quite so sure about this – that he also might have had some idea as to what the motive for killing Mrs Buckley might have been.'

'Why didn't he tell us, then?'

'Guilt, I dare say. No, I don't mean that he killed her himself, but he certainly feels badly now about the position between them.'

'You may be right. And about the weapon, as you pointed out, it should be easy to trace. But about the details of the prosecution's case, I dare say I can hurry them up a bit into giving me an idea on the telephone of exactly what evidence they'll be producing. The question is, what are *you* going to do?'

'You mean, am I going to indulge in what Uncle Nick calls meddling? You know, Geoffrey, I think I am.'

'Is that because you have a settled belief in Mr Buckley's innocence, or is it just a piece of damned obstinacy?' asked Geoffrey bluntly.

'Now, why should it be the latter I wonder?'

'Because we've all been warning you about getting mixed up in anything Chief Superintendent Briggs has the slightest connection with,' Geoffrey told him.

'Well, I don't think it's the latter,' said Antony positively. But later he was to think over what Geoffrey said and wonder about it. It wasn't in his nature to pass by on the other side if there was the slightest chance of Leonard Buckley's innocence. But to interfere for purely selfish motives would have been a worse crime than he felt he could contemplate.

Geoffrey had a luncheon engagement so Antony made his way to Astroff's alone, and found his uncle sitting in solitary state at their usual table. 'Are you waiting for someone, Uncle Nick?' he asked, 'or may I join you?'

'Do so by all means, my dear boy,' said his uncle cordially. He gave his nephew a hard look as he seated himself and didn't much like what he saw. 'I thought you might have Geoffrey with you,' he went on.

'No, he had someone to meet. And –'

'And you're glad enough to be rid of him for the time being,' said Sir Nicholas. 'You don't want to talk about this case you've embarked on so rashly, I know that, but all the same there are things I want to know.'

'I've already accepted the brief, Uncle Nick.'

'You know as well as I do, Antony, that wasn't what I meant.' He paused while the waiter took Maitland's order and then went on as though there had been no interruption, 'As you're being so evasive, I take it you've decided there's – what's that phrase you use? – a matter for investigation?'

'If you must have it, yes I do think so.'

'I wonder why,' said Sir Nicholas. 'Not, I imagine, merely because Meg has assured you that Mr Buckley is innocent.'

Antony grinned at that. 'Hardly,' he replied. 'Geoffrey insists that's the conclusion I've come to myself, but I think he's a little ahead of the game. I wouldn't say I'm anything like certain.'

'Does Geoffrey agree with you?'

'No, he thinks it would be a very good case for pleading diminished responsibility, stressing Leonard Buckley's delusion that his wife was trying to kill him.'

'I'd say that might be a good line myself.'

'Yes, but our client doesn't happen to agree. He insists he's not guilty, and who am I to argue?'

'So you're going to try to prove it?'

'Look here, Uncle Nick, all I've decided at the moment is to probe a little and see if I can make up my own mind one way or the other. If I decide that after all Geoffrey's assessment is the right one ... you know as well as I do that there are ways and ways of getting an idea like that over to the court, even without infringing one's client's instructions.'

'I seem to remember,' said Sir Nicholas reflectively, 'that when you first talked to Leonard Buckley you didn't believe that his wife was trying to poison him.'

'I didn't believe there was any proof,' Antony corrected him. 'I haven't really any opinion one way or the other.' He eyed his uncle assessingly for a moment. If Sir Nicholas wanted the whole story he was going to get it one way or the other, and it might be less painful to give him it straight away than to have it extracted bit by bit under cross-examination throughout the meal. 'Geoffrey is rather of the opinion that I'm motivated mainly by dislike for Briggs. And by a pigheaded desire to go against the advice of all my friends and relations.'

'Did he say that?'

'He asked me if I was sure that wasn't the case, which comes to the same thing.'

'And are you?'

The waiter came back then, and Antony paused to sip his drink before replying. 'To tell you the truth, Uncle Nick,' he said then, grinning, 'I examined my conscience on the subject on the way back into town, but I came to the conclusion that I was being falsely accused.'

'I'm glad to hear it. My objections to your participating in this business still stand however.'

'Yes, I'm sure they do.'

'How do you propose to proceed?'

'I phoned Skelton from the lobby as I came in. He's free this afternoon and if I go round to the flat he'll be glad to tell me whatever he learned from the actors at the special rehearsal yesterday afternoon. I shall then go home to tea, and Gibbs will be hovering in the hall and give me an evil look, silently accusing me of slacking. But that won't be the case, because Meg is going to tea with Jenny and I want to know what she can tell me about what went on backstage on Wednesday night. By then, with any luck, Geoffrey will have got a few more details about the prosecution's case. The depositions won't be ready of course, but he seemed to think he might get something by word of mouth.'

'That should be interesting,' said Sir Nicholas thoughtfully. 'I shouldn't be surprised if Vera and I came up to see you later in the evening.'

'No, I rather thought you might. And if you want to know what I'm going to do after all that Uncle Nick, I can't tell you. It will all depend.'

'I shall hope to be enlightened on that point this evening,' said Sir Nicholas. 'Tell me a little about your talk with Mr Buckley.

In spite of your qualifications, I gather you're inclined to believe his story.'

'On the contrary, I think he was lying like a trooper half the time,' said Antony, and buried his nose in the menu and resolutely declined to answer any more questions for the time being. Though he relented a little when they reached the coffee stage, and gave his uncle an extremely succinct account of the visit to the prison that morning.

IV

If he went back to chambers there would be some reproachful looks from Mr Mallory to contend with, like Gibbs he had never entirely approved of his employer's nephew. So Antony walked back to the Skeltons' flat in Avery Street at a pace just brisk enough to keep the cold at bay, resisting the temptation as he crossed Kempenfeldt Square to turn into the familiar door of number five. Jeremy let him in and led the way into a pleasantly furnished living room which would nonetheless have seemed rather bleak and imper-sonal if Anne had not contrived in some way to add a few touches that made it seem like a home. She gave him a rather anxious look as he went in, which puzzled him later, though at the time he was so busy answering Jeremy's questions about his talk with Leonard Buckley that he hadn't time to consider the matter at all. And by the time Skelton's curiosity was satisfied – or, more correctly, when he had given up hope of its ever being satisfied – his wife was again her quiet, unobtrusive self. 'It isn't fair to keep Antony standing about while you fire questions at him, Jeremy,' she said. 'Why don't you both sit down?'

'Yes, of course, I'm sorry,' said Jeremy, but stayed on his feet. Antony took the nearest chair, because he thought his hostess would feel more comfortable if he did so.

'So I've come to see what you've learned about Wednesday night,' he said.

'Opportunity,' said Jeremy in a very business-like way. 'It's not much good asking Anne or myself about motive, because we've only known the people concerned for a few weeks. Unless,' he whirled round to look at his wife, 'has someone been confiding in you, Anne?'

'I think I've talked to them – to the members of the cast at least – a little more than you have, Jeremy. You've always been completely taken up with what was going on on the stage, but I must admit that after about the twentieth time of seeing it even your play, darling, began to pall a little.'

'There you see!' Jeremy turned to Antony with a look of satisfaction. 'Perhaps we can help you there after all.'

'I didn't say that,' said Anne nervously. 'Why don't you tell Antony about the opportunity part, then I'll see what I can do.'

'Well, you know what was supposed to happen after the lights went on again,' said Jeremy. 'There'd be a moment for the audience to take in what had happened, that Andy Murray was lying there dead, and then Victoria would start to scream. That would bring the rest of the cast running, and they'd all enter from the same side of the stage, which I understand is called the off-prompt side, because that is supposed to lead to the hall. The Buckleys – Donald Turnstall and Gladys Turnstall – were staying in the house, and that was why Leonard entered from the prompt side. So there was Meg, and Gordon Hewitt, and Ellie Dorman, all the people who'd appeared already, standing in the wings ready to enter, though not all at once, of course.'

'In what order?'

'Ellie Dorman first –'

'It's all very well for you, Jeremy, you know them by their real names. I'm more familiar with the people they were playing.'

'Well, Ellie Dorman is Paula Nash, do you remember now?'

'Yes, of course, she was in love with Meg's husband, Douglas Carteret, who is really this fellow Andrew Murray,' said Maitland, unconsciously echoing Roger's phrasing.

'Yes, and that gave her a chance for a good deal of emoting, you see, before the other two came on, the other two being Meg and her lover, played by Gordon Hewitt. So they were all standing together when the lights went out, with Ellie a little ahead of the others. That was behind the closed door at the back of the stage that's supposed to lead to the hall, as I told you. But the two men who play the police officers in the second act – you never saw them Antony, they hadn't appeared when the murder took place – were also watching from the wings at that side of the stage, and Meg's understudy was with them. There's one place in the wings where you can watch what's happening quite well.'

'So that's two groups of people suddenly plunged into blackness, though of course they were expecting it. Could any of them have gone on stage without the others knowing?'

'Any one of them I should think. In addition to the points of vantage I've mentioned there is also a garden door, which is standing open because the action takes place in summer. Any one of them could have got on to the stage that way, and Meg says they're all accustomed to moving quietly, because of this business of getting around in a blackout, you know.'

'I should have thought if one of the group left –'

'I said they were standing together, not that they were all locked in a close embrace one with another,' said Jeremy rather tartly.

'I'll take your word for it. You seem to be concentrating on the actors,' Antony observed.

'Yes, and for a very good reason. Two reasons in fact. The first is that they'd be much better able to find their way around in the dark by the marks of phosphorescent paint that have been mentioned than anybody else.'

'Anybody with business backstage could have got at the paint to daub it on Victoria Buckley's dress, however.'

'Yes, I dare say they could. I still maintain that someone who'd never done it before would find it difficult to move around without bumping into something,' said Jeremy. 'Besides, there's my second reason. I did a bit of detective work myself, and discovered where everybody was. In the case of Kevin Elliott, the director in case you'd forgotten, I didn't need to ask any questions because I knew quite well where he was . . . he'd come up to my box to join us, having decided that everything was going well. Bill Kemp, the stage manager, was attending to the lights himself, and I don't think he could have got to the switch and then on to the stage and back again in time. The rest of the understudies were all together in the Green Room, they also had come to the conclusion that everything was going well and there was no need to stand by with bated breath waiting for a chance to come on.'

'There were other people around though. I'm very vague about this, but surely there'd be some stage hands, people's dressers, that kind of thing.'

'It isn't everyone who has a dresser, you know,' said Jeremy, 'and I'm not trying to sound like a know-it-all. I was just as vague myself a couple of months ago. But it was the end of the act, or very nearly, so those there were were in the dressing rooms or in the corridor near them, I gather they didn't even hear the commotion on stage. There wasn't a big scene change to do, so the stage hands weren't standing around either. Most of them, I think, were having a quiet game of poker in the stage doorkeeper's little room. That too was beyond the range of the blackout, so there was no question of any of them leaving and sneaking on stage. The only other person I can think of is the prompter, Leonard must have seen him as he came on.'

'I've a reason for thinking the murderer entered from the other side,' said Antony. He would have left it there, but Jeremy took him up quickly.

'You're thinking, if Leonard didn't do it himself,' he said accusingly.

'I thought you too were in some doubt about that.'

'The thing is,' Anne put in, 'we'd so much hoped you'd believe him innocent. He's really rather a dear.'

'The fact that I'm here at all should tell you that I feel there are a few more questions to be asked, before we take his guilt for granted,' Antony told her. 'That's the best I can do I'm afraid.'

'Don't worry, Anne darling. If there's anything to find, Antony will find it,' said Jeremy with sudden change of front. 'And I suppose you can't discuss tactics even with me. But I'll tell you something, I'll be glad to see him back in his part again. Monica's doing quite well, but David seems completely confused by being made up as an elderly man. He's word perfect but he hasn't got into the skin of the part at all.'

'Did you have your full house last night?'

'Oh yes, indeed we did. And I'm told we're booked up for goodness knows how long,' said Jeremy. 'And I know I sounded pleased about that at first, but now I've thought it over I'd like the play just to stand on its own feet. People should come because they'd heard it was a good evening's entertainment, not because they hoped the cast would go on slaughtering each other.'

'I don't think you need be afraid of that,' said Antony quite seriously. 'It's a good play and will stand on its own feet very well when the sensation-seekers have finished with it. That's all about opportunity, Jeremy, and very well dealt with too. Which I suppose I should have expected from someone in your line of business. And now it's Anne's turn. You thought you might be able to help me on the question of motive, Anne.'

'Not exactly that. Just that I've gathered this and that about the people in the play in talking to them,' said Anne rather diffidently. 'But it's rather a nasty business, isn't it? I mean, whether Buckley is guilty or not, there's no question that someone we know did it. Jeremy pointed that out to me last night.'

Jeremy who had been standing all this time went across to sit on the arm of her chair. 'The thing is, old girl,' he said, putting an arm round her shoulders, 'it's best to get at the truth even when it hurts.'

'Yes, I can see that. What do you want to know, Antony?'

'Anything and everything about these six people who seem the only possible alternatives to Leonard Buckley.'

'It's not so much that I know anything,' said Anne doubtfully, 'nothing definite about any of them. But watching them, and going backstage sometimes when rehearsals were actually in progress, I did get certain impressions.'

'About their relationships with each other?' Antony asked quickly.

'Yes, that's what I meant. I don't know whether that will be any help to Leonard at all.'

'Well, neither do I at this stage but it may give me a start. Come along, Anne, I'll be really grateful –'

'I didn't go backstage after the murder, you know that. But I've heard that Ellie Dorman had hysterics when she realised what had happened.'

'That's true. She was still in full flood when Roger and I arrived. Roger was concerned about Meg, of course, and I just followed him. It was all very confusing, particularly the hysterics bit, but luckily Meg had kept her head and was trying to comfort Miss Dorman.'

'Well, she's quite a quick witted person,' said Anne hesitantly.

'Yes, but what's the significance of that?'

'I think that at the same time she realised Victoria was dead she must have realised that Leonard's position was extremely precarious.'

'I dare say she did, but –'

'I'm telling this very badly. You see, Antony, it was obvious – must have been obvious to anyone – that she was extremely fond of Leonard.'

'Not to me,' said Jeremy.

'No, darling, but you were all taken up by the characters in the play, not with the real people.'

'You're implying she was in love with him,' said Antony slowly.

'Yes, that's what I meant.'

'Do you think he returned her affection?'

Anne smiled for a moment at the old fashioned phrase. 'He was always very correct, you know, always playing the part he'd perfected over the years on the stage. But I think there's a good chance he really did feel something for Ellie.'

'Well, that's interesting, though hardly helpful. What else did you observe, Anne?'

'The two younger men, Claude Aubin and Gordon Hewitt, both obviously detested Victoria and avoided her whenever they could.'

'Are you sure about that Anne,' Jeremy interrupted. 'Victoria was such an old duck I can't imagine anyone really disliking her.'

'Well, I can assure you those two did,' Anne insisted.

'What were their relations with Leonard Buckley then?'

'I don't think Gordon liked him much, though he wasn't so intense about it as he was about his feeling for Victoria. Claude seemed quite fond of him and that's something else that's queer, Antony, he's obviously in love with Frances Cathers, you know, Meg's understudy, but when the rehearsals started she wouldn't have anything to do with him. And then after a while, perhaps they'd just had a lover's tiff, they grew very close again. For some reason that didn't seem to please Victoria at all.'

'Come now, Anne, don't stop there. All this may be very helpful.'

'What is it telling you?' asked Jeremy curiously.

'Something about the dead woman for one thing. Come on, Anne,' he said again.

'There isn't much else really, except that Gordon Hewitt and Dominic Eldred always seem to be very close friends, and Dominic and the Buckleys obviously knew each other very well. Leonard and Dominic were always very polite to each other, but I think there was ... I don't quite know how to put it ... a lingering fondness between Dominic and Victoria.'

'As though they'd had an affaire in the past perhaps?'

'It's odd,' said Anne, 'it's awfully difficult to visualise older people in that light.'

'They were young once,' Antony pointed out.

'Yes, of course. Yes, it could have been that. I'm quite sure there was nothing between them now though.'

'We seem to have discussed everyone, except Andrew Murray.'

'I'd say Andy is a very normal person. His relationship with all these people seems perfectly easy.'

'There's something you're not telling me, Anne.'

She held his gaze steadily for a moment. 'There is something,' she acknowledged, 'but I don't like to say it to *you*.'

'You don't rely on my discretion?'

'It isn't that, of course it isn't that. It's just that there's one person we haven't mentioned.'

88

'Meg?' said Maitland sharply.

'Yes, that's right, and it's nothing that Meg did I want to tell you about, only it's perfectly obvious that Andy's crazy about her. And that certainly can't help you or Leonard,' she added with what sounded like relief.

'I'm afraid not,' Antony agreed. 'Is there anything else, Anne?'

'No, nothing else that I can think of.'

Antony stayed with the Skeltons for about half an hour after that. Anne looked distressed, he thought, and he wanted to reassure her that her observations were a starting point only, and had done no harm to anybody. When he left, Jeremy went out into the street with him, and lingered there a moment in spite of the coldness of the day. 'Anne isn't one to gossip,' he said rather abruptly.

'No, I know that. I don't consider what she told me this afternoon in that light, Jeremy.'

'It's something you taught her yourself all those years ago in Chedcombe,' Skelton informed him. 'Anything but the whole truth may put the wrong complexion on things.'

'Then I'm glad she was so apt a pupil.'

'I didn't say I agree with all she said,' Jeremy retorted. 'In fact I think it may be mostly imagination. But one thing she was right about, I have been seeing all these people as the characters they're playing in *Done in by Daggers*, so I don't suppose I'd have noticed much about them as people in their own right.'

'You needn't worry, you know, Jeremy. What Anne told me may be a guideline at most. I'm not going to call her to swear in court to what's only an opinion.'

'No, of course not.' All the same, Jeremy sounded relieved. 'How was Leonard anyway? You can tell me that, even though you can't talk about the rest of it.'

'Bearing up,' said Antony. And then, more revealingly than he intended, 'I don't think anybody enjoys being kept under lock and key and knowing they can't get out.'

'No,' said Jeremy thoughtfully. It was obvious that his mind had turned to the past for a moment. 'There, but for the grace of God and the assistance of Antony Maitland – ' he said after a pause, with an attempt at lightness. 'That, as I suppose you realise, is why I want to help with his defence.'

'The police aren't always wrong you know, even though they were in your case,' said Maitland, very much as he had told Anne, and again thought as he spoke, with a rather wry amusement, that he was only repeating something that had been said to him from time to time.

'No. Well, we shall see,' said Jeremy and gave a rather artificial shudder. 'I'd better be getting in, it's damn cold,' he said, and disappeared through the front door.

V

There was just the walk down Avery street, and then number five lay three doors from the corner when he turned into Kempenfeldt Square. Gibbs was at the back of the hall, as he had predicted, but Antony sustained his subtly conveyed disapproval well enough, and started up the stairs towards his own quarters. It was too early for Sir Nicholas to be home, but music from the direction of the drawing room told him that Vera was having a private recital of The Magic Flute.

As he had hoped and expected he found Jenny and Meg having tea together in the big living room at the front of the house. Jenny gave him a quick look, hoping he did not notice its anxiety, and saw at once that he was tired and that his shoulder was troubling him. There was a third cup on the tray and he put out a hand rather doubtfully to the tea pot. 'Are you sure you wouldn't like something stronger, Antony?' she asked. Which was as near as she would ever come to expressing her worry.

'No, tea will be fine. How are you, Meg? And how are the understudies progressing?'

'Monica is perfectly splendid,' said Meg. 'You'd think she was really Victoria's age. The make-up seems to bother David a bit, but he may be better tonight. Roger's coming here straight from the office,' she added, 'and Jenny's promised to feed me before I have to go to the theatre, so we've lots of time if you want to cross-examine me.'

'Have I ever done that, Meg?' Antony took his cup and went to sit down in the wing chair that had its back to the window.

'You know perfectly well, darling – ' Meg didn't attempt to finish the sentence, but Antony – casting his mind back a little – only grinned at her in reply.

'There are one or two things I'm curious about,' he admitted.

'Well, tell me first, how is Leonard?'

'As well as can be expected,' said Antony, and closed his eyes for a moment as though by doing so he might shut out the vision of the prison that had stayed with him all day.

'Well, have you come to the conclusion I'm right about him?' Meg demanded. 'He didn't do it.'

'He's pleading Not Guilty,' said Antony, temporising.

'Yes, but what do you think?'

'This and that,' said Antony. 'Meg, *darling*,' he added, parodying her own use of the word rather unkindly, 'as Superintendent Briggs might say, I'm here to ask questions, not to answer them.'

'Chief Superintendent,' said Jenny, rather enjoying being able to make the correction. Usually it was Antony who was reminding her of Chief Inspector Sykes's correct rank.

'Precisely.'

'If I've said it once I've said it a hundred times,' said Meg with dignity. 'You're getting exactly like Uncle Nick.'

'Never mind that. I want to know a lot more than you've told me yet. About your fellow actors, and about what happened immediately after the lights went on again.'

'I don't mind talking about what happened,' said Meg, 'but as for the rest you know I despise gossip.'

'Well, in this instance you're just going to have to make up your mind to it,' said Antony firmly. 'Who was it who told me that Leonard Buckley was innocent?'

'I did, of course, you know that perfectly well.'

'Then it's your clear duty to tell me anything you can that might help to clear him.'

'Antony's right you know, Meg,' said Jenny. 'If you really believe that what you told him is true—'

'Of course I believe it!' Meg sounded a little impatient, which was rare with her when she was speaking to Jenny. 'But as to the gossip, will it help?'

'I've got to start somewhere,' Maitland pointed out. 'I've been talking to Anne Skelton, and she has certain opinions about the various members of the cast. I'd like to know if yours coincide with them, that's all.'

'These people aren't her colleagues,' said Meg, 'she doesn't owe them any loyalty.'

'If Leonard Buckley is innocent, someone else is guilty,' Antony pointed out more patiently than he felt.

'Don't tell me the obvious, darling.'

'And you don't owe that person any loyalty.'

'No.'

'Then, as we don't know who it is, don't you think it would be better if you tell me anything and everything that you know?'

91

Meg glanced at Jenny and Jenny nodded encouragingly. 'You'll forget everything that isn't relevant immediately, won't you, darling?' Meg pleaded, turning back to Antony.

'You have my word,' said Antony solemnly. 'Tell me first, what did you really think of Victoria Buckley?'

'It isn't very easy,' said Meg reluctantly, 'to like somebody who doesn't like you.'

'That was bad taste on her part.' Antony couldn't altogether keep the amusement out of his voice. 'Do you really mean to tell me –?'

'She didn't like any younger women,' said Meg. 'So of course she particularly disliked poor Frances.'

'That's Frances Cathers, your understudy?'

'Yes, that's who I mean. But she didn't like Ellie either. Though I have to admit, from what she told me, she had some cause there.'

'You mean she confided in you?'

'Yes, just about that one thing,' said Meg very hesitantly. 'Do you know, Antony, I think she did it to make me uncomfortable, because she knows I don't like talking about other people. She said, Ellie had once had an affair with Leonard, and I haven't the faintest idea whether that was true or not. But certainly I think Ellie likes him.'

'There you see, it's not so difficult when you get going, is it?' said Antony. 'Now, from what I've heard, Meg, I'm particularly interested in the members of the cast who were gathered together in the wings on the off-prompt side.'

'I suppose I mustn't ask you to explain. Do you realise that includes me?'

'Yes, of course, but I've had enough opportunity over the years to form my own conclusions,' said Antony smiling. 'Andrew Murray was on the stage, but Gordon Hewitt and Ellie Dorman were standing near you in the wings.'

'That's quite right.'

'And you think either of them could have left you without your knowing it in the darkness?'

'Ellie was standing with her back to me, so I couldn't see whether her eyes were shut. And I didn't notice about Gordon either because my attention was fixed on the stage.'

'Wait a bit!' He paused a moment thinking that out. 'That's something that hadn't occurred to me, but I suppose you mean that anyone who wanted to find their way about the stage in the dark would have had to shield their eyes before the lights went out, otherwise they'd be as blind as the rest of us.'

'Yes, of course, I thought you'd realised that. Leonard would be standing in the wings at the other side, and he might even have had his hand over his eyes, as well as keeping them shut.'

'And Andrew Murray, in his character as your husband, wore dark glasses throughout the first act,' said Antony reflectively.

'That's just silly, if you're thinking what I think you are,' said Meg. 'Even his glasses – which are just ordinary sunglasses – wouldn't have shielded his eyes sufficiently from the full glare of the footlights.'

'Not even if he'd been sitting having his conversation with Victoria Buckley with his eyes shut behind them. Nobody would have known.'

'Not even then,' Meg insisted. 'Besides, Antony, he's the one person in the whole cast who had no sort of tension with anybody else. He's a very easy person to get on with and even Victoria seemed to like him.'

'We'll go back to the people in the wings then. You've told me about Gordon Hewitt and Ellie Dorman, but what about the others, the ones who were watching the action from nearer the front of the stage?'

'Dominic and Claude and Frances,' said Meg, reminding herself. 'I expect Frances felt about Victoria much as I did, that it's hard to like someone who doesn't like you. But the queer thing is that Claude didn't seem to like her either, though I can't think why. And that's one thing you might remember, Antony, those two might have been in a clinch.'

'Thank heaven Uncle Nick isn't here,' said Antony piously. 'Do you mean that Frances Cathers and Claude Aubin are lovers?'

'I should hesitate to say that about anybody,' said Meg primly, and with, as Antony knew, perfect truth. 'I don't know whether they are or not, but I think Claude would like to be.'

'And Mr Eldred?'

'Dominic? That's something else Victoria told me,' said Meg unwillingly. For a moment she had seemed to have forgotten her scruples, but now they were back in full force. 'She and Dominic were almost exactly the same in age, and she said he'd wanted to marry her before she married Leonard.'

'But she didn't want to marry him?'

'I think from what she said she might have done if Leonard hadn't come along. He was older, beginning to be established in the profession, and I suppose he seemed to be a more romantic figure to her. Anyway, that's what she said.'

'That seems to cover everybody,' said Antony, getting up and handing his cup to Jenny for a refill. For a moment he stood silent, watching as she poured the tea, then, still without turning, he went on, 'What remains, Meg, is something you won't mind talking about, I hope, though I think most people would find it more distressing to remember than other people's foibles.' He accepted the cup and went back to the fireplace, this time putting it on the mantelpiece near the clock. 'What happened when the lights came on?'

'We were all dazzled for a moment, I suppose, and the first thing I realised was that Leonard was still on stage, where of course he shouldn't have been. Andy was lying motionless with the dummy dagger apparently protruding from his back, just as the plot called for, and it took me a moment to realise that Victoria, far from preparing to go into her screaming act, was also lying on the floor. Then Leonard seemed to come to life and went to her, but you both saw that yourselves.'

'Yes, we did.' He exchanged a glance with Jenny, remembering that he had thought Leonard Buckley to be sincere in his distress. 'For all I knew, of course, the plot might have called for two corpses, it wasn't until Mr Buckley addressed his wife by her own name that I realised something must be very wrong, and Roger called to me to go backstage with him. I have to admit, Meg, that I found it very confusing, too confusing for me to notice anything, as I should ordinarily have tried to have done. What did Andrew Murray do?'

'I don't think he realised for a moment what was happening either. He was just lying there, waiting for Victoria to start screaming, and the rest of us to rush on. In fact, of course, he wasn't supposed to move again until the curtain went down at the end of the act, which would have only been another few minutes. He raised his head when Leonard started to speak, and perhaps he wasn't as dazzled as the rest of us because he still had those dark glasses on. You remember in the play he was supposed to be a very conceited man, who thought they added to his charm. And that's all I saw of what went on on the stage, because Ellie started to carry on and I had my hands full trying to quiet her. Then Roger arrived with you, Antony, and he took Ellie from me and started to shake her. And I looked past you both and saw that detective – Chief Superintendent Briggs, he must have followed you very closely – standing by the garden door staring on to the stage. So I looked round to see what was happening there, and by then Andy had joined Leonard and was kneeling by Victoria. But then I got distracted, I thought in fact that Roger was going to shake Ellie's teeth out of her head, which seemed rather drastic even if she was being an awful nuisance. So I don't remember what happened after that.'

'All right then, Meg, think about that brief glimpse you had of the stage. Did you notice anything, anything at all, that wasn't as it should have been?'

'Well, of course, Victoria should have been sitting in the chair, still alive.'

'I didn't mean that, and I know the whole business must have been horrible for you.'

'Leonard shouldn't have been there either.'

'I know that too.'

Meg seemed to be racking her brains. 'When I first looked Andy was lying just as usual, then he raised his head, and later, when I looked again he was with Leonard and Victoria. But, as I said, he should have gone on playing dead until the end of the act.'

'Yes, that disposes of all the people,' said Antony. 'You've told me before.'

'I'm only trying to help,' said Meg rather crossly.

'I know you are, and I hate making you think back to that night,' Antony assured her. 'Was there anything about the setting, anything misplaced, anything at all that might give us a clue as to who could have gone on to the stage besides Mr Buckley?'

'I see what you mean,' said Meg slowly. 'If any of the furniture had been moved –'

'That's just what I do mean. Think about it, Meg, there's a good girl.'

'Something black,' said Meg slowly, gazing into the middle distance, 'lying just behind Victoria's chair on the pale blue carpet.'

'Now don't go into a trance,' Antony implored. 'You're not the Delphic Oracle,' he added, as tartly as Sir Nicholas himself might have done. 'Something black that shouldn't have been there?'

'You told me to concentrate and I'm concentrating,' said Meg with dignity. 'Of course it shouldn't have been there.'

'What sort of a something? Could it have been one of Mr Buckley's gloves, for instance, the ones that were found in his pocket afterwards. He might have dropped it and picked it up again.'

'I thought you were supposed to be defending him.'

95

'This is all part of it,' said Antony sighing. 'Could it have been a glove?'

'No,' said Meg, after a moment's thought. 'Leonard's gloves were just an ordinary size, because he never had to put them on at all really. This was bigger, sort of shapeless, certainly there were no fingers.'

'How do you think it got there?'

'Antony darling, I haven't the faintest idea.'

'No, I suppose you wouldn't have. Do you know though, what happened to it afterwards?'

'I haven't a clue about that either. We were all bustled off, practically under guard. Well you know all that yourself.'

'What are you thinking, Antony?' asked Jenny urgently.

'Only that it's something I've got to find out about, love. Mr Buckley may have donned the gloves that were found in his pocket and stabbed his wife, or somebody may have wrapped the hilt of the dagger in this mysterious piece of cloth of Meg's, and done the deed himself.'

Jenny grimaced. 'Neither possibility appeals to me much,' she admitted.

'Well, the good lady is certainly dead, and unfortunately the question of who killed her does matter to her husband. Can you remember anything else out of place, Meg?'

'No, I can't.' She sounded hesitant now. 'Antony, do you think this is important?'

'The most important thing I've heard so far.'

'But then ... darling, I couldn't get up and say all this in court. I wouldn't mind it if it was only a silly piece of cloth that you're so excited about, but they'd ask me what Leonard thought about Victoria and don't you see how dreadful that would be?'

'Yes, Meg, I do see how dreadful it would be for you. You're too nice a person,' he said ruefully, and stood a moment looking down at her sombrely. 'If it were a question of Leonard Buckley being convicted or acquitted, how would you feel about it then?'

'Just the same,' said Meg tragically, 'but I suppose it would have to be done.'

'Well, don't worry about it for the moment.' He was suddenly brisk. 'There may be a dozen other people who remember seeing the cloth, and can say what happened to it afterwards. You know I wouldn't do anything to hurt you if I could possibly avoid it.'

'I should like that sentence better,' said Meg with a rather quivering smile, 'if you left out the last bit.' But she wasn't an actress for nothing. 'Tell me how you put up with him, Jenny,' she asked. 'I know I'd go mad within a week.'

VI

Roger arrived a few minutes after that, and Antony went down to the study to phone Geoffrey Horton. His uncle had still not returned, and The Magic Flute was well into the last act. He shut himself in, therefore, confident that he was disturbing nobody, and was lucky in finding Geoffrey still at his office.

'I'm glad you called,' said Horton heavily. 'I've learned a good deal in the course of the afternoon and it's time we had a talk.'

'You don't sound as if it pleased you particularly.'

'It doesn't,' said Geoffrey. 'Where are you now, still in chambers?'

'No, I'm at home, and I've commandeered the study for the moment. Can you leave now?'

'Yes, that would be the best thing. Kempenfeldt Square is practically on my way home,' said Geoffrey. 'I can be with you in ten minutes.'

So Maitland waited with as much patience as he could muster, and Geoffrey, true to his word, arrived a little within the allotted time, and at that hour was lucky enough to find a parking spot almost exactly opposite Sir Nicholas's house. Antony went to the study door to rescue him from Gibbs, who would doubtless have dispatched him upstairs. 'Meg and Roger are upstairs with Jenny,' he explained, 'but if Uncle Nick comes home and he and Vera want to come in here that won't matter. They're interested anyway.'

'I should think they might be interested in what I have to tell you,' said Geoffrey rather grimly. 'To begin with the police know the provenance of the dagger.'

'And it doesn't help?' said Maitland, watching his friend's face.

'I should say not!' Geoffrey gave a short bark of laughter. 'It came from the Buckleys' flat.'

'But Mr Buckley denied having seen it before.'

'Yes, you told me he was lying about some things, didn't you? Anyway there seems to be no doubt about it. Dominic Eldred, ironically enough, is the man who has the part of the detective in Skelton's play, and he says he gave it to Victoria Buckley many years ago.'

97

'How many?'

'About thirty, he thinks.'

'In that case, is he sure it was still in her possession?'

'Quite sure, unfortunately. He says they had a desk in the living room, and she kept it there to use as a letter opener. Andrew Murray has seen it there too.'

'Have they both identified it positively?'

Horton gave him a long look. 'You've got something to tell me yourself,' he predicted.

'Yes I have, but your story first. We may as well have all the bad news at once.'

'Well then, they're quite sure. To begin with, dagger is apparently the wrong word for it, it's an Italian stiletto, believed to date from the seventeenth century. Eldred says he wanted to give Victoria Buckley something as a memento – he doesn't say of what – he hadn't any money at the time so there was no question of buying anything, and that was the only valuable thing he had. It's an unusual piece because the stabbing blade is particularly sharp but the handle is made purely for decorative purposes and must have been a positive hindrance in its day to the weapon's serious use.'

'Those will be two dangerous witnesses.'

'I got all this from the chap who was preparing the brief, Lamb is getting the prosecution I understand. And if you think you've heard the worst yet, Antony, you're mistaken. When the police searched the Buckleys' flat they found a book on anatomy there.'

'Are you sure?' asked Maitland incredulously. 'You don't mean *The Anatomy of Melancholy*, or anything like that?'

'Don't be silly, Antony. If I'd meant that I'd have said so. A perfectly straightforward book on anatomy, such as a medical student might possess. In fact, it was by no means new, and had probably been picked up at a secondhand bookshop.'

'More work for Cobbolds.'

'I don't see where they could start,' Geoffrey objected.

'Charing Cross Road, for example.'

'It might have been purchased anywhere in the country. Leonard Buckley might have owned it for years!' Geoffrey's voice rose slightly at the unreasonableness of the demand.

'Why should he have? I don't suppose that was a subject that interested him particularly. And if this crime was planned, as it obviously had to be, it wasn't until the murderer had read the script of *Done in by Daggers*.'

'The police will be on precisely the same tack.'

'Oh, I doubt it. I think they'll be content with the maxim that possession is nine points of the law. But to go back a little, Geoffrey, is it seriously suggested that Mr Buckley sat down and studied quite cold-bloodedly and in his wife's presence where to put the dab of paint on her dress so that he would know where to drive in the stiletto?'

'It was a clean blow,' Geoffrey reminded him.

'Yes, but – ' Maitland was striding about the room now. 'If he could have studied the matter, so could somebody else.'

'The book was found in his flat.'

'And the dagger came from there. But the same person who removed the one could have planted the other,' Antony pointed out.

'That's stretching things a little, isn't it?'

'No, I don't think so.'

'I haven't quite finished,' Horton warned him. 'That wasn't all the police found.'

'What else, for heaven's sake?'

'An empty bottle that had contained Vitamin A tablets in Leonard Buckley's dressing room at the Alhambra.'

'Lots of people take vitamins. No, wait a bit! That's the stuff that's supposed to help people with bad night vision, isn't it?'

'It is.'

'What's the idea? That our client took a course of it, to help him find his wife in the dark and stab her?'

'That, or that he took a massive dose that evening for the same purpose. The expert they've got, Dr Larrow, a nutritionist, inclines to the latter view, I gather, but won't commit himself because of lack of experience of what the effect would be. Taken in such a quantity there are dangers, so naturally no reputable doctor would prescribe it.'

'All the same .. well, we'll have to see what our client has to say for himself. Were there fingerprints on the bottle?'

'Nary a one.'

'Come now, that's encouraging, isn't it? Besides, you haven't heard what I've been doing since we parted,' said Antony, and proceeded to give Horton a detailed account. 'It's obvious that there were tensions among the cast, to say the least,' he concluded, 'but it's what Meg had to say about this piece of black cloth that really intrigues me.'

'I think you're proposing to place too much weight on it, Antony,' Geoffrey warned him.

'Do you really think so? *I* think it's the best indication we've had yet ... I mean, what was it doing there? Mr Buckley would have had no need of it, being provided with gloves.'

'I should say myself you'd have to talk to Jeremy Skelton again. You may find there's some quite simple explanation,' said Geoffrey dampingly.

'You don't think it indicates our client's innocence?'

'I think the points I've just outlined to you are much more convincing,' said Geoffrey. 'And if you want my opinion now, the plea of diminished responsibility, even if he would have agreed to it, would have been wrong.'

'If you were on the jury you'd find him guilty of premeditated murder?'

'On the evidence as it stands,' said Geoffrey stubbornly. 'Think of it, Antony.'

'I am thinking of it. Well, I'll speak to Jeremy, of course, but I'd take a small bet on Mr Buckley's innocence now.'

'And I'd take you up on it,' Geoffrey assured him. 'What are you going to do about it if Skelton says this black cloth shouldn't have been there?'

'Of course it shouldn't have been there, Meg would have known about it. But Jeremy's an observant fellow, he may have noticed it himself.'

'If he says it shouldn't have been there,' repeated Geoffrey patiently, 'and you can't find anyone else who saw it, what are you going to do? Insist on calling Meg as a witness?'

'I don't want to do that.'

'No, I thought you wouldn't,' said Geoffrey. 'She knew all about the trouble between the two Buckleys, didn't she? I can't see Lamb missing *that* point in cross-examination.'

'It might be worth it from our point of view, but it would upset her frightfully,' Antony explained. 'I'll think about it Geoffrey. When do you suppose we'll get the depositions?'

'In a day or two, I should think. I'll be able to give you a complete list of prosecution witnesses then.'

'There's one thing you might tell me right away. Sykes appeared in the magistrate's court as investigating officer. Will they be calling Briggs to back up his testimony?'

'No, they don't need him.' He glanced at his watch. 'Joan will wonder where I am,' he said, 'so I think I'd better be going. I'll get Cobbolds started on the quest for the bookshop, Antony, if that's what you want, but don't get your hopes up.'

VII

It wasn't until much later, when Roger returned from taking Meg to the theatre, that he voiced his disquiet to Jenny and Antony. 'Meg's been telling me about the talk you had with her this afternoon, Antony,' he said. 'Do you really think there's something in this story of a piece of black cloth?'

'I think it may be the most important thing to come to light so far.'

'You mean you want to bring it out at the trial?'

'In view of the amount of evidence the prosecution has succeeded in putting together,' said Antony, 'and the scarcity of the points we can make to refute it, we shall be absolutely bound to introduce it.'

'Does that mean calling Meg? She thinks you may do that, and she's very upset about it. I dare say you can guess why.'

'I don't need to guess, she told me,' said Antony. 'And I promise you, Roger, I won't call her unless it's absolutely necessary. In fact I've been thinking it over while you were gone – ' He was interrupted there by the entrance of Sir Nicholas and Vera for whom he had left the front door hospitably open. For once he forwent a formal greeting, about which, where Vera was concerned, he was generally particular. Instead he looked rather defiantly at his uncle and announced, before they were half way across the room, 'I was just going to tell Jenny and Roger that I'm thinking of calling Chief Superintendent Briggs to give evidence for the defence.'

VIII

He hadn't been able to resist the temptation towards drama, which he said to Jenny later he must have caught from Meg. The result, as might have been expected, was an explosion of objections, though Sir Nicholas only said languidly, 'Have you gone mad, Antony?' and took his usual chair. Jenny's protest was incoherent, but Vera said bluntly, 'Can't do that. He's bound to be appearing for the prosecution.'

'Geoffrey says not. I know he was present at the preliminary enquiry, but after that he retired from the case, except in that he is Sykes's superior. It would have been beneath his dignity to continue as investigating officer, don't you think?'

'Suppose so,' said Vera grudgingly. 'All the same, unwise.' Her speech was even more elliptical than usual, a sign, as Antony knew, that she was really perturbed.

'You see,' said Jenny, quite ready, now that the shock of his announcement was over, to back his point of view, 'Meg saw something that may help but Antony doesn't want to call her.'

'And I don't want him to,' said Roger, 'but—'

'The thing is, Roger, she also told me that Briggs was practically on our heels when we went backstage that night, and that he stood for a moment or two looking at what was happening on the stage. He's a trained observer—'

'Thing is,' said Vera, in her gruff way, 'what is this important piece of evidence?'

'I feel sure,' said Sir Nicholas very gently indeed, 'that Antony is about to enlighten us.'

That gentle tone was a danger signal, as Antony knew well enough, but he went into his recital quite firmly in spite of that. 'So you see – ' he said when he had finished, but Sir Nicholas prevented him from completing the sentence.

'I see that you've quite made up your mind as to your client's innocence,' he said. 'Now Halloran informs me that the gossip is that the case against Leonard Buckley is quite watertight.'

'It certainly is a good one, I'll tell you about that later, Uncle Nick. But don't you think this is a valid point? If we can draw the prosecution on into making a fuss about the gloves that were found in Mr Buckley's pocket, we can at least throw a little ridicule on that bit of evidence.'

'It convinces you?' asked his uncle insistently.

'Yes, it does.' Antony was quite positive about it. Though he knew well enough that if he woke in the middle of the night some doubts would be bound to creep in.

'Chief Superintendent Briggs will not be exactly a willing witness,' said Sir Nicholas thoughtfully.

'Then I shall ask the court for permission to treat him as hostile,' said Antony.

'You've quite made up your mind to this rash act?' Sir Nicholas queried.

'Well . . . if I can't find anybody else who saw what Meg saw.'

'He may not have seen anything himself.'

'If it was there, and I think we all know we can take Meg's word for that, he must have seen it,' said Antony. 'Anyway, I think it's worth taking the risk, if I can't find anybody else among the few possible witnesses the prosecution has left me with who saw the same thing.'

'And I think you're insane,' said his uncle cordially. 'However, as there are ladies present I think we'd better go into that at greater length tomorrow. Jenny, my dear, I don't often have to remind you of your duties as hostess, but I think in the circumstances we could all do with some reviving cordial.'

That meant the finest cognac. Jenny gave one despairing look at her husband and hastened to obey.

After breakfast the next morning Antony took a walk up Avery Street and was lucky enough to find both the Skeltons at home. If they were surprised to see him again so soon neither of them showed it. Anne offered coffee, which he declined so soon after his morning ration, and Jeremy said acutely as they seated themselves, 'There've been some developments.'

'Yes, there have. Some good, some bad,' Antony admitted. 'Well, only one favourable one, actually, so naturally I'd like to make the best of it.'

'Can I help?'

'You went backstage too after the murder, though by a different route,' said Antony. 'I want to know whether, before you went, you saw anything lying behind Victoria Buckley's chair.'

Jeremy frowned over that. 'I didn't,' he said at length. 'But I don't think I could have done. Even looking down on the stage from the box, it was a high-backed chair, as you must have seen for yourself.'

'Then later, when you arrived backstage?'

'I saw nothing that shouldn't have been there, except poor Victoria's body, of course.'

'There was nothing in the play –'

'Not a thing. The gloves in Leonard's pocket would have been part of the evidence against him, when Dominic, in the character of Inspector Murchison, decided that he was the guilty party.'

'Would you be willing to give evidence to that effect?'

'Naturally.'

'We shall need every bit of ammunition we can get, you see,' said Antony rather apologetically.

'Don't worry, I'm more than willing to help.' And there they left the matter. There was a little more desultory talk, after which Maitland took his leave.

He wasn't looking forward to lunchtime – on Saturdays he and Jenny traditionally had their midday meal with Sir Nicholas and Vera – and events proved that his instinct had been right about that. It was one of those days when Gibbs insisted on serving, right up to the point where he placed the coffee before them, and in view of his known contrary disposition it was likely that some instinct had told him that his employer was wishing him a hundred miles away. However, the four of them were alone at last, a small silence developed, after which Sir Nicholas spoke his mind. Ladies present or no – any of them could have told you that he wasn't always consistent – he didn't mince his words, and Antony was left in no doubt at all of what his uncle thought of the idea of calling a member of the police force – and a Chief Superintendent in the C.I.D. at that – as a witness for the defence. 'You say he's a trained observer,' Sir Nicholas concluded. 'Who knows what he may have observed that will injure your client?'

'My point is, sir, that Mr Buckley is innocent, and that therefore anything anybody observed behind the scenes must be helpful to him.'

'A pretty thought,' said his uncle disparagingly. 'Have you heard from Geoffrey yet what the prosecution's case is?'

'Yes, as a matter of fact I have. Didn't Gibbs tell you he came here yesterday afternoon, just before you got in I suppose.' He outlined briefly what Geoffrey had told him, and watched the danger signals mount in his uncle's face. Which wouldn't have troubled him over-much if he had been quite firm in the point of view he was arguing. 'You'll agree with me, Vera,' he said finally, 'this makes it all the more imperative that we use every weapon we've got.'

'Don't like the sound of it,' said Vera frankly.

Antony sighed. 'No, I was afraid you might not,' he said. 'Anyway, Uncle Nick, if I can find anybody else who saw this bit of cloth –'

'I can see it might be important,' his uncle conceded, 'but not at the risk of issuing a *sub poena* to Briggs. You'll be launching into your examination-in-chief with no idea at all what his answers may be ... at least, I hope you're not considering having an interview with him beforehand.'

'No, that hadn't entered my head,' said Antony. 'I think it would be worse than useless. But in court, where the judge, whoever he may be, can instruct him to answer my questions ... that may be quite a different matter.'

'I suppose I should admire your optimistic nature.' Sir Nicholas had turned to sarcasm. 'But I tell you again it's foolhardy. And another thing, Antony ... are you quite sure you don't welcome the opportunity of crossing swords with Briggs in court?'

Antony considered. 'I honestly think my main motive is to spare Meg any distress,' he said at last. 'But the other is attractive, too. After the number of times he's asked me questions –'

'That has nothing whatever to do with it,' said Sir Nicholas coldly. 'May I ask whether you have communicated this decision to Geoffrey yet?'

'No, I know quite well his reaction will be exactly the same as yours, sir. However, there are three people I have to see, unless I learn they're being called by the other side, there's just a chance they may be able to help me. Besides, I dare say Geoffrey will have talked to Mr Buckley today, and I want to know what *his* answer is to these new facts that have emerged. After that there will be time enough.'

'Too soon,' said Sir Nicholas, stirring his coffee in an ominous way. 'I can only hope your instructing solicitor has the knack of talking some sense into you, I have to admit I find myself entirely lacking in it.'

Antony and Jenny got away as soon as they decently could, and when they reached their own quarters the telephone was ringing. 'I'll get it,' said Antony, 'I expect it's Geoffrey.' And when he picked up the receiver, he was glad to hear Horton's voice.

'I got those addresses you wanted,' Geoffrey told him, 'and confirmed that the prosecution don't need them. Gordon Hewitt, Claude Aubin, and Miss Frances Cathers,' he added, as though Antony might have already forgotten the arrangement they had made. 'There's a matinee this afternoon, and even though the girl is only understudying Meg she'll have to be at the theatre. So I arranged that we'd see them tomorrow.'

'There's plenty of time,' Antony agreed, 'but I'll be glad to get it over.'

'Meanwhile we can go out to the prison this afternoon. I think it would be a good idea if you come with me,' said Geoffrey.

Antony hesitated a moment, and then agreed. 'It's not so much what Mr Buckley may say it's how he says it,' he said. 'And you must admit he has some explaining to do.'

'I'm the one who thinks that ... remember?'

'What you really mean is that you're taking a more sensible view of things than I am,' said Antony, with a humourous inflection in his voice. 'All the same, Geoffrey, I'd really like to hear what he has to say for himself.'

'I'll pick you up then. In about three quarters of an hour?'

'That will do splendidly.' It was obviously not the time to break to Geoffrey the news of the further *sub poena* that might have to be issued. Though after the interviews that were scheduled for tomorrow, it might not be possible to delay any longer the evil day.

Geoffrey, who was a steady, even a staid driver, still somehow had the knack of always arriving when he said he would, whatever the traffic problems might be. That afternoon was no exception, and they drove down to Brixton mostly in silence.

So all the familiar routine was gone through again, depressing Maitland as much as ever it did, and at last they were in the interview room and Leonard Buckley was coming, rather hesitantly this time, through the door. As soon as it closed he halted, and said, looking from one of them to the other, 'I'm surprised you want to see me again so soon, gentlemen.'

'I felt it was necessary,' said Geoffrey non-committally. 'Come and sit down, Mr Buckley, there are some questions that have to be asked.'

'And answered,' Maitland put in. This time he didn't attempt to sit down, but waited until the other two men had seated themselves, observing his client as they did so. Even in the short time since they had seen him Buckley seemed to have aged, to have shrivelled into half the man he had been before. Am I right, or is Geoffrey? Antony thought. But he felt the familiar unwelcome stab of sympathy, and knew that he wouldn't be happy now until that question was answered one way or the other.

'I dare say we shan't need to keep you very long, Mr Buckley,' Geoffrey was saying. 'You know that the prosecution are bound to disclose details of their case to me, and I've had some preliminary discussions with the solicitor on their side. In the course of those I learned certain things – '

Leonard Buckley's shoulders sagged. 'I know, Mr Horton,' he said, 'I should have trusted you when you talked to me before. You want to know about the dagger?'

'That's it exactly. You told us you'd never seen it before,' Geoffrey pointed out.

'And I lied, that's what you're saying, isn't it? You're quite right and I can't explain it except by saying that I panicked.' This time his eyes moved to Maitland's face. 'I think perhaps you might understand about that,' he said.

'I understand only too well.' Antony's tone was strained. 'I believe that the dagger – or rather I should remember to say the stiletto – belonged to your wife, and was in your flat as recently as ... how long ago, Geoffrey, was it seen there?'

'Andrew Murray says he visited you on the Monday before the play was due to open, the twelfth of February,' Geoffrey said. 'He's quite sure the weapon was in its usual place then.'

107

'Well, that's more than I am. You know how it is when a thing is so familiar to you, you don't notice whether it's there or not.'

'And you can't say that it went missing before the murder?' asked Maitland.

'I can only say that it must have done,' said Leonard, 'but I don't know when. What I'm trying to tell you is that I didn't put it in my pocket that evening ready to commit the murder myself.'

'Had anybody else a key to your flat?'

'No, I'm quite sure of that.'

'Well, would the superintendent of the building let anybody in for any reason? Can you remember such an occasion?'

'No.' But then he thought better of the reply. 'Well, yes, Mr Moffat did say that some flowers had been delivered for Victoria on opening day while we were out. He said the man who delivered them was very insistent that he must put them in place himself in case they needed rearranging, he supposed he was someone from the flower shop.'

'Wouldn't it have been more usual to send them to the theatre?'

'Yes, of course, I was surprised about it, but there they were when we got home.'

'Who had sent them?'

'That's funny, because in spite of the florist's care no card had been included. Do you think ... do you think somebody took the dagger then?'

'We shall have to find out whether the so-called florist was ever alone,' said Antony, glancing at Geoffrey as he spoke. Horton had his notebook out and wrote something down. 'But meanwhile, Mr Buckley,' said Antony, who seemed to have taken over the questioning now – as Geoffrey would have told you he generally did – 'I understand Mrs Buckley had the stiletto for a very long time.'

'I can tell you exactly,' said Leonard. 'Dominic Eldred gave it to her thirty-three years ago.'

'You're very precise about that.'

'I ought to be. It was the beginning of our estrangement.' He smiled rather wanly. 'Rather longer ago than I led you to believe, Mr Maitland, you may put that down to cowardice too.'

'Mr Eldred told the police he gave it to her as a memento. Do you know what he meant by that?'

'Yes, I know only too well. It was to celebrate the birth of their son.'

'I ... see,' said Maitland a little doubtfully. 'This was – what? Ten years after you were married?'

'Yes, that's right. I told you – didn't I? – that Dominic had wanted to marry Victoria, but she chose me. Afterwards she must have regretted it.'

'But she didn't leave you?'

'No, though I know Dominic urged her to. She wanted to go on just as we were, bringing up the child as our own. I think now I was very much to blame, I wouldn't agree to that. He was adopted by some friends of Dominic's, and I don't think Victoria ever saw him again ... until recently.'

'Let me guess. One of the two young men in the play?'

'You're dead right, Mr Maitland, Gordon Hewitt.'

Maitland paused a moment. 'I've been told that he got on reasonably well with you, but seemed to dislike Mrs Buckley intensely,' he said then. 'Did he know the truth about his parentage?'

'Yes, he did.'

'How –'

'It's a little complicated. For one thing, his adoptive parents were killed in an air crash only about a year ago. He'd known Dominic all his life, of course, but not that they were related. I think that Dominic had still a great tenderness for Victoria, and when rehearsals started Gordon seemed to take an instinctive dislike to her, and that upset him. So he told him the whole truth, hoping it would change his attitude, but unfortunately it had just the opposite effect. I talked to him myself about it, not that it seemed to distress Victoria at all but the whole thing seemed so unnatural. The odd thing was, everything was my fault really, but he didn't seem to blame me at all.'

'I don't think you should blame yourself either, Mr Buckley. You can hardly say the original affaire between your wife and Mr Eldred was your fault.'

'No, that's true.' Again there was that rather wan smile. 'I'm afraid all this will only convince you that the relations between Victoria and myself were very bad indeed. In fairness though, I'm going to tell you that it was only after I learned that she was pregnant, that I was unfaithful to her myself. I knew I couldn't be the father, you see.'

'You must have been very discreet about it,' said Antony in almost a flippant tone, and earned a sour look from Geoffrey. 'May I make a further guess and suggest that one of your – shall we say partners? – was also a member of the cast, Miss Ellie Dorman?'

'I don't think on the whole I want to answer that, Mr Maitland.' Something of Buckley's former dignity had returned. 'I have a very great regard for Ellie.'

'So much regard that she may have believed you would marry her under different circumstances?' Maitland insisted.

'Ellie Dorman is not a murderer,' said Leonard flatly.

'Very well, we'll leave it at that. That brings us to Mr Horton's second question.' He glanced at Geoffrey. 'Your witness,' he said.

'It's about a book that was found in your flat,' said Horton. At that moment his disapproval of Maitland and all his works was very evident, but Antony didn't worry too much, knowing that any stiffness between them wouldn't last. '*Stubbs on Anatomy*,' said Geoffrey. 'A book of that name was found in your flat. Is the study of anatomy an interest of yours, Mr Buckley?'

'Good heavens, no! Not of Victoria's either. I'm sure no such book should have been in our possession. Perhaps somebody left it after a visit.'

'Mr Maitland thinks that's what happened, perhaps at the same time as the flowers were delivered,' said Geoffrey in a tone that conveyed neither belief nor scepticism. 'You will see however –'

'Mr Horton means,' Antony interrupted, seeing the prisoner's bewildered look, 'that the prosecution will maintain you used this book to decide where the stiletto could be used with the most deadly effect.'

'Good heavens!' said Leonard again. 'Do I seem like that sort of person, Mr Maitland? I'm grateful for your frankness, of course,' he added, 'but it makes me rather sick to think about it.'

'I take it then that you deny all knowledge of this particular book.'

'I do indeed!'

'There's one other material point. Do you take vitamins, Mr Buckley?'

'No. Why do you ask?'

'A bottle that had contained Vitamin A tablets was found in your dressing room. What can you tell me about it?'

'Nothing. I don't understand why it should be considered important.'

'Because Vitamin A is good for night blindness.'

Leonard thought that out for a long moment. 'I know nothing about it,' he said at last, firmly.

'Can we rely on that? No more prevarication?' He heard

Geoffrey click his tongue disapprovingly, but ignored him and pressed on almost immediately. 'Then can we go back, Mr Buckley, to the time when the lights came on again, finding you still on the stage.'

'I told you what happened. I suppose you don't believe me,' he added despondently.

'I didn't say that. It's just that we need a little more detail. Please tell me again exactly what happened.'

'The lights came on. I told you why I was still standing there. I was rather bewildered, and the first thing I saw was Andy, lying on the floor just as I expected. But I think I knew straight away that something was wrong, or why should someone else have been on the stage, the person who brushed past me? So I turned, and then I saw Victoria.'

'Wait a bit! You were to make your exit on the prompt side, the right side as viewed from the audience. But Andrew Murray was on the other side of the stage, you should have been facing away from him. How was it you saw him first?'

'I'll try to tell you. I'd fixed the dagger, and Andy gave the sighing moan that we'd rehearsed so often he'd got it off to perfection, and I felt him fall away from me to take up the position that had been agreed on the floor. Then I turned to go back, to tell you the truth Mr Maitland I don't find moving about on the stage in those conditions as easy as some of my younger colleagues. So I was taking my time, but I knew I had plenty of it so I didn't worry. And when I got – I think from what was said later it was centre stage but I didn't notice myself – someone brushed past me, catching my shoulder as he went so that I was spun round.'

'Quite a collision then.'

'To tell you the truth, I got the impression of a hand on my shoulder, forcing me to turn. But I'm not really sure about that, so I didn't mention it.'

'Well, I think you'd better forget about the word "brushing". What happened then?'

'I was so startled – I told you this – that I just stayed where I was until the lights came on.'

'This person, could it have been a woman?'

'I never thought of that.' He took his time over the rest of his answer. 'I can only say that I think it was a man,' he said then. 'I got the impression of somebody taller than myself, and it had to be somebody in the theatre –'

'One of the actors, we think,' said Maitland, and heard Geoffrey

111

mutter something that sounded like, 'If it was anyone', under his breath.

'Well then, Meg and Ellie are both much of a height, about the same height as I am myself.'

'And the understudy, Frances Cathers?'

'She's a little taller, but not I think as heavy as the person that brushed by me.'

'Thank you, that's very clear. Go back to the point when you first saw Mrs Buckley.'

'She was lying on the floor too. She shouldn't have been there,' said Leonard. 'You know they say in books – at least they used to – I was rooted to the spot. I thought that was a stupid phrase, until it happened to me. Then I was able to move again and I went to her and called her name. I think she was dead already.'

'Then, or within a few moments,' said Geoffrey. 'If you're worried, Mr Buckley, I don't think she can have known what happened or have suffered at all.'

'Thank you, Mr Horton,' He turned back to Maitland again. 'Why are you asking me all these things?' he enquired.

'Because I want to know the answers,' said Antony simply. 'Try to put yourself back again on the stage, visualise everything that was there. Was there anything out of place? A chair moved? Anything?'

The silence lengthened. At last, 'I was only conscious of Victoria,' said Leonard Buckley, 'that something had happened to her and perhaps somehow I was to blame. If I hadn't spoken so freely ... but that's water under the bridge now. And I thought too what a pretty girl she'd been and how we'd laughed together when we were young.'

'Did you by any chance drop one of your black gloves and retrieve it later, before the police found them in your pocket?'

'Of course not. There was no need for me to take them out at all.'

'You told us before that you couldn't think of any reason for anyone to kill Mrs Buckley,' said Antony.

'Yes, and that still remains true.'

'Gordon Hewitt?'

'His resentment against her couldn't have been sufficient motive. As for Dominic – I suppose you're going to bring him up next – I think he was still devoted to her.'

'Then I think that's all we need to know. What about it, Geoffrey?'

'I think you've covered everything,' said Horton, half amused, half reproving. He made his way towards the door to summon the warder, saying over his shoulder, 'I'll be in touch, Mr Buckley. I hope our questions this afternoon haven't been too upsetting.'

Again they made the journey almost in silence, but, 'You really are enough to infuriate a saint, Antony,' said Geoffrey, drawing up to allow his friend to get out of the car outside the house in Kempenfeldt Square.

'What is it this time?' said Antony, resigned.

'The kind of questions you ask.'

'I know.' This time he sounded sympathetic. 'I believe the man, and don't mind upsetting him in an attempt to find out the truth. You're getting as bad as your revered father-in-law.' (Mr Bellerby, also a solicitor, a man well known to believe in kindness to clients.) 'I suppose it must be catching. Meg keeps telling me I'm getting like Uncle Nick,' he added and grinned.

'I wish you had half his sense of decorum,' Geoffrey retorted. 'I might have fewer headaches then.'

It was time, Maitland thought, to turn the conversation. 'What time is our first appointment tomorrow?' he asked.

'In the morning, eleven o'clock. I'll pick you up at half past ten, if that's all right.'

'Quite all right. And the other two in the afternoon?'

'Yes.'

'Then I'll tell Jenny to expect us both to lunch, shall I?'

'That would be a pleasure,' said Geoffrey sincerely. 'Good night, Antony, and try not to get any more bright ideas before then.'

He drove off, leaving Maitland wondering just how much of his intentions Geoffrey had already divined. On the whole it seemed unlikely ... but with Geoffrey you never knew.

As was perhaps natural, of the three people he intended to see that day, Antony was most interested in Gordon Hewitt, and he was therefore glad when he found that Geoffrey had arranged that interview for the morning. It meant going out to Streatham, however. 'Not too convenient for the theatre,' said Gordon, leading the way up to his room, which proved to be no more than reasonably comfortable and no more than reasonably warm. 'However, who knows how long the run will be, I want to put by every penny. And there's always the chance we'll come off with a couple of weeks at the Streatham Hill Theatre, that's only round the corner.'

He was an engaging young man, as Antony had already observed from his place in the stalls on the night the play opened, and though of course he was far too young for Meg, on the stage there was no difficulty in believing in a romantic attachment between them. Even in the strongest daylight Meg looked no more than a girl; in makeup on stage she could have played Juliet with ease if she'd wished to. The thought set Antony smiling, her comments on the ill-fated lovers, when one day she had been persuaded to give them, had been stringent in the extreme.

Now he said amiably, as soon as the door was closed behind them and while Gordon was setting chairs, 'Jeremy Skelton seems to think you're in for a long run.'

'Yes, I hope so. I think, to tell you the truth, it would have been a long one anyway, but now with all the excitement ... that's one good thing Victoria did at least.'

'Nothing in her life became her like the leaving of it,' Antony suggested, and was amused to see the expected look of horror spread across the actor's face. 'Yes, I know I mustn't quote *Macbeth*, but we aren't in the theatre and it was actually a paraphrase.'

'Let's hope that makes a difference.' Hewitt paused and looked from one to the other of them. 'Mr Horton explained who you are,' he said, 'though of course I've heard of you from Meg, Mr Maitland, but I don't understand how I can help you.'

114

'It's a matter of being thorough,' said Antony rather vaguely. Geoffrey gave him a cold look and proceeded to elaborate on the statement.

'We want to find out as much as we can about what went on backstage at the time of the murder,' he said. 'We can't approach Miss Dorman, or Mr Eldred, or Mr Murray, because they're all being called by the prosecution.'

'Do I understand by that that you mean to call me for the defence? I'd be only too glad if I could help, but I don't really know anything.'

'Well, if you don't, of course we shan't call you. But meanwhile there are one or two matters –'

'You were standing in the wings when the lights went out,' said Antony, who had been following his own train of thought and seemed quite unaware that he was interrupting. 'I understand that you and Meg and Miss Dorman were due to go on stage soon after they came on again.'

'Yes, that's right. Ellie was due on first, it was a delicate matter of timing actually because there wasn't any real cue, only Victoria was supposed to be screaming. Then after a moment or two Meg and I would have gone on together, the inference being that we'd been together all the time in one of the other rooms.'

'So Miss Dorman was standing a little ahead of you?'

'Yes, of course. None of us was standing very close together though. Obviously we couldn't talk so there'd have been no point in that.'

'Did you notice anything at all while the lights were out?'

'No. I'd been looking on to the lighted stage, so of course I was quite blind for a minute or so. It was only just before the lights came on again that I could even see the phosphorescent marks that Leonard had to follow. By that time Andy must have been lying on the floor, and I dare say Victoria was too, though I didn't know it then.'

'I can quite understand that you couldn't see anything, but did you hear anything, sense anybody moving around?'

'I heard Andy's very realistic dying gasp, and Leonard didn't progress absolutely noiselessly, he wasn't meant to, the audience was supposed to have the feeling that something was going on, but not to be able to see what it was.'

'That sound of his moving about must have broken off earlier than you expected.'

'Yes, I suppose, now you mention it, it did.'

115

'Could any of your group have left it, gone on stage themselves?'

'There was the garden door a few feet away which was open. It was night you know – in the play, I mean – which explains why there was no light from that either.' He thought for a moment. 'Yes, I suppose any of us could have gone on stage that way without the others knowing,' he admitted. 'But I thought–'

'You thought Mr Buckley was guilty and that was the end of it?'

'Yes, I'm afraid I did. Of course, when it's someone you know it's difficult to believe they could do a thing like that, but I can't help seeing if *he* didn't some other member of the cast probably did. Which is even harder to credit, because he was the one with the motive after all.'

'Tell us about that, Mr Hewitt.'

'But you know already. He thought Victoria was trying to kill him.'

'Was that general knowledge among the actors?'

'Oh, yes. Of course we never talked about it in front of either of them, it was supposed to be a dead secret. But you couldn't help seeing they practically hated each other, it's no good trying to hide anything in a theatrical company anyway.'

'The question arises, do you believe it was true?'

'I shouldn't think so. Not that I hold any brief for Victoria, rather than a rather nebulous feeling that I shouldn't speak ill of the dead, but I don't believe that of her. I'll tell you who does, though.'

A thoroughly nice, talkative young man, thought Antony, and exchanged a glance with Geoffrey, from whose expression he gathered that the solicitor was thinking exactly the same thing. 'Who believed it?' he asked.

'Why, my – Dominic Eldred,' amended Gordon quickly. 'I know that's true because he told me, and he was pretty unhappy about it I can tell you.'

'You're telling us he was fond of her?'

'I don't understand it, but he was.'

'You also nearly told us that he's your father.'

'Yes, he is.' Gordon's tone was a little defiant.

'How long have you known that?'

'I always knew I was adopted, of course, and I've known him all my life. But it was only after rehearsals began . . . this is a bit difficult,' he said, and it was obvious it was the first time it had occurred to him where his frankness might lead.

116

'I know it is,' Antony sympathised, 'but now you've gone so far—'

'Yes, I suppose I may as well tell you. I never did like Victoria, though I'd never seen a lot of her before. I think Dominic told me because he thought it might make for better relations between us.'

'Told you, yes, but told you what?'

'That he was my father, and she was my mother. I'm afraid — I know it's illogical, because I had a perfectly happy childhood — that it just made me dislike her even more. I could understand about Dominic, it's difficult for a man, and he had always kept in touch and seen I was all right. But she was married, if she didn't want a divorce she could at least have taken me in and pretended I was Leonard's child.' He paused, brooding, and then added belligerently, 'I suppose you're thinking I might have been a little more original. That's a very standard reaction, isn't it?'

'I think probably a very natural one in the circumstances,' said Maitland, though he did pause for a moment to wonder why Leonard hadn't been included in the witness's ill will. Perhaps it would do no harm to ask about that. 'Mr Buckley — ' he began.

'Oh, you couldn't help liking Leonard. Not that I think he ought to have killed her,' Gordon explained carefully, 'but I don't care what he did, he's a nice chap fundamentally.'

'And in spite of the passage of — what is it, thirty years? — Mr Eldred still had a fondness for Victoria Buckley?'

'Thirty-three years actually,' said Hewitt precisely. 'And yes, I think he was still very fond of her indeed.'

Antony started to say something and stopped himself, so that Geoffrey gave him a curious look. After a moment, 'You've been very frank with us, Mr Hewitt, and I'm very grateful,' he said formally. 'There's just one more question ... a matter of fact this time, not of opinion. When the lights came on again, did you notice anything out of place on the stage?'

'Victoria was supposed to be sitting in the chair—'

'Yes, I know all that. I meant, was there anything else there that shouldn't have been? Or was any of the furniture disarranged?'

'My attention was pretty well rivetted on Victoria, it was such an extraordinary thing. I certainly didn't notice anything then, but later — the curtain was down but the lights were still on — I thought her chair wasn't standing exactly where it should have been. But that was natural enough, after all.'

'Yes, I think so. Nothing else?' Maitland persisted.

'Nothing at all.' They chatted for a few moments after that, it

117

seemed the least they could do after such a friendly reception, and then left.

'An ingenuous young man,' said Geoffrey thoughtfully as they made their way back to the car.

'I wonder,' said Antony, but couldn't be persuaded, even on the drive back to town, to amplify that remark.

II

After lunch they visited in turn Claude Aubin, and Frances Cathers. Claude was a well set up young man, not exactly handsome but with an attractive smile, and a mop of fair, curly hair. He seemed unaccountably nervous and Antony thought that a little small talk to start with wouldn't do any harm. Therefore, when Geoffrey had finished his careful explanations he remarked casually, 'I saw from the programme that your part in Jeremy Skelton's play is that of Sergeant Draper, but I never got round to seeing the second act.'

'You ought to, it's a good play,' said Claude judiciously. 'Not that the part is anything much, of course, Dominic gets all the good lines. But in these days one must be grateful for anything.'

'I'd like to, but I think my wife has reservations about going again. She's said once or twice,' said Antony, improvising freely, 'that she wondered how any of you could carry on, so soon after Mrs Buckley's death.'

'Well, there's nothing in that,' said Aubin airily. 'It's a tradition you know. And apart from that, it isn't as if any of us really liked Victoria.'

'That wasn't quite the impression I got.'

'Wasn't it?' said Claude, and dried up as though realising he had said too much.

'I understood that Mr Eldred was devoted to her.'

'Oh, Dominic! Everyone in the profession has known about that for years.' (And Meg must be one of the original three monkeys, Antony thought, half amused, half exasperated.) 'And Andy gets on with everybody, I shouldn't have included him. Or Meg, of course,' he added thoughtfully, 'she seemed to pull off the difficult feat of liking both the Buckleys equally. I don't know how she did it. But, I say, if you're Leonard's lawyers, you must think he's innocent.'

'People will tell you ours is a cynical profession,' said Antony gravely, 'but that's what we should like to prove.'

Claude Aubin seemed to be quite satisfied with this rather

118

equivocal answer. 'I should have thought – I read a lot of detective stories, you know – that you could have quite easily proved the old man was insane, suffering from delusions, something like that. I mean, I didn't like Victoria myself, but the idea of her going around with a vial of poison trying to get rid of him … it's too ridiculous for words.'

'Quite frankly, I don't know what to think myself about that,' said Antony, sounding just as ingenuous as Geoffrey had accused their previous witness of being. 'I expect before all this happened you thought murder was quite out of the question among anybody you knew.'

'Well, that's true enough. All the same –'

'I think you must leave Mr Buckley's defence to us, Mr Aubin,' said Antony, his smile robbing the words of their sting. 'You said you didn't like Mrs Buckley, can you tell me why that was?'

'So that you can try to prove I killed her?'

'Not necessarily.' He smiled again, trying to win an answering amusement from Claude. 'All these mysteries you read, you must know it's essential to find out exactly what the victim was like.'

To his surprise this explanation too seemed to go down well. 'Yes, of course,' said Claude quite eagerly. 'Well, if you want my opinion she was a meddling old woman, and malicious at that.'

'Could you explain that a little further?'

'There's a girl I've met, she's understudying Meg –'

'Miss Frances Cathers?' said Antony.

'Yes, that's right. I met her before this play, and we got on like a house on fire. Then after rehearsals started – for *Done in by Daggers*, you know – she began to cool off and I couldn't make out what was wrong. Finally it all came out, Victoria had been making mischief, telling her I don't know what about me.'

'I've a feeling that last statement isn't quite correct, Mr Aubin. I think you do know very well.'

'Yes, but I get so mad when I think about it,' Claude admitted, 'that I'd really rather let the whole matter drop.'

'Do you think Mr Buckley's guilty?'

'Yes, of course. Although I like the old boy.'

'But you will admit the possibility that you're mistaken. In that case, don't you think you should help us as much as you can to get to the bottom of Mrs Buckley's character?'

'Oh, all right!' This was said rather ungraciously, but when he started to speak his embarrassment seemed to leave him. 'She told Frances that she'd known me for years … which wasn't true, I'd heard of *her*, of course, but we'd never met until the rehearsals

119

started. She said I was ... you know ... gay, and that my parents had been worried about me and confided their worry to her. A very circumstantial story. And she said that going out with Frances was just to try to persuade them that I'd changed.'

'Why do you think she did that?'

'I haven't the faintest idea, the way women's minds work is beyond me. But Frances says she was frantically jealous of all younger people, girls in particular. I think she talked it over with Meg and that was the conclusion they came to.'

'It must have been an interesting confrontation,' said Antony thoughtfully. 'You finally got Miss Cathers to admit what was troubling her.'

This time Claude did answer his smile, in fact he laughed aloud. 'You may well say so,' he agreed. 'I cornered her one day and demanded an instant explanation, and finally it all came out.'

'And how did you convince her–'

'That there wasn't a word of truth in it? I told her the story of my life,' said Claude cheerfully. 'My love life that is. To tell you the truth I didn't really think that would mend matters, but anything was better than having her believe what Victoria had told her. Everything has been just fine between us since then. In fact,' – he paused and threw a glance in Geoffrey's direction, perhaps a little unnerved by his continued silence – 'if the play goes on running, as it seems to be doing, we're looking for a flat to share.'

'A thoroughly modern young woman,' said Antony with nothing in his tone to convey either approval or disapproval. 'Do you know of anybody else whom Mrs Buckley treated in a similar way?'

'Not to say know,' said Claude. 'Well, it stands to reason they wouldn't tell me. She was rather prone to make snide remarks, Ellie Dorman was often a target, but I don't know whether she spread any special tales about her.'

'All right then, we've come to the matters of fact,' said Antony, 'and I'm grateful to you for being so frank with us.'

But it was no use, Claude Aubin hadn't noticed anything out of order on stage – 'except Victoria's body,' he added, as Gordon Hewitt had done – and as far as he was concerned any of the people who had been standing with him in the wings – Frances Cathers and Dominic Eldred – could have taken a few steps to the left to the open garden door and gone on stage without his seeing them. And he liked Leonard, didn't want to see him in prison for what in his case would probably be the rest of his life, but there was nothing else he could tell them to help. After a while they gave it up, and took their leave.

The room Frances Cathers rented reminded them irresistibly of Claude's, large, with uncomfortable-looking, old fashioned furniture, and none too clean. It was obvious they were both trying to save money, and Antony took a moment to wonder whether they were suffering from the delusion that if they moved in together two could live as cheaply as one. However, that was none of his business. He let Geoffrey say his piece, and then he embarked on his own questions. But there was nothing to be learned, if she had noticed anything out of the way it had gone from her mind by now, and though she did say that Claude couldn't possibly have gone on stage during the blackout, he wasn't inclined to believe her. 'You were holding his hand, I suppose,' he suggested, and she agreed with him eagerly. He didn't believe that either.

However, what she had to say about Victoria Buckley coincided exactly with what Aubin had told them, though she hadn't anything to add to his opinion. As for the stage just after the murder, her only thought had been of some ghastly practical joke; about the setting she had noticed nothing at all. She was a pretty young thing, taller than Meg, fresh faced, and as fair as Claude, but Antony hoped he would never have to see her play Meg's role of Mary Carteret. 'In which I may be wronging her,' he said to Geoffrey, having confided his thoughts to him as they went down to the street again. 'She may be perfectly capable, but somehow –'

'Meg's special,' Geoffrey agreed. 'If we ever find the car again – do you remember where we left it, Antony – I'll take you home, shall I?'

'Not on your life. Mallory has me fully booked up tomorrow and I want to finish this,' said Antony firmly.

Geoffrey glanced at his watch in a marked manner, and then at his friend's face; but seeing no sign of relenting there shrugged resignedly and said, 'Very well. What do you want to do?'

'Matters arising,' said Antony vaguely. 'From our talk with our client, I mean. You know as well as I do, Geoffrey, what we need.'

'Yes, of course,' Horton agreed. 'But Cobbolds –'

'Can find the bookseller if they can,' said Antony. 'We can also talk to Victoria's dresser … unless the prosecution are calling her?'

'For some reason, they're not. I don't know why, because someone from Cobbolds has already talked to her and all she can say is, of course Mr Buckley had by far the best opportunity of daubing his wife's dress with paint.'

'Yes, I was afraid of that. So it's no use our duplicating the effort. And Leonard Buckley –'

'He used a sort of communal dresser. The men share his services, except for Dominic Eldred and Andrew Murray, whom I suppose consider themselves to be stars. It wasn't up to him,' said Geoffrey, obviously quoting, 'to search through Mr Buckley's things to see what he kept in his dressing room. He'd no idea whether he usually took Vitamin A or not.'

'Helpful!' said Antony bitterly. 'But that still leaves us with one call I think we might well make ourselves.'

'The superintendent of the building where the Buckleys lived,' said Geoffrey in a resigned tone. 'I might have known you wouldn't let me get home to tea.'

'Cheer up,' Antony exhorted him. 'Jenny will give you some if you really want it, as soon as we've finished with this chap – what's his name? Moffat? – but I should think by that time you'll be in the market for something stronger.'

III

'But it didn't really help,' Maitland confided to his audience later. Geoffrey had decided to go straight home, but Meg and Roger were having tea with Jenny when he arrived, as were Sir Nicholas and Vera. 'This Mr Moffat is quite old, and when he spoke of a young man delivering the flowers for Victoria Buckley the day of the opening, he might have meant somebody of any age up to about seventy, I should think.'

'He wasn't a Yorkshireman by any chance?' asked Meg. 'You know the way they call everyone Young Man?'

'No, he wasn't. Well, perhaps what I said was a bit of an exaggeration, he's quite convinced it was the florist himself who delivered the flowers, a rather effeminate man, very thrilled by anything concerning the theatre. That's why he insisted on delivering the flowers to the room himself, and seeing that they were properly arranged. But we have to remember all the people concerned are actors.'

'What about an identification? Or are you afraid he'd pick on your client?' said Sir Nicholas, not without malice.

'No good. I've given you Moffat's impressions, but he's far too shortsighted to be asked that question in court, counsel for the prosecution would make hay of his testimony.'

'But did delivering the flowers give the man who brought them the opportunity of planting the book and removing the stiletto?' asked Sir Nicholas, putting his finger accurately on the point at issue.

'Yes, as a matter of fact it did. Moffat is inclined to be grumpy, not that the chap, whoever he is, could have known that, and he left him to it – arranging the flowers, I mean – saying he hadn't time to stand around watching. He says it was quite ten minutes before he heard the man let himself out of the house.'

'Could he tell you the name of the shop that supplied the flowers?'

'He didn't know, and he didn't care.'

'And the Vitamin A might or might not have been planted in Mr Buckley's dressing room,' said Sir Nicholas in a meditative tone. 'I don't like it, Antony, the weight of the evidence is all against you.'

That brought an outcry from Meg. 'You're not going to stop trying, darling,' she protested. 'You none of you knew Leonard, but I'm absolutely certain –'

'I know,' said Antony bitterly. 'He wouldn't have done a thing like that.'

'Well, I know, darling, that phrase is the bane of your life. You've told me so often enough. But I don't care what you say, I won't believe it of him.'

'We haven't exactly given up,' said Antony, relenting. 'Geoffrey has still got that firm of enquiry agents of his on the job, in due course I'll be studying my brief, and then we'll see what we can make of things when we get into court.'

'Will you be calling these people you saw today?' asked his uncle.

'I think we might, the two men anyway. It might be helpful for the jury to have a picture of Victoria Buckley that wasn't that of a saint walking the earth.'

'Depends whether they repeat what they told you in court,' said Vera gruffly.

'I think they will. Geoffrey called Gordon Hewitt ingenuous, he's certainly a talkative young man, and I think he may quite enjoy a good gossip. I admit I have a few qualms about that though, he has obviously put a different interpretation on what he told us than I did.'

'You've got a theory,' said Sir Nicholas almost accusingly.

'A sort of idea,' said Antony, very vague. 'Young Hewitt is obviously very fond of his father, and thought by telling us how devoted he was to Victoria Buckley that he was removing suspicion altogether from Dominic Eldred.'

'Wasn't he?' asked Meg, fascinated.

'Not to my mind, though I'd be the first to admit I'm probably putting the wrong construction on things. He also told me, you see, that Eldred was quite convinced Victoria was really trying to poison Leonard. Don't you think he might have wanted to save her from herself?'

'Seems a bit far fetched,' said Vera.

'My view exactly, my dear,' said Sir Nicholas cordially.

'I can present you with another idea, Antony, if you like,' Roger offered.

'What's that?'

'Hewitt disliked Victoria because he found out she was his mother, he may have really disliked Dominic Eldred though he was at pains to deny it. Suppose he was being incredibly subtle –'

'My dear Roger, not even a serpent could have anticipated the convolutions of Antony's mind,' Sir Nicholas informed him. 'But what about the other young man, Claude Aubin?'

'He's in love with the girl to whom Victoria Buckley detracted him,' said Antony. 'I suppose that gives him a motive, and her too for that matter. I also think, Meg *darling*, that when you were pretending to come clean with us the other day you were still holding a good deal back.'

Sir Nicholas closed his eyes in wordless protest. Meg looked back at Antony steadily without speaking, but Jenny jumped quickly to her defence. 'Antony, you've known Meg all these years, surely you've realised by now –'

'That she can't stand gossip. Yes, of course, I've realised it,' said Antony a little crossly. 'But all this isn't helping us frame our defence.'

'So nobody saw the black cloth except you, Meg,' said Sir Nicholas.

'I didn't imagine it,' she flashed back at him.

'No, I don't suppose you did. Tell me, Antony, have you broached this insane idea of calling Superintendent Briggs to the witness stand to Geoffrey yet?'

'Yes, I told him after we left old Mr Moffat this evening,' said Antony. 'That's why he didn't come home with me, he's far too annoyed. We sat in the car and argued for what seemed like an age, and then he drove me home and said he'd think about it.'

'He'll come round,' said Vera, as though she thought her

nephew might be in need of some consolation. Antony grinned at her.

'I expect he will,' he agreed. 'And you may pray, both of you,' he added, looking from Roger to Meg and then back again, 'that Briggs is as observant as his profession ought to make him. Otherwise, Meg, I'm afraid you're for it.'

This time Sir Nicholas was again moved to faint protest, but for once in his life nobody – except perhaps Vera – seemed to be paying any attention to him.

Easter was late that year, and – as Antony and Geoffrey had both expected – the trial was not due to come on until after the recess. It was, however, high on Mr Justice Bellman's list, so though the matter was of no great urgency it couldn't be overlooked altogether. One Tuesday Roger called to say that he had succeeded, with some difficulty, in getting tickets for *Done in by Daggers* that evening, and would Jenny and Antony accompany him? Meg was very keen that they should see the play in its entirety. Antony agreed, guessing that that was what Jenny would have wished him to do. Her feelings were mixed, he knew, but perhaps curiosity triumphed over distaste.

By a coincidence it was that same afternoon that Detective Chief Inspector Sykes telephoned him. Antony had just been presented with a cup of tea, with two soggy Marie biscuits in the saucer, and his concentration having already been broken was ready enough to talk to his old friend. That was, he thought, the best word to use for the relationship that had grown up between the two of them, even though they had more often been adversaries. Sykes was a fair-minded man with a strong sense of justice and was ready enough to acknowledge a sense of obligation when he felt one was owing.

When he talked to Maitland there was often a tinge of amusement in his voice, and when anything moved him he was all too liable to slip back into his native dialect. This afternoon both the amusement and the broad Yorkshire vowels were very much in evidence. 'Nah then, lad,' he said, as soon as he was quite sure the call had been put through and he was addressing the right person, 'what's to do then?'

'You've been talking to the dear Superintendent,' said Antony, amused in his turn.

'Detective Chief Superintendent Briggs,' said Sykes impressively. And then, his voice rising a little on a note of protest – a thing Antony had never heard from him before – 'You can't do this you know, it's unheard of!'

'I haven't done anything,' said Maitland virtuously.

'Don't tell me you're not behind this *sub poena* he's received,' said Sykes. 'I never heard of such a thing.'

126

'We live and learn,' said Maitland sententiously. 'And I'm not at all sure, Chief Inspector, that we ought to be talking to each other at all. In the circumstances,' he pointed out.

'We're not talking about the case, just this mad idea of yours –'

'That's what Uncle Nick says too,' Antony sighed.

'What does he say?'

'That it's an insane idea. At least, I think he said insane but whatever it was it came to the same thing. But even Uncle Nick admits there's nothing improper about it. You're the investigating officer. Briggs happened to be there, but he's merely a witness now.'

'But what on earth do you hope to gain by it?'

'Now that, Chief Inspector, is something I can't tell you.' If Sykes could but have seen him he would have noticed that Maitland's humourous look was very marked indeed at this moment. 'Do you realise,' he went on dulcetly, 'that you're trying to influence my conduct of the case?'

'I'm doing nothing of the sort,' said Sykes, horrified. 'Though I suppose,' he added thoughtfully, 'that if you wish to make an issue of the matter in court –'

'You know me better than that.'

'Yes, I do. And you know I'm only trying to stop you from making a fool of yourself,' said Sykes bluntly. 'If the Chief Superintendent knew anything –'

'He got backstage before you did, Chief Inspector.'

'If he knew anything,' said Sykes doggedly, 'he'd have told me. And I'd be calling him myself. You're just trying to raise the devil –'

'Nothing of the sort. I'm just trying to do the best for my client,' said Maitland.

'You know something that I don't know,' said Sykes accusingly.

'If I did, you'd be the last person I'd tell. And if I did I shouldn't be calling Briggs,' pointed out Antony reasonably. 'But you must admit,' he added gently, 'it should enliven the proceedings considerably.'

This brought nothing from the other end of the line but an exclamation of annoyance and a moment later the gentle replacing of the receiver. Antony was left to reflect that for the first time in all their long acquaintance he had spoken to Sykes and not been cross-examined carefully as to the health and well-being of every member of his family, his own included.

127

He'd been right about Jenny's feelings in the matter of an evening at the theatre. She went with him eagerly and Roger joined them within a very few minutes of their arrival. It was a full house, which he said was nothing out of the ordinary, and the seats he'd been able to obtain were well to the side but still with a good view. 'I thought this would give you the chance of observing some of the witnesses you will be up against in court,' said Roger, slipping into his seat.

'Yes, that was well thought of. I don't see Jeremy and Anne here though,' said Antony, looking about him and seeing the empty box where the author and his wife had been sitting on the first night.

'No, I think he feels it's well launched now. Meg says he's in the middle of another book.'

'Geoffrey will be glad of that I should say. Whatever Jeremy's lost interest in it isn't in Leonard Buckley's case, he telephones every other day for news.'

'The old boy seems to have had a great capacity for making friends. I wish you could get him off Antony, it will make Meg very unhappy if you don't.'

'Who lives may learn,' said Antony lightly.

'And I also hope,' said Roger, not seeming to notice the comment, 'that you'll be able to do it without her intervention. We haven't talked of the matter again when we've been with you –'

'No, I thought it was better to let it rest.'

' – but I know it's preying on her mind that she might have to give evidence herself.'

'Tell her she's being illogical,' said Antony, and heard Roger's smothered laugh as the curtain went up.

The first act of course was familiar to them, but this time Maitland looked at the actors themselves with more interest. Meg, of course ... if something was indeed preying on her mind there was no evidence of it. She was a beautiful and witty Mrs Carteret, dallying oh-so-gracefully with a man whom nobody would have dreamed to be her junior. The man in question, played by Gordon Hewitt, Antony had already met and talked to at some length, so here too there was not so much to interest him. But when it came to Andrew Murray, playing Meg's husband and due to meet a sticky end at the end of the first act, he was glad of the chance of observing him in greater detail.

Murray was one of those men who at forty-five – perhaps even fifty – are still almost nauseatingly handsome. That suited the role he was playing, an actor who broke everyone's heart, and Meg was quite equal to the task of conveying to the audience the fact that in spite of her own dalliance hers might be one of them. Mentally Maitland went over what he knew about Andrew Murray. Somebody had said he was a man who got on with everybody which might or might not be true, but on the whole it didn't seem likely. He didn't look like a nonentity. He had also been the first person to tell the police of the rift between the two Buckleys, but as everyone seemed to have known of it in spite of Meg's insistence on secrecy it was likely that they would have heard the news in any case before the investigation was over. Meg said she had known Andy for years, and somebody had said that Andy was in love with her. That started a train of thought, but he put it aside for further consideration and fell to studying the actor as intently as if he had him already in the witness box. Murray was more than competent, he was brilliant, Antony decided, quite in Meg's class. That being so it was a little surprising that he should meet his doom so early, but then Maitland began to see that the character of Douglas Carteret, cleverly drawn by Jeremy Skelton, was an integral part of the plot and would probably play its own part in the solution of the mystery. Exactly what he had told his own witnesses about Victoria Buckley. Could it be an omen? He smiled to himself at the thought, but rather annoyingly it remained with him.

There was Ellie Dorman, too, to consider, an attractive enough woman in her own way; not, to his mind, Meg's equal, but another good actress who succeeded in conveying well enough an attraction that could well have been the downfall of the character Andrew Murray was playing, even if it hadn't been made clear already that he was unfaithful to his wife every chance he got. But watching the actors, watching the setting in which they moved, another idea began to take hold of him. Something that might be of help to him, something incidentally, that made him lose a little interest in the female members of the cast. He felt in his pocket surreptitiously for one of the envelopes he carried about with him, and scrawled something across it. Uncle Nick might say, another insane idea, but much he cared for that.

So the act wore on to its inevitable conclusion. Jenny clutched at his arm as the lights went out and he patted her hand consolingly if absent-mindedly. But all was well. When they could see again there was only one body on the stage, and Andrew Murray remained where he had fallen on the floor while the scene played itself out.

During the interval they made their way to the bar, where Roger had had the forethought to make arrangements for their drinks to be awaiting them. 'What did you think of the two understudies?' he asked idly.

'I thought it was positively gruesome seeing them there,' said Jenny. 'They aren't the Buckleys, of course, but I think they're doing pretty well now.' But Antony had to admit that he'd hardly noticed either of them, his attention had been so taken up with the people who might have been concerned in the murder.

'There's some idea or other that's come into your head,' said Roger shrewdly, watching his face.

Antony might have said, 'Two ideas as a matter of fact,' but he confined himself to admitting that the other man was right. 'I decided to *sub poena* the chair that Victoria Buckley was sitting in immediately before she was killed,' he said.

'But I thought – ' Jenny objected.

'Don't take me literally, love. To be absolutely accurate, to introduce it as an exhibit.'

'I can't see that it would be much use now,' said Roger. 'After all, people have been pulling it about for weeks. And if it had any evidence to give, the police would have found it.'

'If you are talking about fingerprints, Geoffrey says it was absolutely covered with them, pretty well all the stagehands had handled it at some time or another. Anyway, we're postulating that the murderer used a cloth to hold the handle of the stiletto. That isn't the point,' said Antony, but when Roger pressed him about it he declined to say anything more.

In the second act Claude Aubin revealed himself as a good enough actor, perhaps even a little too good for the rather small role he was playing. But it was, of course, Dominic Eldred who took Antony's attention. He had been told that Eldred was Victoria Buckley's age, though if anything he looked younger. He had iron grey hair, rather close cut but which curled tightly, an impressive manner, and a good grasp of the part he was playing. It made Antony reflect with a little wry amusement that if anybody knew exactly how a police inspector would behave towards a suspect it was Jeremy Skelton. The book, he recollected, had been written before the unpleasant events that preceded Jeremy's marriage to Anne, but in turning it into a play he had doubtless drawn somewhat on his own experiences.

The evening wore on, the murderer was exposed, and Meg, witty to the last, so that Antony had the further thought that perhaps the part had been rewritten with her in mind, fell with a glad cry into Gordon Hewitt's arms. The applause was tumultuous and there were at least five curtain calls, after which Roger went backstage to wait until Meg had succeeded in removing her makeup and was ready for ordinary society again.

They had decided to eat after the theatre that night, and Jenny had prepared a cold buffet for them at home. When they got to Kempenfeldt Square, however, the parking situation was completely out of hand, which was unusual at night because three sides of the square housed offices now. Roger dropped the two women off at the door of number five, but Antony stayed with him until they found a spot for the car, glad enough of the opportunity to speak to him alone. 'I don't think,' he said, as they turned across the square, 'that Meg is the only one who's been trying to hide things from me.'

Roger didn't answer immediately, and though his stride didn't falter there was all at once a sort of stillness about him. 'I wonder what you mean by that,' he asked warily.

'An idle thought that came to me while I was watching the play.'

'Yes, I thought there was something,' said Roger rather sharply.

'Oh, I was telling you the truth about the chair. But I thought this was something we might keep between ourselves. It concerns you ... and Meg.'

'What has Meg got to do with anything?'

'Roger, you've known me long enough and well enough to realise I'd do anything in the world for her,' Antony assured him. 'I just think you're making a bit of an ass of yourself, that's all.'

'Perhaps you'll explain that,' said Roger, mildly now.

'I've every intention of doing so. You know we've been told, even Meg admitted it, that Victoria Buckley resented growing old. No, I don't think anybody put it exactly in those words, but that's what they meant, and she particularly resented younger women. You've been behaving like a cat on hot bricks ever since Meg took this part—'

'You know all about that, Antony. You warned me about it yourself.'

'I warned you you'd never keep her away from the theatre, and over the years you've done pretty well in putting up with it,' said Antony. 'But this time was different. Jenny said it was almost as if you'd made it a test of some kind in your own mind, whether she took the part or not. Was that true?'

There was a very long silence. 'In a way I suppose it was,' admitted Roger reluctantly.

'But why? Why on this particular occasion should you feel like

131

that?' Another silence. 'It was because of something Victoria Buckley said to you, wasn't it?' Antony persisted.

'How the devil did you know that?'

'As Uncle Nick isn't here I may as well tell you I was guessing,' said Antony. 'But I'm beginning to feel I knew the lady pretty well. I can almost hear her saying to you, "Meg and Andy Murray have always seemed to me a perfect couple. They've known each other for so long it seems as if it was meant that they should be acting husband and wife now."' His mimicry of the dead woman's voice and manner were wickedly exact, so that Roger, who had forgotten for the moment his friend's facility in that direction, gave him a really startled look.

'That's almost exactly what she said to me,' he admitted. But then he sighed. 'Your guesswork was always pretty good, wasn't it?' he said. 'As I should know if anybody does.'

'Well, the thing is,' said Antony, 'you've learned just as much about Mrs Buckley as I have. Don't you see now there was no foundation for any of these stories of hers?'

'Yes, I suppose I do.' Roger laughed, but not as though he was amused. 'You think I should stop worrying and concentrate on being a good husband to my famous wife,' he added.

'That's it exactly.' He knew perfectly well that this was one aspect of the situation that had never caused Farrell the slightest difficulty. 'Not that you'll ever be good enough for Meg,' said Antony earnestly, and halted as they came to the bottom of the steps outside number five. 'But then' – he smiled suddenly – 'she'll never be anywhere near good enough for you either, Roger, so I'd call it quits if I were you.'

132

PART TWO

REGINA *versus* BUCKLEY

Easter Term, 1973

TUESDAY, The First Day of the Trail

I

Mr Justice Bellman had only recently been raised to the Bench and this happened to be the first time that Antony had appeared before him. They were members of the same Inn however, and therefore knew each other quite well in a casual sort of way, even though the judge was a somewhat older man. It was not without a feeling of foreboding that Maitland went into court that morning, he suspected that Bellman was a man completely without humour, and Derek Stringer – also a member of Sir Nicholas's chambers, who was acting as his junior – had told him that the judge was a stickler for all the small points of etiquette which must sometimes be waived if a trail is not to drag on indefinitely. It seemed unlikely that he would allow any tactics on the part of the defence that didn't comply with his own idea of orthodoxy, or any line of questioning whose relevance he himself could not understand. And Maitland wondered, looking up at the scarlet-clad figure on the bench, just what the harvest of that would be for his client.

Leonard Buckley was in the dock by now, listening to the indictment, and Maitland's first thought on seeing him had been that the prisoner had shrunk still more during the last weeks of his incarceration. But then Buckley seemed to pull himself together, almost as though the watching eyes were in some way a tonic, so that Antony was reminded that his client was, after all, an actor. That sent his mind scurrying back over the years to the last time he had seen a member of that profession in a similar position. The case had been Sir Nicholas's and he himself a witness, but it had been obvious at the time that if one were to get mixed up in anything criminal it was most undesirable that in private life you should have anything to do with the stage. The most sincere statement could be discounted with the single phrase, The man's an actor, and if he wasn't very careful that's what the jury would be thinking about Leonard Buckley too. His worst fears were confirmed when he looked down and saw a note that Derek had pushed in front of him. 'He likes an audience,' Stringer had written, with an exclamation mark emphasising the point. 'I suppose that's only to be expected, but it won't help us.'

135

Maitland read the note, and gave its author the briefest of smiles in acknowledgement, and then hid the paper under his brief. The preliminaries, which really didn't need his attention because they were so familiar, were over by now, and his opponent, a man called Lamb, who had once been solicitor-general, was getting to his feet to make his opening speech for the prosecution. This was a moment Maitland hated, particularly when, as now, he believed his client to be innocent; a view he held to rather stubbornly, knowing well enough that neither his instructing solicitor nor his junior agreed with him, any more than his family did. With the exception, of course, of Jenny; but Jenny, bless her, had not a legal mind.

It was soon obvious that his discomfort on his client's behalf was well justified; Lamb had the story of the crime off pat, and described Leonard Buckley's part in it in convincing detail, none of which could have made good hearing for the man in the dock. Maitland slid down in his seat and closed his eyes, a small indication of lack of interest which no longer deceived anybody, though at one time it would have set Geoffrey, seated behind him, to poking him in the ribs to make sure he missed nothing. This time he was allowed to remain undisturbed, listening to Lamb's sad account of infamy, which seemed to depress him so much that he sounded not very far off tears.

Sir Gerald Lamb was a scholarly looking man of middle height, with straight hair, still very thick, and pince-nez perched on an aristocratic nose. Even when he was wearing his gown, the odd way he carried his shoulders was very evident, and Maitland was always reminded by the sight of him of a large, melancholy bird hunched against the wind. But he was a formidable opponent, quick to see the drift of opposing counsel's questions, and only too ready to spike his guns if at all possible. His other outstanding attribute, a passion for thoroughness, was very apparent at the moment. Every point must be hammered home, it wouldn't do to ask the jury to take anything for granted.

By the time he had finished the morning was far advanced, and Maitland was beginning to hope for an adjournment. But Mr Justice Bellman was evidently made of sterner stuff than some of his colleagues, he made no move in that desirable direction, but instead the first witness was called. Maitland roused himself to listen, though it was doubtful whether at this point anything would be said to which he could take exception. Beside him, Derek's pen moved steadily, taking notes. Lamb had chosen to begin with purely technical evidence. A scale model of the stage, including

136

that part of the backstage area immediately surrounding it, was introduced and the man who had made the model and taken the measurements was called on to swear to their accuracy. The fingerprint experts followed; they had found nothing abnormal, nothing at all unexpected. There was nothing here for the defence, the fact that there were no prints on the Vitamin A bottle having been brought out in direct examination. Nothing else was under dispute, except that Maitland asked, after the condition of the stiletto had been cited as evidence that the murderer had worn gloves, 'Might not a cloth round the handle have served his purpose as well?' The answer to that, of course, was yes, but it didn't prove anything.

After that, mercifully, the recess was called. 'We needn't have commandeered the chair after all, Geoffrey,' said Antony as the defence team left the court together. 'That model is perfect for our purpose, and as the prosecution introduced it themselves not even Briggs is going to accuse me of any trickery.' But after that they talked of other things. There would be more arguments later, when the case for the prosecution really got under way.

II

After lunch there was a stir of interest in the court when Detective Chief Inspector Marmaduke Sykes of the Criminal Investigation Department at Scotland Yard took the stand. He was a square-built man with an air of content about him, and Antony reflected as he watched him take the oath that in all the years they had known each other he had never seen Sykes rattled. The examination-in-chief took some time. Sykes had never been a man to rely on quotations from his notebook, written in stilted and officially acceptable language, and Antony had observed before that most judges seemed to prefer this. It turned out however, that Mr Justice Bellman was the exception; he interrupted repeatedly, demanding that a statement be rephrased, and the wonder was that Sykes's placidity didn't seem to be ruffled. His evidence was, of course, to a great extent a confirmation of facts already stated to the jury and Sir Gerald Lamb, growing more melancholy by the moment, did not allow him to spare the court from their repetition. In addition, the prisoner's original statement to the police was admitted in evidence. There was some skirmishing about that, but the prosecution prevailed. Still, at last it was over. Sir Gerald, who could be trusted to observe the courtesies, handed the witness over to the defence with a polite word of thanks.

Maitland was already on his feet. 'I don't think, Chief Inspector, that my questions will detain either you or the court very long,' he began. 'But there's one thing in particular that I should like to ask you. You have cited a number of points seeming to indicate the guilt of the gentleman who is my client, but for the most part these had not come to light when he was placed under arrest. Can you explain the rapidity with which you reached the conclusion that that step was justified?'

For the first time he thought he detected a shade of discomfort in Sykes's expression. 'In the course of the interviews that were held in the theatre on the evening of the murder two things came to light,' he said. 'We were told of the motive—'

'Ah yes,' Maitland interrupted. 'This idea that the deceased had resorted to poison in an effort to ensure that her husband should be the victim, not herself.'

'That is accurate as far as it goes, Mr Maitland,' said Sykes in his careful way. 'I don't know whether Mrs Buckley was trying to poison her husband or not, and at this stage there seems to be no possibility of obtaining proof either way. But the accused certainly believed that she was doing so, or said he did. And the ill will between them was well known to other members of the cast of the play.'

'That is one point, Chief Inspector. Is that all you had to go on?'

'No, but it seemed expedient to interview Mr Buckley again. It turned out that he had in his pocket a pair of black cotton gloves, which he explained by saying that they were one of the props of the play. They were to be found in his possession during the second act, as part of the proof that he was the murderer.'

'Didn't you believe this explanation?'

'I made enquiries later and found it to be true.'

'You're not trying to tell us, Chief Inspector, that the fact that the role he was playing in the play was that of the murderer somehow makes it more likely that he killed his wife?'

Sykes was incautious enough to permit himself a smile. 'Come now, Mr Maitland,' he said, his accent broadening a little. 'You know better than that.'

Mr Justice Bellman leaned forward. 'Sir Gerald,' he said.

'M'lud?'

'Your witness seems to have very little idea of the seriousness of these proceedings.'

'I beg your lordship's pardon,' said Lamb. 'Perhaps if my learned friend, Mr Maitland, will confine himself to matters concerning the evidence – ' He broke off there, apparently too unhappy to continue any further.

'If your lordship pleases,' said Maitland quickly. He had no desire to see Sykes castigated because they were by way of being friends. 'That is two pieces of evidence, or so-called evidence, that you have cited, Chief Inspector. Was that all you had to go on when you made the arrest?'

'It seemed sufficient,' said Sykes placidly.

'To you, or to one of your superior officers whom I understand was also present at the play that evening?'

'Chief Superintendent Briggs was present, certainly, but it wasn't fitting that a man of his rank should continue as investigating officer,' said Sykes, sidestepping the question neatly.

'No, that's obvious. I'm still waiting to hear which of you decided that an arrest was the next appropriate move?'

'It was a joint decision,' said Sykes.

'Mr Maitland!' Mr Justice Bellman leaned forward again. 'I understand you will be calling the Chief Superintendent as one of the defence witnesses. Are you trying to discredit him in advance?'

'Indeed no, my lord. That is the furthest thing from my thoughts. But I have found in the past, as I am sure your lordship must have done, that where there is a preconceived notion on the part of the police, the consequences may not always be completely desirable.'

'This is no time to address the jury, Mr Maitland,' said the judge coldly. 'And I think this line of questioning has proceeded far enough.'

'If your lordship pleases,' said Maitland again. He sounded resigned, but he wasn't altogether dissatisfied. 'May I be permitted to ask the witness, however, whether he attaches any importance to this pair of black cotton gloves?'

Sykes glanced at the judge, but receiving no sign answered the question. 'I think in the circumstances they are very important indeed,' he said firmly.

'The circumstances being that no fingerprints were found on the hilt of the dagger?'

'That is so. If you listened to the previous evidence, Mr Maitland,' said Sykes solemnly (but there was amusement underlying the statement as Maitland well knew) 'you'll have heard that, as there was of course no real fingerprint-taking in the play, there was no reason for anything to be handled carefully.'

139

'But the dagger – I believe we should be saying "stiletto", Chief Inspector – was not one of the properties.'

'No, but unless our expert told a completely different story in court this morning to the one he told me, the surface was such that, if it had been handled without gloves, a very clear impression of the murderer's hand would have remained.'

'I see. Thank you, Chief Inspector.' Sykes looked a little bewildered for a moment at this unexpected and obviously heartfelt gratitude. 'So we will return to the other points, the things that came to light after you formed what I can only think was this rather rash decision to proceed to an arrest.' He caught the judge's eye and added hastily, 'Precisely, my lord, that is a point the members of the jury can very well decide for themselves.' (He had no better an opinion of the collective intelligence of juries than most other barristers, but it didn't do to say so. This one looked a good average bunch.) 'You've examined the model stage setting for *Done in by Daggers*,' he said then with a note of enquiry in his voice. 'Both today in court, and probably at an earlier time.'

'I've examined it very carefully,' Sykes agreed.

'Could you tell me then whether the furniture is placed exactly as it was when you first saw it?'

'I have to qualify my answer to that a little,' said Sykes. 'I didn't myself take the measurements. But as far as I can tell, and I did observe the setting very carefully, the model is exactly right.'

'Including the position of the chair in which Victoria Buckley was sitting before the lights went out?'

'Naturally I looked at that most carefully.'

'And the model shows it as you first observed it?'

'It does.'

'Then to turn to the other items of evidence that have been adduced against my client. The stiletto for instance?'

'I was informed by a colleague of the accused that it belonged to Mrs Buckley. If I may repeat myself–'

'There's no need for that.'

'– Mr Buckley's statement was introduced into evidence during my examination-in-chief. He had stated categorically at the time he made it that he had never seen the dagger before. Or the stiletto, since you seem to prefer that word.'

'I believe it is more exact. At the time my client gave the statement, I understand he had not seen his solicitor.'

'No, that's true, though it had been suggested to him that it would be advisable for him to do so.'

140

'I see.' He put as much sinister meaning as he could into the words. 'This Mr Eldred now –'

'If you're going to ask me, Mr Maitland, if he could make a positive identification, the answer is that he could. He himself purchased the stiletto, gave it to Mrs Buckley many years ago, and had since then seen it continually in her possession. In the flat she shared with her husband,' he added, not wishing there to be any mistake about that.

'Thank you, Chief Inspector,' said Maitland, rather ironically this time. 'I didn't suppose she was in the habit of carrying it about in her stocking. Another point of yours is the book on anatomy that was found in the Buckleys' residence.'

'*Stubbs on Anatomy*,' said Sykes in his exact way. 'I did not have the opportunity of questioning Mr Buckley about that, as you can understand, but it seems a strange sort of reading for a man of his type.'

'Forgive me, but I think you know very little about my client,' said Antony, allowing a little sharpness to come into his voice. 'However, he will himself give evidence about this when the time comes. In the meantime I have no desire to enter into a controversy with you, but I think you will agree that both these matters are circumstantial only. For instance, some unauthorised person gaining access to the flat could have introduced the one while he removed the other.'

'That's possible of course,' said Sykes, unmoved by the suggestion.

'And the bottle of Vitamin A, on which you seem to set such store, doesn't the same thing apply to that? It could have been introduced into Mr Buckley's dressing room by a third party.'

'It could. If you are willing to accept the fact that someone was deliberately trying to frame your client.'

Maitland ignored that. 'You'll forgive me if I say I find the introduction of this empty bottle into evidence a little puzzling. Many people take vitamin supplements today.'

'The contention is –' Sykes began.

'Yes, I know what the prosecution contends. They say that a large dose of this particular vitamin enables the person who takes it to see better in the dark; to make the adjustment from light to dark more quickly, I should say. You'll forgive me if I tell you that I find that a little far-fetched.' Sykes said nothing to this, though he may have felt there were a good many requests for his forgiveness flying about. 'As I understand it,' Maitland went on, 'any actor required to plunge on to the stage in pitch blackness would prepare himself by keeping his eyes shut for a few moments, perhaps by covering them with his hands as well, so that the sudden darkness would be no problem and he would be able to see the phosphorescent paint placed on the furniture to guide him.'

'That is all true, of course,' Sykes agreed. 'The Vitamin A would be an added precaution, understandable enough in somebody with murder in mind.'

'Yes, I agree with you there. Where we disagree is on the identity of the murderer. May I ask you whether you observed anything strange in my client's appearance when you questioned him shortly after his wife's death?'

Sykes frowned over that, as though the question puzzled him. 'He was nervous and upset,' he said at last.

'Not unnaturally, innocent or guilty.'

'No, not unnaturally.'

Perhaps Antony found this answer satisfactory, in any event he switched course again. 'You're familiar with the properties of Vitamin A, Chief Inspector, since the prosecution has made it one of the planks of their case against Mr Buckley.'

The judge intervened at this point. 'Mr Maitland, do you not feel these matters might be best gone into when the doctors take the stand?'

'Indeed I do, my lord. I, or my friend Mr Stringer, will be bringing the subject up with them, of course. But there is one point I should like to make here and now. Whether the police consider the murder to have been premeditated or a matter of impulse.'

'And the properties of Vitamin A have something to do with this?' asked the judge sceptically.

'If you'll permit me, my lord –'

'Very well, Mr Maitland, you may proceed.'

'I'm obliged to your lordship. To be brief then, Chief Inspector, what I'm about to say can be verified when the medical evidence is given. A massive dose of Vitamin A, which might be expected to have an immediate effect on the night vision of the person taking it, could not be repeated without danger to the said person's health. You'll tell me, no doubt, that in Leonard Buckley's case he might have been taking the stuff regularly ever since the parts were allotted to him and his wife and he knew what the play called for. Can you produce any witness to the fact that he had been taking this vitamin at least during the period of the rehearsals?'

'As far as I know, nobody had seen him taking it.'

'Thank you, Chief Inspector.' Maitland paused to smile at the judge, who had been about to intervene. 'We are therefore left with

142

the assumption that Leonard Buckley took the massive dose I spoke of in preparation for that night's doings. May I ask you why he of all people should have needed to do so, when he was standing in the wings able and indeed expected to take such precautions as would enable him to see the phosphorescent paint easily when the stage was darkened? In anybody else the act of covering their eyes would have caused comment, and indeed suspicion.'

'That is true, of course,' said Sykes, ever willing to be fair. 'But I don't feel myself qualified to comment on the state of mind of a man about to commit murder.'

There was dead silence for a moment. Maitland was staring at the witness as though he had never seen him before, or perhaps wasn't even conscious of his presence. After a moment the judge said sharply, 'Mr Maitland!' Antony blinked and looked all round the room before his eyes came to rest again on the witness.

'Thank you very much indeed, Chief Inspector,' he said with a fervency that sounded exaggerated. 'I have no more questions, my lord,' he added and sat down.

Geoffrey was shaking his shoulder, though fortunately he remembered to make it the left one. 'You've thought of something,' he said, almost accusingly.

'Yes, I have, indeed I have,' said Antony without turning his head. 'Didn't you see it too, Derek?'

Stringer shook his head. Maitland did turn then and gave Horton an encouraging grin. 'I think I need some Vitamin A myself,' he said in an amused tone. 'I ought to have seen this before. Leave it for now, there's a good chap. Lamb is just going to re-examine.'

When the court adjourned for the day Chief Inspector Sykes had been on the stand for the whole afternoon, but still remained imperturbable. 'You'll tell me now,' said Geoffrey grimly as the court emptied around them. 'You've had some idea that will help our client.'

'I told you I had,' said Antony. He was piling books and papers together and then pushed them towards his clerk with a smile. 'Do you mind taking these back to chambers, Willett?' he asked. 'I think I'll go straight home when Mr Horton has finished cross-examining me.'

Willett bent to scoop up the pile. 'Yours too, Mr Stringer?' he asked.

'If you please,' said Derek. 'And I bet he's as curious as I am,' he added, as the clerk departed.

'Yes, Antony, what's all this about?' asked Geoffrey impatiently.

Maitland took time to look all round the court, and made sure no one was within earshot. 'Merely that I know now who killed Victoria Buckley,' he said aggravatingly.

'If you're only going to tell us for the hundredth time that our client didn't do it – ' Horton began, but was interrupted without ceremony.

'Nothing of the sort. Anyway, what I tell you three times is true,' said Antony, smiling. 'You really ought to have believed me.'

'Tell us what this inspiration of yours is and we'll see,' said Geoffrey.

'You'd better do so, Antony,' Derek advised. 'Geoffrey's patience is exhausted.'

'If Lamb hadn't kept Sykes for so long –'

'Yes, I know you couldn't help that. But now you're being deliberately annoying,' said Geoffrey. 'Out with it!'

'Well, all I set out to do was to emphasise that Mr Buckley probably needed Vitamin A less than anybody else. We haven't talked to all the suspects, but we have talked to someone from each group, and if anybody had been shielding their eyes just before the lights went out that would have been noticed and commented upon. But it never occurred to me before – fool that I was! – that there is one person to whom that argument doesn't apply.'

'So?' said Geoffrey, rather coldly.

'Think about the murder for a moment,' Maitland urged. 'It was done by somebody with a strong sense of drama ... well the suspects are all actors so that doesn't help us much. But the sort of person to kill by stabbing is not the sort of person with a deliberate temperament. I say it was a sudden decision made by the sort of impulsive person who couldn't have decided weeks before what he was going to do and prepared himself for the act by cold-bloodedly dosing himself with Vitamin A over a period of five or six weeks.'

'I'm inclined to agree with you,' said Derek Stringer. Horton gave him a reproachful look.

'I'm not saying you may not be right,' he said, 'and I dare say you can convince the jury of that. But where does it leave us?'

'There was one man who could have kept his eyes shut without the fact being apparent.' He was speaking quickly now, taken up with his idea and almost unconscious of his companions. 'Don't you remember, Geoffrey? You didn't see the play but you've heard all the evidence, and taken a good deal more notice of it than I have

144

I dare say. Andrew Murray, in his role as Meg's husband, was wearing dark glasses.'

'But he was on the stage!' Geoffrey objected. 'The man Leonard Buckley was supposed to murder.'

'Yes, I know,' Antony agreed. 'That's why I say he of all people might have needed the Vitamin A. He'd been sitting in the full glare of the footlights, and even with the dark glasses I think he'd have been more blinded than the others by the sudden darkness.'

'Too blind to see those paint marks we keep talking about. Yes, you may be right about that,' said Geoffrey. 'But let's consider the other aspects of this idea of yours. He was on stage, and certainly in his own chair when Mr Buckley reached him because he affixed the dagger and heard Murray's groan, and was aware – I don't know which of his senses told him this – that the other man had fallen to the ground. Would there have been time for Murray to do what was done and be back in his own expected place by the time the lights came on?'

'The lights were out for a minute and a half,' said Antony slowly.

'There's also the fact that he collided with Mr Buckley on his way back to his chair.'

'Yes, we'll take that into account too. I don't suppose the murder of – what was his name in the play, Douglas Carteret? – took more than thirty seconds, and Mr Buckley told us particularly that he knew he'd plenty of time so wasn't hurrying back into the wings. There can be no doubt that Andrew Murray in addition to being devilishly handsome is extremely agile, much more agile than our client, just as he's a much younger man. He hadn't to come all the way from the wings as Mr Buckley had, just to cover the distance between the two chairs, which he could have accomplished in the first instance flat on his stomach. The stage was carpeted if you remember . . . sorry, Geoffrey, I keep forgetting you didn't see the play. Anyway, there was quite a thick carpet and it would have deadened the sound. As I see it, he'd have taken off his glasses and resumed them again before the lights came on. He'd have to stand and get behind the chair to stab her, you know my ideas about that. And that accounts for the fact that he was off course when he encountered our client.'

'That couldn't have left him with much time,' Derek put in. 'All the same the point about the sunglasses and the Vitamin A is a valid one.'

'Dr Yarrow is one of the most distinguished nutritionists in the

145

country,' said Geoffrey. 'He'll certainly testify to the properties of the vitamin, but I gather he's never seen anyone who's taken a really large dose.'

Antony brushed that aside. 'Honestly, I don't think that matters,' he said. 'He's Lamb's witness, but we may have more good from his testimony.' And then, looking from one to the other of his companions with a half smile, 'I've given you something to think about, haven't I?'

'What do you propose to do about it?' asked Geoffrey.

'I think we should see our client. Do you suppose we can get hold of him before they take him away, Geoffrey? That would be much more convenient.'

'I dare say we can, they usually wait until the crowds have cleared away,' Geoffrey assured him.

'Then don't argue, there's a good chap, just go and see if you can find him. And if I may take a guess at what he'll tell us, it will be that Andrew Murray had a motive for getting rid of him, as well as of Victoria. We mustn't forget there's been an obvious attempt to frame him.'

Geoffrey scowled at him, but he went.

III

The interview with Leonard Buckley in one of the rooms below the court was short and to the point, and would have been even briefer if it hadn't been for the prisoner's initial reluctance to answer Maitland's questions, even though these were put with a directness that verged on incivility. He started out with a blunt statement, 'I think you haven't been altogether honest with us, Mr Buckley,' and went on from there.

'In what way?' asked Leonard, obviously taken aback.

'Do you still maintain that you don't know anybody, anybody at all, with a motive for killing your wife?'

'I told you about Gordon Hewitt, who did seem to resent her. But he's a nice young man, he would never have carried his dislike to those lengths.'

'I'm not talking about Hewitt now. I'm talking about Andrew Murray.'

'But he was on stage, I'd just stabbed him,' said Buckley ingenuously, and then added quickly, 'in the play I mean.'

'Mr Buckley, you're evading the question. How long had you known Andrew Murray?'

'Oh, for many years.'

'How did you first meet?'

'A play we were doing that had been a great success in the West End was taken on tour. We haven't really done that sort of thing for some time, but the inducement that was offered was one we couldn't refuse. Andy was still playing the provinces then, we met him at a party someone or other was giving, I can't quite remember.'

'And –?'

'Oh dear, this is very distressing.'

'It will be still more distressing if you don't tell me,' said Maitland grimly. 'All we've been doing so far, Mr Stringer and I, has been running round in circles.'

'But I promised him ... and anyway it doesn't follow –'

'You know something about Murray that you have been keeping silent about. It may interest you to know, Mr Buckley,' Maitland added with calculated brutality, 'that he isn't willing to extend the same courtesy to you.'

'What on earth do you mean?'

'You haven't been putting two and two together, Mr Buckley. Murray gave evidence at the magistrate's court hearing.'

'Yes he did, but he was bound to answer the questions put to him.'

'And how did the prosecution know what questions to put?' Antony demanded. 'Because he had gone into the whole sorry story of the relationship between you and your wife as soon as he got in to see them the evening before.'

'I wouldn't have thought that of Andy, I wouldn't indeed.'

'Well, you can believe it. Mr Horton can confirm that I'm telling you the truth.'

'Of course I'm not doubting you, Mr Maitland. Only I think –'

'Something you know to his detriment,' said Maitland inexorably. 'Something that Mrs Buckley knew as well. And now I come to think of it, is it loyalty to her or loyalty to him that's keeping you silent?'

'Victoria was sometimes ... impulsive,' said Leonard miserably.

'I think from what I've learned of her that she was the main threat to him, but I'm sure he had no objection to getting rid of you at the same time.'

The silence lengthened while Leonard Buckley absorbed this statement. Perhaps he was thinking of the evidence that had been piling up against him. At length, 'I suppose I'd better tell you,' he said, but still with some reluctance. 'There was a girl he'd been living with, in Manchester this was. She w s trying to make a go of it on the stage herself, and she was a nice little thing, pretty, but with no personality whatever. She obviously hadn't a hope.'

'So far a common enough story,' said Antony. 'Even ... how long did you say this was ago?'

'About fifteen years, I suppose, I don't remember exactly. And of course that wasn't all the story.'

'Tell us the rest of it then,' Antony invited.

'The inevitable happened, she had a baby. I don't necessarily believe that marriage should inevitably follow in cases of that kind, where no genuine love is involved, but he left her without a penny, apparently without a qualm. Victoria visited her in hospital, and the girl showed her a letter. I believe it was quite unnecessarily unkind.'

'There are steps the girl could have taken in a case like that,' Geoffrey put in, his legal blood obviously boiling.

'Yes, but the baby died you see. And it seems the girl had leukaemia, poor little thing, and after a year or two she died as well. That was when Andy came south, while she was in hospital, so in a way you could say it was the beginning of great things for him. But Victoria was the only one who knew exactly what had happened, except that she told me, and that sort of publicity wouldn't have been at all good for him professionally. A love affair is one thing, deserting a helpless girl quite another.'

'I can imagine that. But this is fifteen years ago, you say, did something happen to bring the matter to a head at this late date?'

'I'm very much afraid that Victoria did that herself. She wasn't very happy with the way rehearsals were going, particularly with the scene she had with Andy, just before he's killed in the play. She thought he was making things difficult for her deliberately, and came in one evening announcing that she'd settled his hash and things would go better from now on.'

'Did she tell you how she had ensured that?'

'Yes,' said Leonard, and paused for so long that Antony thought he wasn't going to continue and was about to prompt him when he added of his own accord, 'I'm afraid she told him a lie. She said she had the letter in her possession, and that she would tell the whole story, using it as proof, unless he mended his ways. I remonstrated with her of course, but there wasn't ever any arguing with Victoria. She was as pig-headed as a mule.'

'I see.' Maitland was up from his chair and pacing the narrow

148

room for a few moments before he spoke again. 'And he thought he could trust you – you nearly proved him right about that – but all the same he'd be happier if you were safely out of the way in prison.' Then he stopped pacing and whirled round, to speak directly, and very forcefully to his client. 'I don't want this to come out during your direct examination, Mr Buckley. Do you understand that? We'll confine ourselves to your denial of the facts that the prosecution are citing against you. And in cross-examination you won't be asked questions about Murray, because Lamb doesn't know anything about all this.'

'But –' said Derek and Geoffrey together. Antony swung round to answer them. 'If things go as I hope we'll get an opportunity to recall Murray, then we can ask *him*.'

'You're taking a chance,' said Geoffrey disapprovingly. 'I think you ought to attack him in cross-examination before the prosecution close their case.'

'No, I won't do that. It will be much more effective to get some backing for our story first.'

'You're thinking of Superintendent Briggs,' said Geoffrey accusingly, 'and you don't even know what he's going to say.'

'No, I don't, but . . . bear with me, Geoffrey. I really do feel this is the right way to go about it.'

Geoffrey, recollecting suddenly the impropriety of arguing on such a matter in front of their client, said no more. Derek, as was his custom, had fallen silent as soon as he realised the futility of arguing with his leader. They left Leonard Buckley shortly after, a rather bewildered old man, but Maitland was under no illusion that the matter was closed so far as his instructing solicitor was concerned.

IV

After that Antony was naturally late home, and Sir Nicholas and Vera had already joined Jenny upstairs for their regular Tuesday evening dinner together. Jenny got up when he went in to fetch another glass of sherry, Vera said in her gruff way, 'Had a long day,' but Sir Nicholas gave him time to greet them before saying in his most dulcet tones, 'Halloran tells me you've got some bee in your bonnet about Vitamin A.'

'How on earth does he know?'

'Mr Halloran always knows everything,' Jenny put in.

'If you are suddenly struck dumb in the middle of cross-examination you must expect some comment,' his uncle told him.

149

'I gather you were in the act of trying to persuade the court of your client's innocence on the grounds that he wouldn't have needed it.'

'It's backed by some perfectly respectable medical opinion, plus a little elementary psychology,' Antony protested, accepting a glass and placing it in its usual place on the mantelpiece. He was tired that evening and far too restless to sit down immediately. 'Besides,' he added and looked from one to the other of them in a deliberately tantalising way, 'it gave me an idea.'

'If it's on a par with your ideas so far about this business, I don't suppose it's much help,' said Sir Nicholas roundly.

'Well, I'll tell you.' He expanded obligingly on Leonard Buckley's story.

'Motive,' said Sir Nicholas judiciously when he had finished. 'That doesn't prove anything.'

'I know that, and it's why I won't have the matter brought out until we have some other evidence before the court,' said Antony. 'Geoffrey is all for attacking Murray as soon as we get him on the stand, or rather, as soon as Lamb has finished with him, but I vetoed that.'

'Geoffrey has come round to your way of thinking, then?'

'I suppose he has. You know, Uncle Nick, it's true when you think about it that Murray is the only possible alternative to Mr Buckley.'

'Still a toss up,' said Vera. 'Don't think I don't sympathise with you, wanting to get your client off. But are you sure you're going about it the right way?'

'Of course I'm not sure!' said Antony, who was unfortunately prone to having three-o'clock-in-the-morning doubts at any time of the day.

'As I understand it, you're taking chances on two of your witnesses,' said Sir Nicholas. But though they went on considering the pros and cons of the course he proposed to take until Jenny announced that dinner was ready, Maitland refused to abandon his position.

Later, when Roger arrived, the talk was general; but something in his friend's manner must have alerted him, because when Antony went down to the front door of number five with him – he left a little earlier than the others because of fetching Meg from the theatre – he lingered a moment on the top step and said bluntly, 'Something's happened.'

'How do you know?' asked Antony a little taken aback.

'You've been in a state of simmering excitement all the evening,'

150

Roger told him. 'I suppose,' he added thoughtfully, 'it's something that arose in court today.'

'Not exactly. I had an inspiration, that's all. And whether I'm right or whether I'm wrong I just don't know,' he added frankly.

'Tell me about it,' Roger invited.

If there was one thing he could rely on it was Roger's integrity. Antony told him briefly what he'd already told Sir Nicholas and Vera, and in much the same words. 'But I'd rather you didn't mention this to Meg just yet,' he concluded.

'Why not?' Roger's tone was unexpectedly sharp. 'Antony, do you think this could possibly be the reason she doesn't want to give evidence? That she knows this story about Andy Murray, I mean?'

'No, I don't, and you're a fool to think it,' Antony told him, not mincing his words. 'That's just why I don't want her told. If she did know it would be awkward for her, appearing on stage with him.'

'Well ... I can't let her go on acting with the fellow,' Roger objected.

'I think you must, but if we're lucky it won't be for more than a couple of nights longer.'

'But –'

'Don't rock the boat,' Antony urged.

'Oh, all right! How sure are you about this anyway?'

'When I first thought of it, and when I heard what Leonard Buckley had to say, I was absolutely certain. Since then some doubts have crept in, but they aren't strong enough to influence my course of action.'

'You've told me often enough you won't attack a witness in court on a matter as serious as this unless you're sure you have cause.'

'That's true. I suppose that's another reason I won't say anything to Murray in cross-examination, won't commit myself to this theory until some independent evidence has been produced. And as Uncle Nick points out it's very doubtful whether it ever will be. Don't forget, Roger, not a word to Meg.'

'She may know already,' said Roger in a rather dismal tone, obviously reverting to the first thought that had come to his mind when he heard the story.

'Nonsense! She'd have told you if she had.'

'Oh, no, she wouldn't. She's quite serious about this hatred of gossip thing you know.'

'I know that,' said Antony, and forbore from reminding Roger that he had known Meg a good deal longer than he had. But he was very thoughtful as he went upstairs to join the others, and for the first time he was wondering exactly how much Meg knew that she hadn't told him.

I

The day started slowly, from Maitland's view at any rate, because these were witnesses whom he had decided Derek could deal with more capably than he could himself. Not that the point they wished to make was unimportant, but he had a shrewd suspicion that his junior was more familiar with the medical aspects of the case than he was himself, so that if anything unexpected came up . . .

About the cause of death, there was, of course, no dispute, and after that came the evidence of the finding of a small quantity of phosphorescent paint on the dress Victoria Buckley had been wearing when she died, intermingled with her blood.

'But there was not sufficient bleeding to have marked her murderer?' asked Lamb in his despairing tones.

'That's very unlikely. The stiletto was extremely sharp and driven well home. There would have been no spurting of blood at all.'

When Sir Gerald Lamb sat down again Derek Stringer came to his feet. 'I'm going to ask you to step down from the witness box for a moment, Doctor, and look at the model of the stage which is on the table in the body of the court with the other exhibits. With your lordship's permission,' he added, and Mr Justice Bellman inclined his head graciously.

There was a pause while the witness complied with counsel's request. When he was standing in front of the exhibit Stringer went on, 'Do you know which chair Victoria Buckley was sitting in, Doctor?'

'I've never seen the play, but I imagine it's the one with the chalk mark in front of it, which I take to represent her body.'

'That's right. As you look at the stage it is on the right and fairly near the front. Will you describe the chair to us?'

'I'm not an expert on furniture, but in style at least I think it's Victorian.'

'Mr Stringer,' said the judge. 'If we require evidence on this point, surely the defence will, in due course, call its own expert.'

'It's not a matter of the age of the chair, my lord, but the shape has a bearing on a matter which I think the doctor can elucidate for us. May I proceed?'

'If you have no objection, Sir Gerald?'

'None at all, m'lud.' Perhaps Lamb had his own quota of curiosity. Hearing his tone Antony thought of his opponent's nickname in legal circles, Poor Lamb, and smiled to himself.

'It's the height of the back of the chair we're concerned about, Doctor,' said Stringer turning back to the witness. 'Remembering that Victoria Buckley was not a tall lady, does anything strike you about that?'

'Indeed it does. Unless she was sitting well forward in the chair it would have been impossible for the blow to have been struck exactly where it was. Impossible, too, for the murderer to see the paint. And even if she were sitting like that,' the doctor added in a doubtful tone, causing Maitland to silently call down blessings on his head, 'I doubt if the killer's hand could have been drawn back far enough to strike the very violent blow that she received.'

'Thank you, Doctor. Now will you look at my client?'

The witness turned to look at Leonard Buckley. 'Yes?' he said questioningly.

'Perhaps you will be kind enough to stand up, Mr Buckley.' Leonard complied. 'It may be difficult for you to judge from where you stand, Doctor, but I can assure you my client is a short man, not more than five foot three. I'm sure you can judge that for yourself if you compare his height with that of the warders standing near him.'

'He's certainly a short man,' the witness agreed.

'Very well then, with his lordship's agreement I will again ask for your opinion, Doctor.' But he went on without waiting for Bellman to speak. 'If you had been creeping onto the stage yourself to commit this murder, how would you have proceeded?'

'The deceased made no sound?' It was obvious that the doctor was becoming fascinated by this unexpected line of questioning.

'No sound at all.'

'I think it would have been necessary to jerk the victim to her feet and hold her while I plunged the knife into her back,' said the witness with unprofessional relish.

'And – assuming this unlikely course of events, Doctor – how would you prevent her from making an outcry?'

'By hooking my arm round her throat.' He demonstrated rather graphically as he spoke. 'By holding her in the crook of my elbow

I could ensure that she was silent until the stiletto was plunged home.'

This time Lamb did come to his feet. 'M'lud,' he moaned.

'I think I must disallow the objection, Sir Gerald,' the judge told him. 'You have called this witness as an expert, and on this point at least I believe the defence has a right to use him as such.'

'If your lordship pleases,' said Lamb and sank back into his place again.

'Thank you, Doctor.' It was obvious to Maitland at least that Derek was pleased with himself. 'A hand over her mouth might have accomplished the same thing?'

'But it would have left her more opportunity to wriggle,' the doctor objected. 'And if he had already observed exactly where he wished to strike—'

'I understand. There is just one point more and then I won't trouble you any further. Remembering that the prisoner was very little taller than his wife, remembering that he is a man of seventy years, in good condition admittedly, but not of an abnormally strong physique, do you think he could have acted in the way you have described?'

Before he answered the witness glanced doubtfully at Sir Gerald Lamb. 'I don't think the answer to that question falls within my competence,' he said, forestalling another objection, one that the judge would certainly have upheld.

Lamb re-examined, which was only to be expected, and being a sharp-witted man, in spite of his melancholy, succeeded in casting a good deal of doubt upon the reconstruction. Even so, glancing over his shoulder Maitland observed that Geoffrey was grinning, and when he turned to his learned junior there was the same sign of jubilation on Derek's face. 'I almost convinced myself,' he admitted *sotto voce*, leaving his leader to wonder whether, after all, the matter was quite as clear as it seemed to him.

Dr Yarrow, who specialised in nutritional matters, was called next, and looking back on it afterwards Maitland couldn't see that his evidence had advanced the prosecution's case in the slightest. Unfortunately, the defence hadn't profitted either. When asked about the effects of Vitamin A in counteracting night blindness he talked learnedly about the formation of visual purple in the eye and the sensitive rods in the retina which govern the eye's adaptation to the dark. Brought down to earth by Lamb he repeated all this in words of one syllable and went on to discuss recommended daily dosages; higher in the United States, he said, than in this country.

He himself would not recommend more than 3000 international units a day, and some authorities, he believed, set the amount still lower.

Pressed by the defence about the effect of an (unspecified) massive dose he became a little huffy. One such dose might or might not be harmful, certainly it should not be repeated. Naturally, he would never prescribe the vitamin in any large quantity owing to its possible toxic effects, and therefore could not speak from experience. He doubted whether anyone could, for that reason. But – if it was clearly understood that this was merely a personal opinion – such a dose must certainly have increased the night vision of the taker by an appreciable extent.

The next witness was Ellie Dorman, and it took Maitland a moment or two to reconcile the woman he saw going into the box with his memory of the one he had seen on stage. He might have put her down as a typical spinster, but in *Done in by Daggers* she had been playing up to Andrew Murray to the top of her bent, a vibrant, attractive woman. If anything Lamb's dejection seemed to increase as he went through the preliminary questions. 'Rogues and vagabonds, he doesn't like them,' said Derek in Antony's ear.

All in all her story didn't advance them very far. She described what had been happening on stage before the lights went out, her own station during the blackout period and complete lack of consciousness of anyone else's movements, and her shock at the unexpected scene when the lights came on again. She was obviously reluctant to testify that there had been any friction at all between the two Buckleys, though it was quite apparent that she had no time for Victoria, and even said a little waspishly, 'As for Leonard thinking she was poisoning him it seems very unlikely. But it's the sort of thing I wouldn't put past her at all.'

With that counsel for the prosecution had to be content, if indeed that word could ever be applied to him. He turned his witness over to the defence with a mournful gesture.

Again it was Stringer who came to his feet to cross-examine, and his first questions were directed to discovering whether she had noticed anything unusual about the stage when the lights came on again. The answer was an unequivocal 'no'. He didn't think there'd be any shaking her on that, and went on to other matters.

'How well did you know the Buckleys?' he asked.

'Very well indeed, for quite a long time. We miss them terribly in the theatre you know, they were such a perfect couple.' She paused, obviously remembering the evidence she had just given. 'At least, that was their public image,' she added.

'Then you're just the person we need,' said Derek enthusiastically. 'I'm sure the court will be interested to hear the views of a lady of your discernment.'

'One moment, Mr Stringer. How are we to know that the lady has discernment?' asked Mr Justice Bellman, obviously enjoying himself.

'She's a well known actress, my lord,' said Derek, thinking quickly. 'That requires perception, a degree of ability in being able to understand other people's views. I'm sure your lordship will agree with me.'

'Perhaps I do and perhaps I don't,' said Bellman noncommittally. 'However, you may proceed.'

'I'm obliged to your lordship. What I want you to tell us, Miss Dorman,' said Stringer, turning back to the witness again, 'is what you know about my client's character and reputation.'

'I think all the world knows what a wonderful actor he is,' said Ellie. 'His reputation couldn't be higher.'

'In spite of these ... shall we say disagreements with Mrs Buckley?'

'They were a very well kept secret,' Elly confided. 'Some of us who were close to them knew there was a little trouble, but I think matters had only come to a head recently. The members of the cast may have guessed – well I know most of them did – but as far as the public was concerned there was no scandal.'

'Let's forget about this public image for a moment. Tell me about his character as you knew it from your friendship with him and his wife.'

'He's a very fine person,' said Ellie, picking her words and emphasising them too. 'And if you're going to ask me if he could have done such a thing as murder Victoria, that's impossible, quite impossible!'

'Thank you, Miss Dorman, that was to be my next question. But I can see that my learned friend for the prosecution has a few more questions for you, so I will just ask one more: that last answer is the result of your own observation, is it not?'

'Oh yes, of course it is. I told you I knew them both very well.'

'Thank you, Miss Dorman.' Derek sat down, Sir Gerald Lamb was already on his feet.

'This is something you feel very strongly about, madam,' he said.

157

'Strongly? I don't quite understand I'm afraid.'

'It's quite obvious that you have a very high opinion of the accused.'

'Oh yes, of course I have.' She paused there, obviously thinking how to make what she said more telling. 'But he well deserves my good opinion, I can assure you of that.'

'You had known the Buckleys for a long time, I believe, at the time of Victoria Buckley's death?' said Lamb. The idea obviously depressed him, but Maitland was quite well aware that he had some special reason for the question.

'I said I couldn't remember exactly how long. I suppose at least twenty years.'

'In spite of the fact that you didn't altogether like Victoria Buckley?'

'I didn't say that,' said the witness hurriedly.

'I think, madam, that you will agree that you implied it. In spite of this fact you maintained a friendly relation with both of them?'

'Yes, that's quite true.'

'But you knew about the situation between them, you admitted that, I think.'

'I guessed . . . something,' said Ellie.

'You admired Leonard Buckley?'

'Oh yes, I did.'

'And in order to continue seeing him it was necessary that you should maintain your friendship with his wife as well.'

'I suppose that's a fair way of putting it.'

'I wonder then' – Lamb still sounded in the depths of despair, but it was obvious that he was nearing his point – 'were your feelings for the prisoner perhaps not even stronger than you have admitted. Were you . . . are you . . . in love with him?'

A slow flush spread over Ellie Dorman's face, leaving Maitland wondering how she managed if that happened when she was on stage. Perhaps the makeup would hide it? Or perhaps this was a special occasion. 'Are you in love with Leonard Buckley?' Lamb insisted.

Her chin tilted. There was no getting away from it, you had to admire her. 'I was and I am,' she said firmly. And her tone added for her, make what you like of that.

'I wonder then, madam – you'll forgive the question but the inquisitiveness of my learned friend for the defence has made it necessary – did the matter perhaps not go even further?'

'I don't know what you mean.'

'I think you know very well. I'm asking you if you and the accused were ever lovers?'

This time there was no betraying flush, but her hands grasped the rail in front of her until the knuckles showed white. 'Twenty years ago,' she said. 'It didn't last very long, but you're quite right, I've loved him ever since.'

'Then I think you will agree, Miss Dorman, that your opinion as to his probity is of very little value.'

'Why?' She flared up immediately. 'Because he seduced a young girl? It wasn't like that at all. He said he had a right to do what he liked, because Victoria had been unfaithful to him first.'

If Lamb was pleased by this admission he gave no sign of it. 'I didn't mean exactly that, madam,' he said, 'though the jury may care to take that matter into consideration. But your opinion of a man you say you have loved for years is not likely to be an unfavourable one.' He paused a moment, but Ellie had nothing to add. 'Thank you, Miss Dorman,' he said, and seated himself again, having completely wrecked any small advance the defence had made during the cross-examination of the witness.

II

After that, and not before time, Antony thought, came the luncheon recess. Again there was no sign of Sir Nicholas when they got to Astroff's, which was a good thing when you considered his opinion of the defence strategy; on the other hand, it laid the way open for another attack by Geoffrey on that very point.

When they got back to court, the next witness to be called was Dominic Eldred. This time Maitland had no difficulty in reconciling his real-life appearance with the impression he gave on stage, though his personality seemed to have undergone a complete change. He was quietly spoken, obviously respectful of the court's authority, but the thought crossed Antony's mind that his demeanour might be just as much acting as his interpretation of the part of Inspector Murchison on the stage.

Lamb left the direct examination to his junior, a man named Haliburton who was young and already making a name for himself, though it seemed doubtful if this particular case would enhance his reputation much, his leader not being over-fond of delegating authority. This was merely a matter of going over what had happened during the blackout again – and like the people Antony and Geoffrey had seen the witness could tell nothing to the point – of identifying the stiletto as one he had given to Victoria

Buckley some thirty years before, and stating that he knew it had still been in her possession very shortly before the murder. There wasn't very much to be done about that, but Maitland rose to cross-examine. To tell the truth he hadn't yet decided whether it would be expedient to emphasise to the jury that Victoria Buckley had not been perhaps the perfect wife the public had believed her to be. They must have gathered this already, from Leonard Buckley's contention that she'd been trying to poison him, and also from what Ellie Dorman had said. Perhaps the facts should be stressed, however, or perhaps they shouldn't. He found himself in an unaccustomed state of indecision.

'Concerning the blackout on the stage, during which Victoria Buckley was murdered,' he said, aware as he spoke in this rather roundabout way that he was still playing for time, 'there is one thing my friend for the prosecution did not ask you. When the lights came on again, was there anything odd about the stage?'

'I ... don't think so. I was blinded for a moment, you know.'

'Yes, I realise that. But only for a moment,' Maitland insisted. 'After that ... for instance, was any of the furniture out of place?'

'Not so far as I remember.'

'And nothing was there that shouldn't have been there. That wasn't present when the lights went on at the same time at the dress rehearsal, for instance?'

'I didn't notice, I was too horrified by what I saw.'

'You were expecting to see Mr Andrew Murray playing dead. What did you think when you saw that Mrs Buckley was also lying on the ground?'

'Just for a second I thought perhaps she had fainted, and then I saw the handle of the stiletto. I think Andy realised what had happened before I did, he raised his head and then he got up and went across to her. Leonard was already standing by her side. I know it's a trite expression but I can't think of any other, I seemed to be rooted to the spot.' (Somebody else had said that, or something very like it. Perhaps it was a valid concept after all, though Antony, with his instinct towards movement in any unexpected or distressing situation, found it hard to understand.)

'You were very fond of Mrs Buckley, am I right about that?'

'Very fond indeed.'

'How long had this affection of yours endured?'

'For many years.'

'Can you not be a little more specific than that, Mr Eldred?'

160

There was a brief pause. 'If you must know, I wanted to marry her before she met Leonard,' Dominic said. 'We were exactly the same age, you know, or almost, and I think she thought I was too young for her. Besides he was already making a success, and must have seemed a more glamorous figure.' Just for a moment his eyes strayed towards the man in the dock. 'That was forty-three years ago,' he said.

'So after that you maintained the role – over forty-three years, as you pointed out – of a friend of the family?'

'Yes, I did.'

'Were you in the habit of giving Mrs Buckley expensive presents?'

'No, not at all. A bottle of wine when I went to dinner with them perhaps, that sort of thing. A gift for them both, not just for her.'

'Then I wonder what the occasion was that prompted the gift of the stiletto. It must have been of considerable value.'

'More now than then perhaps,' said Dominic.

'Precisely. But also you would be better able to afford it now than then. I understand it was given thirty-three years ago.'

'I said ... about thirty.' He halted again, eyeing Maitland closely, as though trying to weigh up the extent of his knowledge.

'You are on oath, Mr Eldred,' said Antony quietly.

'I don't think it will help you at all,' said Dominic rather hesitantly, 'but Victoria and I were – were very briefly intimate at about that time. The stiletto was a memento of something that had given me great happiness.'

'Was there any talk of her obtaining a divorce and marrying you? You were still unmarried yourself I believe.'

'Yes, I was still unmarried, still am for that matter. And of course I asked her to do that. But their image was already established for the public, Leonard's and Victoria's, as the Ideal Couple. I'm an actor too, remember, I understand all about the hopes and ambitions ... and disappointments besides. I could very well understand her attitude.'

'Did you continue to be lovers?'

'Not more than ... about a month or five weeks I suppose in all.' His tone was fainter now and the judge asked him rather sharply to speak more loudly. 'And looking back,' said Dominic, 'I can't even remember whether it was she or I who called a halt to that. We were of the same generation, you know, old fashioned I suppose we should be called nowadays. If there was no hope of the

161

affair ending in marriage, I don't think either of us felt it was right to go on.'

'Did my client know what had happened?'

'I think he did, though he never said anything.'

'So you slipped back into the same role of family friend as before?'

'I did.'

'Then there is just one more question I should like to ask you, Mr Eldred. And perhaps you are in a better position to answer it than anybody else. Do you think Victoria Buckley was trying to poison her husband?'

That brought a much longer silence than any that had gone before.

'You reminded me just now that I was on oath,' said Dominic ruefully. 'So I have to say I did believe it, I knew how she had begun to feel about him, how they felt about each other. But I don't think when she did it that she could have been in her right mind.'

'Have you any special reasons for saying that?'

'Only that I've known her so long, it wasn't in her nature to do a thing like that.'

'And are your reasons for believing that she was using poison equally vague?'

'I suppose they are,' the witness admitted. 'Only I began to think of one or two rather strange things she'd said, asking me if I should still be her suitor if she were free.' He shook his head as though to clear it. 'Nothing that you could call proof,' he said.

'Thank you very much, Mr Eldred, I've no further questions.' He would like to have added, I'm sorry to have brought all this into the open, but it wasn't the moment for that. Something in Eldred's dignity had touched a sympathetic chord in him. He sat down, Lamb declined to re-examine, and Andrew Murray's name was called.

With his new knowledge (or would suspicion be a better word?) Maitland looked at the actor with even greater interest now than he had done when he saw him on the stage. As had been the case with Dominic Eldred, physically there wasn't much change to be seen, his good looks had been the most visible thing about him then, and they still were. But, again like Eldred, his personality had undergone a complete metamorphosis. From the happy-go-lucky ladykiller of *Done in by Daggers* (if you could use that word to describe someone who was himself to be the murderee) he had become a serious, thoughtful man, obviously only too conscious of his part in the prosecution's case, and equally obviously not liking it at all.

As far as Sir Gerald Lamb was concerned the witness came up to proof admirably. His description of the ill-feeling between the two Buckleys was drawn out reluctantly, but was twice as convincing because of that. He had known them both for years, but not well until rehearsals for this play began. (Maitland noticed Leonard Buckley raise his head when he heard that, and took a moment to hope that his client would remember his injunctions to silence when it came to be his turn to give evidence.) All that time, until this recent encounter with them, the witness had thought that the public image of the pair was the true one, it had surprised and pained him to see how they really felt about each other. The last time he visited them had been on the twelfth of February, that was a Monday, two days before the opening. He noticed the stiletto then on the desk in the living room.

Being Lamb's witness, and a vital one at that from the prosecution's point of view, all this had to be repeated not once but several times until there was no chance that the jury hadn't taken in every point. Geoffrey Horton, all the more eager because he was a convert to Maitland's point of view, occupied his time in writing a series of notes, urging that Leonard Buckley's story of their previous acquaintance, and of what had happened recently between Murray and Victoria Buckley, should be put to the witness in cross-examination. Antony could have done without that particular bit of reiterated advice, his decision had been made on instinct of which he had a profound distrust. As for his junior, there was no telling what Derek was thinking. He would go along without argument with whatever was decided, but whether he agreed or not was quite another matter.

At long last Sir Gerald Lamb sat down again, Maitland wrote NO in large letters across Geoffrey's latest note and passed it back to him, and stood up in his turn. Andrew Murray turned slightly to face him, his look politely enquiring. 'Your role in the play *Done in by Daggers* called for you to wear sunglasses?' Maitland began.

'Yes,' said the witness, visibly startled, but then he recovered himself and began to elaborate on his answer. 'I argued about that with the author several times, because you can't say they're exactly becoming. But he was quite adamant about it. He had some idea that it would make my being murdered more convincing, even though the deed was to be done in the dark, and as Kevin agreed with him there was nothing I could do.'

'That is Kevin Elliott the director?'

'Yes. Of course, his decision was final.'

'Just ordinary sunglasses?'

'Why, yes. I didn't need a prescription for them, if that's what you mean.'

'How often was the scene rehearsed in darkness?'

'Just once, at the dress rehearsal.'

'In anticipation of the darkness, did you perhaps play your scene with Victoria Buckley with your eyes closed behind the dark lenses?'

'There was no need. By the time the lights came on again I should be lying on the floor, and I was supposed to stay like that for the rest of the scene. I didn't need to see anything in the darkness, just to wait until Leonard tapped my shoulder as a signal that the dagger was fixed, and then tumble on to the ground.'

'You told my learned friend that this tap on your shoulder came rather later than expected. Are you sure about that?'

'Quite sure.'

'And yet the scene had only been once before rehearsed in darkness.'

'It's only an estimate of course,' said Murray rather hurriedly, 'but that time Leonard seemed to reach me much more quickly.'

'But we all know – don't we – how difficult it is to judge time's passage without actually looking at a watch or clock.'

'Yes, it is, but I still think . . . oh well, I don't suppose it matters either way.'

'I rather think my learned friend for the prosecution doesn't altogether agree with you about that,' said Antony, smiling. 'But we'll leave the point for one that is perhaps of greater interest. When you became conscious that something was wrong . . . how did you do that by the way?'

'I heard Leonard calling Victoria's name.'

'I wonder what your impression is about that. Did he sound genuinely concerned?'

'Yes, at the time I thought so. But he is an actor after all.'

'As are several other of the witnesses in this case,' said Antony, rather as though he was speaking to himself. 'So you raised your head –'

'Leonard was standing beside Victoria, I didn't see the dagger for a moment, I thought she must have fainted. And then I scrambled to my feet and went across to join him and of course it was obvious very quickly that there was nothing we could do for her.'

'So you informed us in your evidence-in-chief and so the medical evidence confirmed,' said Antony. 'The thing I meant to ask you, Mr Murray, is this, did you at that time notice anything wrong about the stage setting?'

'Nothing but the very terrible wrongness of Victoria's death.'

'That was not what I meant. We have heard from the doctor at great length about that. What I meant was, was all the furniture in place? Or was there anything present that should not have been?'

'No, no I'm quite sure about that.' This time Andrew Murray was quite definite. 'We'd been rehearsing for some time with the full set, I'd have been bound to notice if there was any change.'

'Thank you, Mr Murray, that's all I have to ask you. But I believe Sir Gerald – ' he added with an enquiring look at his opponent. And sure enough Lamb was already on his feet.

'Perhaps we could do an experiment, Mr Murray,' he suggested. 'If you will close your eyes I will time you with my watch and you can tell me exactly at what point in the one and a half minutes of darkness Leonard Buckley touched your shoulder.'

The witness complied. 'It was exactly,' said Lamb, for all the world as if he had just received bad news, though in fact he must have been elated, 'one minute and twenty seconds before the sign came. Would you not say, Mr Murray, that this might well explain the fact that the accused was still on the stage when the lights came on?' he added, and was interrupted by a furious objection from Maitland which the judge upheld.

After that Andrew Murray was allowed to go. Antony was rather hoping for an adjournment when Sir Gerald Lamb announced that he had no further witnesses to call, but in the absence of any sign by Mr Justice Bellman he had no choice but to get to his feet again and open his own case.

If he made these opening remarks brief it was not altogether from the feeling that when he had finished Bellman would be bound to adjourn, but in keeping with his general policy. In this case though, perhaps more than ever, he had the feeling that the least said at this stage the better; he poured a little gentle scorn on the very circumstantial nature of the prosecution's case, 'And as for the motive they cite, members of the jury, thirty odd years ago when he learned of his wife's betrayal would have been the time at which this gentleman might have resorted to violence if such was his nature. Not now, not after forty-three years of a successful partnership.' After that he went over in some detail Derek's cross-examination of the prosecution's main medical witness. 'The murderer must have been strong, and considerably taller than the deceased. A man, certainly, but a man with attributes that Leonard Buckley does not possess.' After that it was merely a matter of promising to refute the evidence that had been presented. 'You will hear my client's story, members of the jury, from his own mouth, and other witnesses beside who will help you to arrive, I have no doubt, at a true verdict of Not Guilty.' But he exchanged a rather rueful grin with Derek as he sat down again and, 'Words, words, words!' muttered Geoffrey in his ear.

But Mr Justice Bellman had finally had enough. 'For which we may all be truly thankful,' said Derek, standing respectfully as the judge went out. They left in a body and Geoffrey said as they reached the street outside, 'I only hope you're doing the right thing.'

A cheerful thought to take home.

III

Maitland saw nothing of Sir Nicholas that evening, a fact for which, to use Derek's words, he was truly thankful. Vera, he knew, would have talked the matter out sympathetically, but Sir Nicholas would have condemned his strategy in no uncertain terms, leaving him feeling more insecure than ever. Roger, however, came round at about the usual time, and Antony surprised him, a little before the hour at which he usually left for the theatre, by saying, 'If I take a cab will you let me fetch Meg this evening?'

'Yes, of course, but it's easier for me to take the car. Why on earth –?'

'I just want to ask her again about this story of hers about the black cloth on the floor behind Victoria Buckley's chair,' said Antony. 'It may help when I'm questioning Briggs,' he added vaguely.

'Well, I suppose it may.' Roger sounded doubtful, and the look he gave his friend wasn't altogether free from suspicion. Still, he said nothing more, and Antony left a few minutes later, leaving him to talk the whole mystery out with Jenny, which he had no doubt was what they would do in his absence.

He persuaded the stage doorman to let him in, and even to give him some pretty comprehensive directions as to how to get to Meg's dressing room from this unfamiliar point. She called 'Come in,' when he knocked, and was in the act of taking off her makeup. Her startled eyes met his in the mirror through a barrier of cold cream. 'Antony?' she said, and there was no mistaking the quick flare of anxiety. 'Is Roger all right?'

'Perfectly all right. I just wanted to talk to you, Meg, that's all.'

'I don't see – ' But she turned to her dresser who was hovering, obviously uncertain what to do in the face of this unexpected visitor. 'Just pass me the tissues, darling,' she said, 'then I shan't need you again tonight.' By the time the door was closed and they were alone together she had removed the cream and makeup from the right side of her face. 'Why didn't he come with you?' she demanded.

'Mainly because I wanted to see you alone.'

'That sounds ominous.' The stained tissues went into the waste paper basket. 'I've got to change you know, darling,' she added, 'I'm still in costume under this.' She indicated the wrapper she was wearing. 'Won't it wait?'

'I think,' said Antony honestly, 'I'd rather get it over with.'

'As bad as all that?' Meg's tone was still not wholly serious. 'When you look like that, darling, it generally means you're in an Uncle Nickish mood and want to lecture me. What is it this time?'

He looked at her for a long moment and thought that if there were any truth in Victoria Buckley's story it would be more than he could bear. Meg and Roger were something more than mere friends, and apart from his own feelings, Jenny loved them both. Anything that hurt her ...

'Don't play your tricks on Roger, Meg,' he said abruptly. 'He's too good a chap.'

'I don't know – ' But her instinct of honesty was too great to allow her to persist in a denial. 'You know I adore Roger.'

'That might mean anything in your jargon, Meg.' He watched her flush and added gently, 'If I'm being impertinent I'm sorry.'

'I don't believe you're sorry at all.' Meg's chin went up. 'But if you must have it ... I love him. Will that do?'

'Then why is he worried about your feelings for Andrew Murray?'

Meg stiffened. 'Did he tell you that?'

'Victoria Buckley told him that there was something between the two of you, and you know I've been trying to find out as much as I can about the lady. So I guessed what had happened and asked him. Do you think he'd discuss you in the ordinary way, Meg?' He grinned suddenly. 'The last time we talked about you was on the *Susannah*, and you must admit the circumstances were exceptional. I asked him his intentions as far as I remember and read him a lecture on not interfering with your art.'

'Did you, darling?' There was no levity in her tone. Her eyes were fixed on his face with an expression at once anxious and a little puzzled.

'You must admit he's played fair about that. I don't imagine it's been easy.'

'But he couldn't have believed ... really, Antony, that clothes horse!'

'Is that how you see him? Then why the devil, Meg, don't you let Roger know it? Does it never occur to you –'

'Whatever Victoria said he shouldn't have believed her.'

'Don't you see he thought she was a nice old lady, telling him something that upset her for his own good?'

'Didn't you tell him it was nonsense?'

'Of course I did, and I thought I'd convinced him. But then last night he came up with the idea that perhaps your not wanting to give evidence was because it might harm Murray in some way.'

'But it couldn't ... Antony you're not going to tell me –?'

'I wasn't going to tell you anything,' said Antony ruefully, 'in fact, I specifically told Roger *not* to tell you the conclusions I'd reached.'

Meg was still almost speechless. 'That Andy killed Victoria?' she said incredulously.

'It's a long story, Meg, and I haven't time to go into it. But that made me realise that Roger was still half believing what Mrs Buckley had told him, so I thought that perhaps you –'

'If I'd known she was spreading a story like that I'd have stuck a knife in her myself,' said Meg viciously. 'Had she been maligning Andy too?'

'No, what she knew about him was a story she didn't spread, but according to Leonard Buckley it's true.'

'Something that happened recently?'

'I told you, Meg, it's too long to go into. But no, something that happened quite a long while ago.'

'Then why should he want to harm her now?'

'She was thinking of trying her hand at a little blackmail.'

But her mind had already slipped away from him, back to her own affairs. 'What do you want me to do, darling?' she asked. 'Give up the stage?'

'No!'

'Well then –'

'Just play fair in your turn, *darling*. Don't leave Roger in the dark about things no mere man can be expected to know.'

'But ... *you* believe me, don't you, Antony?'

'For one thing, Meg, I'm not your husband. For another, Roger would never have asked you about this story.'

'I suppose not.'

There was a flatness in her tone. He said, 'I'd better go.' And then, 'I should apologise, shouldn't I, for interfering?'

'Not that, darling, never that.' There was a silence while they looked at each other and then she shivered. 'What's going to happen?' she said.

'That's up to you, Meg.'

'No, I ... of course I'll do anything you say. You know I adore Roger.'

'*I* know it.'

'All right ... all right. I'll make sure he does too. But ... Antony, that wasn't your only reason for coming here, was it? You're worried about something.'

'Is it so obvious?' he asked bitterly. 'I may have made an error of judgement, Meg, and if I have I've let my client down badly.'

'Poor Mr Buckley, I was almost forgetting about him. But I don't understand you, Antony.'

'Geoffrey wanted me to attack Murray while we had him on the stand, to try to force some admission from him. I think ... I thought, anyway ... that it would be more effective to get the evidence against him first.'

'You mean from Superintendent Briggs?'

'From him and from another man. It's taking a chance, I know that, because I haven't the faintest idea what either of them will say.'

'And you're not quite sure about Andy, are you?' she asked shrewdly. 'You're always said you wouldn't attack anyone in court unless you were sure.'

'That's what Roger said. And for at least three quarters of the time I *am* sure,' he admitted. 'The other quarter ... that's when my doubts start up. So I wondered –'

'Whether I'd give evidence after all if Chief Superintendent Briggs doesn't come up to scratch. I told you I would, darling.'

'Yes, but I promised not to call you.'

'I'll come to court tomorrow,' said Meg. 'I shall be a possible witness, that means I have to wait outside, doesn't it? But I'll be there if you need me. And I should think,' she added in a

169

considering tone, 'that will convince Roger if nothing else does. I'll ask him to come with me,' she decided.

Suddenly Antony was laughing at her. 'Darling Meg,' he said, and for once there was no stress of sarcasm upon the word, 'I should think you're quite capable of convincing Roger without any help at all.'

She smiled back at him and got up purposefully. 'We'll see,' she said. 'I'm going to change now, but I meant it, Antony, I'll be there tomorrow.'

IV

So he escorted her back to Kempenfeldt Square. 'I won't come up, darling,' she said, 'I'll just wait by the car. I expect Roger will come down straight away.'

'I expect he will,' said Antony; he had no doubt at all about that. He summoned his friend and stood a moment watching them drive away together. Then he went rather heavily up the stairs, tired to the bone and with the worried feeling not very much diminished. Jenny took in the situation at a glance, but as usual forbore to mention it directly. 'Is Meg being difficult?' she asked.

'On the contrary, she'll give evidence if Briggs doesn't tell me what I want to know.'

'About the black cloth on the stage?' Jenny asked.

'Yes. Even so, I'm very much afraid I've made a mess of things, Jenny. If Briggs didn't see it, why should they believe Meg?'

'I don't believe for a moment that you've taken the wrong decision. Come and sit down and tell me about it.'

So he sat beside her on the sofa and repeated the gist of his talk with Meg, insofar as it concerned the case. 'I thought for a moment she was going to tell me not to worry, I'd done my best,' he concluded.

Jenny turned to look at him. 'Why do you hate that phrase so much?' she asked.

'Didn't I ever tell you?'

'No.' She looked at him then more closely. 'You're going to say it was something that happened during the war. You never have talked about those days.'

Antony nearly said, and I don't want to now, but that would have been too unkind. 'There was an occasion,' he told her, choosing his words with difficulty, 'when twenty-seven people died because of an error of judgement on my part. That's what my colleagues told me: you did your best.'

170

'Yes, I see. I'm sorry I asked,' said Jenny contritely. 'I can quite understand, darling, it must just have made matters worse.'

'And how long is it since you called me that?' Antony demanded, trying for a lighter tone. 'Darling?'

'Not since Meg adopted it as an affectation I dare say,' said Jenny, treating the question seriously, as she sometimes did. 'That was the time you wanted to get out of Intelligence, wasn't it?'

'It was. And I suppose thinking about Leonard Buckley ... to my eyes he's a pathetic figure and the fact that he's retained his dignity only makes matters worse. If I've let him down as I let them down –'

'I don't suppose for a moment that you have. And anyway,' said Jenny wisely, 'there's always the Court of Appeal.'

Antony stared at her for a moment as surprised as if she had suddenly bitten him in the ankle. Legal talk from Vera, he expected, after all she'd been a member of the profession. And Jenny had heard enough of it over the years between him and Uncle Nick, that was true. But as for advising him!

'Yes, love, there's always the Court of Appeal,' he agreed weakly.

THURSDAY, *The Third Day of the Trial*

I

So the next morning they were able to proceed directly to Leonard Buckley's evidence, and Geoffrey, after one look at Antony, forbore from mentioning again what he considered the errors of the day before. Maitland looked round the court as the prisoner was being sworn. Chief Inspector Sykes was sitting sedately among the witnesses who had already given their evidence; and Andrew Murray was at the other end of the same bench, still playing to perfection his role of concerned bystander; but Antony got a nasty jolt when his eyes strayed to the place where those of his brethren who were not directly concerned with the case, but might find some interest in it, sat. Sir Nicholas met his incredulous look with a bland one, and then turned back to the discussion he was having with a man beside him.

The court was waiting, the judge coughed and then said, 'Mr Maitland!' in rather a peremptory tone. So Antony got to his feet and faced his client and thought with compunction that he was looking older every time he saw him.

The preliminaries were quickly gone through with no stumbling on the prisoner's part. Geoffrey had told him what to expect, of course. 'And you were married to Victoria Buckley for forty-three years?' Maitland concluded.

'A little more than that. Forty-three years last September.'

'Mr Buckley, before you tell your story to the jury there's something I should like to ask you. You took the oath just now.'

'I swore to tell the truth, yes.'

'Would you tell us, if it is not too impertinent a question, exactly what that means to you?'

'I swore by Almighty God. To do so falsely would be a great sin. I know that nowadays that is an unfashionable point of view, but I'm an old man and it's what I have believed all my life.'

So far so good. And the jury will be thinking, as I thought of some of the prosecution's witnesses, after all the man is an actor. 'I'm grateful to you for speaking so frankly, Mr Buckley,' he said aloud. 'Will you tell me then, did you kill your wife?'

'No, no I didn't. I would never have done such a thing.'

'Before we go on to your account of what happened on the stage the night Mrs Buckley died, I should like to take one by one the points which the prosecution have raised against you. First there is the question of motive.'

'What I said in my statement is true. There had been ill-feeling between us, sometimes I thought hatred. But when I saw her lying there I found I hadn't hated her at all. She was lying so still, and then I saw the stiletto. I recognised it at once, of course, though I'd thought of it for so many years as nothing more than a letter opener. But to see Victoria dead ... all that I could think of was the malice of my thoughts towards her, and I hoped she knew that now all that was washed away.'

'My learned friend who appears for the prosecution has made great play with the fact that the stiletto came from your flat.'

'It's perfectly true, but I can't explain it.'

'There was also a book introduced into evidence. *Stubbs on Anatomy*. That was also found in the flat.'

'It was certainly not Victoria's,' said Leonard with the slightest touch of humour in his voice. 'I don't think she had any interest in the subject, and I'm sure I didn't. But I have thought, Mr Maitland, that the book couldn't have been there very long. If she had thought me interested in the subject, I'm quite sure she would have got rid of it somehow.'

'I see.' That was something the prisoner had thought of for himself, quite bright of him. 'But there is an even simpler explanation, Mr Buckley; whoever introduced the book to your flat could have removed the stiletto at the same time.'

That brought a protest from Lamb, apparently saddened by his opponent's duplicity in trying to get a point over to the jury other than during his final speech. Mr Justice Bellman agreed with him, of course, Maitland wouldn't have expected otherwise. When the judge had given his decision Antony said meaninglessly, 'I'm obliged to your lordship,' and turned back to his witness again. 'Another point of which the prosecution has made much is the finding of an empty bottle that had contained Vitamin A tablets in your dressing room, Mr Buckley. Have you ever taken Vitamin A?'

'No, I'm not much of a one for pills really.'

'But it is true, I'm sure, that in the rather confusing atmosphere backstage it wouldn't be difficult for someone to have introduced this bottle to your room.'

'It isn't really confusing,' said Buckley annoyingly. 'But there are lots of comings and goings, anyone could have put it there.'

173

'I thought as much. And there were no fingerprints on the bottle,' said Maitland thoughtfully. (This time Lamb made no objection, perhaps his spirit was broken.) 'Now I should like you to tell us, Mr Buckley, in your own words, first how you came to think that Mrs Buckley was trying to poison you, and then exactly what you did on the stage during the blackout on the night she died.'

There was something to be said for having for a client a man who was used to appearing in public. Mr Buckley went through his story again, and it contained no surprises for the defence. But none of them were under any illusion that the matter would be allowed to rest there. When Maitland relinquished the witness Sir Gerald Lamb rose to his feet and said in a shocked tone, 'Mr Buckley, I believe you made a statement to the police.'

'I did. That was before I talked to Mr Horton, my solicitor,' added the prisoner ingenuously.

'You are not telling us, I hope, that nobody pointed out to you the desirability of having your lawyer present?'

'Oh no. Chief Inspector Sykes told me quite clearly that I should do that, but I didn't know any solicitors, and I hadn't done anything wrong, so I couldn't see the necessity.'

'But later you asked to see Mr Geoffrey Horton?'

'Yes, I found his name and telephone number written on a piece of paper in my pocket.' This business of taking an oath to tell the truth cut both ways, Maitland thought rather despondently.

To his relief, however, and even greater surprise, Lamb let that point go without any further questioning. 'To get back to this statement of yours, Mr Buckley,' he said. 'You have made a great point about the sacredness of your oath, but I'm afraid you were not quite so particular when talking to the police.'

'They didn't ask me to swear to the statement, and I didn't think that would ever arise.'

'You admit then that it contained one or two ... inaccuracies shall we say?'

'Not on any important point,' the accused insisted.

'Come now, Mr Buckley, was not the ownership of the stiletto an important point?'

Leonard considered that. 'I'm opposed to lying even when no oath has been taken,' he said at last. 'But in this case I felt it was justifed. Perhaps that belief was prompted by fear, I don't know. I felt that since I did not use the dagger myself its provenance could be of no interest. Since then my solicitor has disabused me of that idea, as has my counsel. Smaller truths may lead to larger ones.'

Lamb looked a little taken aback by this apparently quite sincere speech. 'You really expect us to believe – ' he began, but his voice trailed into silence as he met the witness's innocent look. 'There's another point on which I believe you misled us when you made your statement to the police.'

'I don't think ... perhaps you could remind me,' said Mr Buckley courteously.

'That,' said Sir Gerald Lamb despairingly, 'is why I am here.' The thought of the human duplicity that had led them to their respective places in the courtroom seemed for a moment almost to overwhelm him. 'I am speaking of what you told Chief Inspector Sykes that night about the duration of the – shall we say enmity? – between you and the deceased.'

'I don't much care to hear Victoria referred to that way,' said Leonard Buckley irrelevantly. 'We were very much in love when we married, you've heard me tell Mr Maitland that. As for the date when the honeymoon was over – '

'No later, I imagine, than the time when you learned that Mrs Buckley had been unfaithful to you,' said Lamb with a little sharpness in his tone that was very uncharacteristic.

'I suppose you might say that disillusionment began to set in at that time,' Leonard conceded. 'But I think Mr Maitland had a valid point you know, when he said – '

'Mr Maitland was out of order,' said Lamb, interrupting him.

'I was just going to point out that I might have felt murderous then, but after all these years the impulse had worn off. Surely you can see that.'

'That is a very specious argument, Mr Buckley. You're fortunate in your counsel,' said Lamb, obviously not intending a compliment. 'To twist your words a little, surely *you* can see that this recent delusion of yours concerning the deceased provides a very good and rational motive.'

'You mean because she was trying to poison me.'

'If she was,' Lamb corrected him.

'Oh, I'm quite sure about that, but I was taking my own precautions, preparing my own meals, there was nothing immediate to worry about on that score. And you must see, Sir Gerald,' – Leonard Buckley had been sitting throughout the trial with his chin sunk on his chest, apparently not attending, but Maitland realised now that he must have absorbed every word – 'I could have taken care of that matter by leaving her, if I hadn't wanted to preserve our professional partnership. But killing her dissolved that even more irrevocably.'

'I see you are an apt pupil,' said Lamb and left the subject for a moment. 'I believe, Mr Buckley, that you were not being as inattentive as you seemed during this trial.'

'Do you think I'm not interested?' asked Buckley almost humorously.

'You have every reason to be,' moaned Lamb. 'You heard the evidence of Mr Andrew Murray did you not?'

'Of course I heard it.'

'And observed the demonstration of the time he believed to have elapsed between the lights going out on the stage and your tapping him on the shoulder to indicate that the dagger was in position. One minute and twenty seconds is a long time, merely to cross the stage. What have you to say to that?'

'That Andy – that Mr Murray is mistaken.'

'Now I put it to you, Mr Buckley, is that likely?'

'I couldn't possibly have taken so long to reach him, and affixing the dagger was the work of a moment.'

'Exactly. But if your first objective was the chair where your wife was sitting, and your intent to murder her, would not that explain perfectly the discrepancy in time?'

Leonard thought about that for a while. Maitland was beginning to realise that he had a logical mind, for all his woolliness on some points. 'I suppose it would,' the prisoner admitted after a moment. 'But as it didn't happen that way it's really quite irrelevant.'

'How then do you account – ?'

They were off on a long trail, Maitland realised, and his client was acquitting himself well but by the time Lamb had finished with him he doubted whether he would seem so confident. And he was quite right about that, Leonard Buckley tired visibly as the morning wore on and the questions became more insistent. By the time Lamb sat down at last all his assurance seemed to have deserted him. Antony got up with a few reassuring questions, doing his best to stress the points that the witness had made in his own favour. But the judge was having none of it, all through the re-examination Lamb was almost constantly on his feet, and each objection in turn was upheld. They adjourned for lunch with the defence team in the lowest of spirits, and Geoffrey only too obviously refraining nobly from saying, I told you so.

II

That being so they were unusually silent over their meal, three

176

men who knew each other very well and consequently had usually plenty to talk about. They were back in court in good time, and as soon as the judge had made his ceremonial entry and the prisoner had been brought up from the nether regions Jeremy Skelton was called as a witness. Antony noticed that his uncle, who had declined to accompany them to Astroff's, was back in his place again.

Jeremy, who of course had been outside the court until now with the other witnesses who had not yet given their evidence, looked around him with interest as he took the oath. Antony took time to wonder whether, in spite of the years he had spent concocting mystery stories for the amusement of the reader, he had ever been in a court before. Except at his own trial, when he had not been in a position to take such a detached view. His evidence was brief and to the point. The gloves in Leonard Buckley's pocket had been there because the play called for them to be discovered dramatically by Inspector Murchison during the second act. Skelton would obviously have been quite willing to recite the plot from beginning to end, with some side details concerning red herrings, but Maitland managed to head him off. Instead he had the witness escorted down from the box to look at the model of the stage, and asked him the now familiar question, whether anything had been moved.

Jeremy studied the model with interest. 'That's very good,' he said appreciatively. Then, 'And everything is exactly as I insisted it should be, except that the chair Victoria was sitting in has been pushed back a little.'

'Straight back?'

'No, not quite. Looking at it from the audience I should say it had been moved a little to the right.'

No use asking him about the black cloth, Maitland knew the answer to that already. 'Thank you, Mr Skelton, that is all I have to ask you,' he said. Lamb didn't even bother to cross-examine.

The next witness too was quickly despatched. He was the superintendent of the block of flats in Kensington where the Buckleys had lived; Mr Moffat, whose first name turned out to be Alexander. He testified to the delivery of the flowers to Victoria Buckley on the day of the opening, the day also of her death, in almost the same words as he had originally told the story to Antony and Geoffrey. Obviously he had been going over it in his mind ever since.

Knowing that his shortsightedness would make him an easy prey for the prosecution, Maitland didn't ask him whether he could identify the man, but Lamb, of course, remedied the omission at least in part as soon as he got the chance. 'This mysterious messenger,' he said, 'was he carrying anything when he arrived?'

'A bunch of flowers, I told *him* that.'

'So you did, Mr Moffat, if by "him" you mean my learned friend. I meant, was the messenger carrying anything else?'

'Not as I noticed. But there,' he added, causing Maitland to call down silent blessings on his head, 'my eyesight isn't too good. A great big thing like a bunch of flowers, well I couldn't miss that. But anything else –'

'You wear spectacles, Mr Moffat. Did you not have them on that day?'

'Oh, yes, I had them on all right. They were my brother-in-law's, I took them over when he died. But they don't seem to do much good.'

After that there was no need to re-examine.

Maitland had twisted round in his seat and was watching his uncle's face when the next witness was called. Sir Nicholas was looking austere, it was obvious that his opinion of Antony's temerity in calling Chief Superintendent Briggs for the defence had not abated one jot. And when he knew that Meg was, as it were, waiting in the wings in case things didn't go as the defence wished, it was likely that his distaste for the whole episode would be even more forcibly expressed.

Chief Superintendent Briggs was a big, burly man of choleric disposition. He marched into the witness box with no attempt to step lightly, and took the oath firmly but rather contemptuously, Antony thought. Maitland wasn't worried about that however. He disliked Briggs probably as much as any man living – some people might explain that kind of thing by saying their chemistry didn't match – but though he had often referred to him on less formal occasions as a pig-headed old bastard, he had never suspected him of double dealing. The detective's view of counsel was even simpler, he both disliked and distrusted him, and now when he turned to face Maitland to be led gently through the inevitable preliminaries, the normal ruddy hue of his complexion had turned rather alarmingly to something much nearer purple.

Maitland began his examination on a low key. 'I believe, Chief Superintendent, that you were in the theatre on the evening of February the fourteenth last to attend the opening performance of a play called *Done in by Daggers* by Jeremy Skelton.'

'I was.'

'Were you alone?'

'Yes. My wife doesn't care for detective stories.'

'You are a fan of Mr Skelton's perhaps?' It is undeniable that Maitland asked that question out of a pure sense of mischief.

'Certainly not!' Briggs snapped. 'Still,' he conceded, 'perhaps I had some interest in seeing the play.'

'A sort of busman's holiday for you, in fact. Where were you sitting, Chief Superintendent?'

'At the back of the stalls.'

'I am sure neither you nor the court want a repetition of what Chief Inspector Sykes has already told us. Let's go straight to the blackout. Obviously you saw nothing during that period, but what did you hear, what were your impressions?'

'I got a vague impression of movement. I heard what I believe was supposed to be the moan of a man mortally wounded.' There was the briefest pause and then he added belligerently, 'Mr Maitland, any member of the audience could have served your purpose in this.'

'I think not, Chief Superintendent. The prosecution had its expert witnesses, and in a sense that is how I am using you. You will not deny, will you, that you are a trained observer?'

'Of course I am!'

'I realise,' said Antony in his gentlest tone, 'that I have seriously inconvenienced you by calling you as a witness in this trial. But you will concede, I know, that my client has his point of view in this.'

'That is nothing to do with my objection,' said Briggs. 'If I had known anything that exonerated the prisoner I should have informed the investigating officer, and no arrest would have been made.'

'That shows how one can be mistaken. I was under the impression that my client was arrested before most of the evidence was in.'

'On very sufficient grounds!'

'Come now, Chief Superintendent, you're my witness and we mustn't quarrel.' Briggs glared at him. 'It is open to me, you know, to ask the court for permission to treat you as hostile, but I don't wish to do that.'

'You may do it and welcome. If this is – ' Maitland stopped him with a raised hand.

'You're going to say "another of my tricks", aren't you?' he said. 'Please understand my reasons for calling you. I'm very far from suggesting that evidence is being suppressed, but what I do think

179

is that you of all people may have been in a position to see, without understanding, something that may be of help to the defence.'

'I have never considered myself deficient in understanding,' said Briggs unmollified.

'Certainly not.' If Antony hadn't been so nervous he might have enjoyed this encounter; but he *was* nervous, and he had a nasty feeling the witness knew it. 'Will you give us your impression, Chief Superintendent, of the time that elapsed between the lights going out and the moan you heard?'

That required some thought. 'I think the answer to that must be I don't know,' said Briggs at last. 'Sitting in the dark it seemed like an age, but—'

'Let's try another way then,' said Maitland rather hurriedly. 'Could you estimate the time between the moan and the lights going on again?'

'Again I'm afraid I can't help you.' Not even if I wished to, said his tone.

'Very well then. The lights went on, you observed on the stage not one body, but two. For a moment I'm sure—'

'M'lud!' said Lamb, saddened by this impropriety.

'You're quite right, Sir Gerald. Mr Maitland, you must not lead your witness.'

'If your lordship pleases. Will you tell us, Chief Superintendent, what you saw when the lights went on again?'

'I saw the two bodies. As I believe you were about to surmise, Mr Maitland, I thought at first that both were part of the play. That was not really a very difficult conclusion for you to reach,' he added spitefully. 'I also saw the accused standing centre stage. The first inkling I had that anything was wrong was when he called his wife's name and went over to her. Her name in the play was Gladys, but he used her own, Victoria. And then I realised from his demeanour that something must be seriously amiss. And I say again' – he turned a little to face the judge – 'and I should like that to be on record, my lord, that any member of the audience might have told you as much as this.'

'But with far less effect on the jury,' said Maitland. 'Perhaps you don't realise your own importance, Chief Superintendent. Will you tell us what you did then?'

'As soon as I realised that something was genuinely amiss I went backstage. There is a door on the left of the auditorium, which leads to the wings where most of the cast seemed to be gathered. And then I went on to the stage to see if anything could be done for Mrs Buckley.'

'To get the record straight, Chief Superintendent, Chief Inspector Sykes was also in the theatre, though in the dress circle I believe. He followed you backstage and arrived a little later. As I've no doubt you felt was proper you turned the investigation over to him.'

'That is true.'

'Otherwise you yourself would have been appearing for the prosecution, and I shouldn't have had the option of calling you.'

'That is also true.' His tone was icy cold by now.

'Then – also in the interests of accuracy, Chief Superintendent – may I suggest that you hesitated in the wings for a few moments before going on stage to join Mr Murray and Mr Buckley?'

'I may have done. The whole place was unfamiliar, and no doubt I hesitated a moment or two to get my bearings.'

'But your main interest was focussed on the stage?'

'As I have told you.'

'Then, in those few moments before you actually made your entrance, what did you see?'

'I saw Mr Murray and Mr Buckley alive, and Victoria Buckley dead, as I found a very few minutes later.'

'Mr Murray was on his feet then?'

'Just getting to his feet.' He paused and then added fretfully, 'I really can't see the point of all this.'

'Surely that is for my friend of the prosecution to say if he has any objection to your testimony.' But Sir Gerald Lamb was happy enough to let the defence cut its own throat. The police case to his mind was overwhelming, and a senior police officer could not be expected to give the lie to it.

Maitland resumed after a moment's silence. 'I must ask you to give your mind to the question of what you saw, Chief Superintendent. When you were a boy, did you never play the Kim game?'

'I am not here to play games,' said Briggs, outraged.

'I ask in all seriousness. If you could put yourself in the place of the boy in the story who was shown a tray of objects and then asked how many of them he could remember –'

'My lord!' That was Briggs, making his own objection. But Lamb was only a moment behind him.

'May I submit, m'lud, that this is not a proper line of questioning.'

'I cannot, of course, allow anything that militates against the dignity of the court,' said Mr Justice Bellman doubtfully. 'I think, Mr Maitland, you must examine your witness without any further – er – playfulness.'

'Even though it is his own dignity he is concerned with, rather than the court's?' asked Maitland mutinously.

'I hope it will not be necessary to find you in contempt, Mr Maitland,' said the judge with ice in his tone.

Antony recollected himself. 'May I apologise to your lordship?' Bellman eyed him in silence for a moment. 'And may I continue with my examination of the witness?' he added hopefully.

'Very well, Mr Maitland. But no more games.'

'Certainly not, my lord. I was asking you, Chief Superintendent, what you saw when you looked on to the stage from the wings.'

'Just what I've told you.'

'Think,' Maitland said persuasively. His tone was urgent, but it did not in any way betray the sudden panic he felt. There was always Meg's testimony in the background but it wouldn't be nearly so convincing as that of a senior police officer. And if this went wrong – he realised as the thought formulated itself that it was a form of superstition – how could he expect anything from the next and even more vital witness?

'I have thought!' Briggs's temper was reaching boiling point.

'Then think again,' Maitland invited. 'Because,' he added – and hoped he was telling the truth – 'the court is quite prepared to wait until you have done so.'

Briggs took a moment to look all round him. Antony had never seen a bullfight, nor ever wished to, but he couldn't help feeling that perhaps the goaded animal looked much the same when first it felt the prick of the dart.

'The stage was furnished as a living room,' the detective said. 'If I remember rightly, the programme said, *Mrs Carteret's drawing room*. There were the two chairs –'

'Just a minute, Chief Superintendent,' Maitland interrupted him. 'With your permission, my lord, I should like the witness to go down into the body of the court and view the model that the prosecution placed in evidence.'

'If you insist, Mr Maitland,' said Mr Justice Bellman resignedly.

'I think it is of the utmost importance, my lord.'

'Very well then. Please do as counsel requests, Chief Superintendent,' the judge added to the witness.

The usher was waiting, a moment later Briggs was standing looking down at the model. 'I see nothing wrong with that as a representation of what we saw,' he said.

'If I could only persuade you to – to transport yourself back in time,' said Maitland. 'You can see the chalk mark where Victoria

Buckley's body lay. Her husband was standing beside her, and Mr Murray just getting to his feet. What else did you see, besides what is before you now?'

'Nothing except ... nothing that could be important.'

'Tell me,' Maitland urged. It wasn't exactly a question, but neither the judge nor Lamb interrupted him.

'It couldn't have been important,' said Briggs, his voice growing slower as he spoke, as though he were trying to convince himself of the truth of his words. 'I never thought of it from that day to this. A black rag, lying behind the chair that Victoria Buckley was sitting in. I supposed at the time that it was something called for by the plot of the play. Mr Murray picked it up and pushed it into his pocket, again a very natural gesture.'

'Such a cloth, in fact – do I echo your thought exactly, Chief Superintendent? – as the murderer might have used to wrap around the handle of the stiletto?'

'Yes, that's exactly it, that's why –'

'But my client's arrest was based on two considerations. Motive, and the fact that a pair of black cotton gloves was found in his pocket. With those in his possession, would he have needed the cloth as well?'

'No, but ... how did you know about the cloth, Mr Maitland?'

'You mustn't ask counsel questions, Chief Superintendent,' said Mr Justice Bellman automatically.

With this unexpected backing Antony ignored the question. 'There is just one more thing I should like to put to the witness. It has been mentioned here in court that the chair Victoria Buckley was sitting in before she was killed was moved a little, backwards and to the right as the stage is viewed from the audience. Will you look again at the model and see if you agree?'

'Yes I do,' said Briggs without hesitation this time. 'But it's quite easily explained.'

'Indeed? I should like to hear the explanation.'

'I watched Mr Murray walk across the stage. When he bent down to pick up the cloth he bumped against the chair, rather clumsily I thought. It wasn't really in his way.'

'Didn't you think that rather odd?'

'No, not at all. He was wearing dark glasses for his part in the play, and when I got a good look at him I saw that they were very dark indeed. Wearing them, I should think it was quite likely he would be a bad judge of distance.'

'I see. I'm sure you're right about that, Chief Superintendent, but you'll forgive me if I don't altogether agree with you that there was nothing strange about his having selected glasses – they were only a prop, after all – so dark as to make him almost unable to see.'

'I should be surprised at anything else!' said Briggs, simmering again.

'Then I won't keep you any longer,' said Maitland, and sat down with a swirl of his gown.

'So far so good,' said Derek beside him.

Sir Gerald Lamb, bewilderment now added to his usual melancholy, declined to cross-examine. Mr Justice Bellman leaned forward. 'Do you wish to recall Mr Andrew Murray to the stand Mr Maitland?' he enquired. 'I'm quite ready to give my permission if you do.'

Antony got to his feet again. 'Take him up on it,' Geoffrey said in an undertone behind him.

'I'm obliged to your lordship, but first I have one more witness to call,' said Antony clearly.

'Hm. You know your own business best no doubt,' said the judge rather huffily. Maitland sat down, and never in his life had he been more uncertain as to whether that were true.

'John Cruickshank,' called the usher clearly.

Again Maitland undertook the examination of the witness himself. If his insistence on handling the matter in his own way was to result in a fiasco, it would be his name only that was associated with it; people would remember Derek's clever cross-examination of the doctor, the failure would be ascribed to his leader. With perfect fairness, thought Antony, almost as dismally as Sir Gerald Lamb might have done.

The witness was a tall man, grey haired, stooping, with an unusually wide forehead and gentle blue eyes. This time the preliminaries were important, and Maitland took him through them slowly. His name, his address, the address of the tiny bookshop which he owned, and which was situated not far from Charing Cross Road but sufficiently off the beaten track to prevent it from being well-known. 'I believe I'm right in saying, Mr Cruickshank, that your interest lies mainly in the field of antiquities?'

'I don't touch anything modern, no.' Like Jeremy Skelton the witness had looked around him with interest, but he seemed in no way daunted by what he saw. 'I have some valuable stuff, of course, but my interests are wide and any secondhand book can find a home with me. In the north when I was young,' he added

184

confidingly, smiling at counsel, 'we used to call such establishments "Mucky Bookshops". That would be a fair enough description of mine.'

Behind him Maitland could sense Geoffrey Horton's tension as if it were a tangible thing; beside him Derek's hand still moved steadily across the pad and just for a moment he envied his junior his detachment. 'I think perhaps I should be right in saying,' Antony said, returning the witness's smile, 'that your work is also your hobby.'

'Oh yes, indeed, that's quite right. There's never a book comes through my doors that doesn't become a personal friend. In fact, I sometimes find it difficult to part with them, I wouldn't sell them at all if it weren't for keeping the wolf from the door.'

'I know,' said Maitland sympathetically. 'With your permission, my lord, I should like the witness to be shown the copy of the book which the prosecution placed in evidence.' A moment later Mr Cruickshank had *Stubbs on Anatomy* in his hands; he looked down at it, beaming, and his long fingers caressed the worn cover.

'Oh yes, I remember you,' he said, apparently addressing the book.

'One old book is very much like another,' Maitland began, but the witness interrupted him eagerly.

'Oh no, you're quite wrong there. I'd know this one anywhere. There was mildew on the spine, I cleaned it up, of course, when it came into the shop but the mark was left. Just look.'

'So you're sure that is the same book that you had for sale?'

'Yes, to tell you the truth I had it for five years or more, I couldn't forget the look of it on the shelf. I was quite astonished when a man came in one day, and after poking around for a little while took it down and wanted to buy it. It's an old book, any medical student would think it out of date, but I believe in its day it was considered very reliable.'

'So you sold the book?'

'I'm not being very precise, am I? Yes, that's what I meant. I was quite sorry to see it go, and I couldn't in conscience charge him much for it. So I didn't really gain anything from the transaction except to lose an old friend.'

'When was this, Mr Cruickshank?'

'I brought my record book with me, may I consult it?'

The courtroom was very silent. Maitland glanced at the judge and received a curt nod in response to his enquiring look. 'My lord,' he said, 'the defence would like to introduce this record book in evidence.' And then, when the formalities had been complied with, 'You may look at the book now, Mr Cruickshank, and then I think his lordship and the jury would like to see it, to confirm what you say.'

'Yes, of course.' The witness did not sound quite so sure of himself now. 'The book just says, Friday the second of February,' he said, 'but I remember that it was in the afternoon.'

There was a pause, another uncomfortable silence, while the usher collected the ledger, waited for the judge to look his fill, and then proceeded with it to the jury box. 'I wonder,' said Maitland clearly, quite aware as he spoke that he was, in a sense, taking his client's life in his hands, 'whether you would be able to identify this man again.'

'I'm quite sure I could, I have a very good memory for faces. They're almost as interesting as books,' said the witness in his confiding way.

'Then would you look around the court,' Maitland suggested, 'and tell us if you can see him here?'

This time in the silence Maitland heard Geoffrey catch his breath, and then his whispered comment, 'Lord help us, he may say anything!' John Cruickshank's eyes moved round the room in a leisurely way, lingered for a moment on the still figure in the dock – Leonard Buckley was no longer pretending to a lack of interest – and then moved on to the seats reserved for the witnesses who had already given evidence. Antony saw his lips moving, and thought for a horrible moment that he was going to identify Detective Chief Inspector Sykes, but then his head turned a little further and he said in a pleased way, 'Yes, he's here.'

'Then one last thing, Mr Cruickshank, will you please point him out to us?' The witness raised his hand, funnily enough even now he seemed quite unconscious of any drama in the situation, though he must have been the only person in the courtroom unaware of it.

'There,' he said, 'at the end of the row, sitting by the wall.'

'Thank you,' said Antony, and his tone was more heartfelt than he had intended. 'Would you mind standing up, Mr Murray, so that there can be no doubt about it?' He waited for a moment while Andrew Murray lurched to his feet, his normal grace of movement quite lost for the time being. 'I want to be in no doubt about this, Mr Cruickshank,' Maitland went on. 'Is that the man to whom you sold the book we have been discussing?'

'Why yes, certainly,' said the bookseller, with no doubt at all in his voice. 'So good-looking, I remember thinking at the time that he must be a film star.'

III

'So you've done it again,' said Sir Nicholas caustically that evening. And when Antony looked enquiring, 'Won your case, but with as much furore as possible,' his uncle amplified.

That evening they were all gathered in the study, and as that night's performance of *Done in by Daggers* had been cancelled – too late to put on an understudy, Meg explained – Meg was with them too. Antony was glad to see that Roger was looking more relaxed; Meg was never one to demonstrate affection in public – except by the indiscriminate use of the word darling, which from time to time grated on him intolerably – so whatever amends she made to her husband would be something between the two of them; but he felt that now all was well.

Vera looked up. 'Seems very unjust, Nicholas,' she remarked, 'considering the verdict was favourable to Antony's client.'

'And I still don't know,' said Jenny plaintively, 'exactly what happened after the bookseller identified Andrew Murray.' She didn't add, though probably all those present were aware, that she had been unwilling to press her husband for details. These affairs always upset him; he was glad that Leonard Buckley was free, but sorry to have been the instrument of somebody else's downfall. 'And Meg and Roger were there, though not in court, so they don't know a thing about it either. I do think you might tell us.'

'I can put it very briefly,' said Sir Nicholas. 'No doubt the newspapers will report it with the word Sensation in brackets.'

'But after that,' Jenny persisted.

'Lamb asked the witness if he liked the theatre, which seemed to offend him. No, he hadn't seen *Done in by Daggers*, and didn't intend to. Had he been shown any photographs, then, of the people concerned in this case. He hadn't ... I'm glad, at least, you avoided that pitfall, Antony. At which point Bellman himself took over and instructed Lamb to recall Andrew Murray, though I think they both still believed there might be some explanation forthcoming.'

'And did Antony cross-examine him?' Meg asked.

'As it turned out it wasn't necessary. He made some show of resistance, but within five minutes was telling the whole story under Lamb's gentle prompting. Not a man of much moral fibre,' Sir Nicholas concluded.

187

'Well, I could have told you that,' said Meg.

'But what story?'

'Victoria Buckley wasn't a nice woman,' said Antony, rousing himself to take part in the discussion. 'She even made a crack to me about you, Jenny, but of course, I didn't take any notice.'

'Do you take me so much for granted?' asked Jenny, exchanging a smile with Meg.

'Far from it, love, but that's the best evidence I can give you for the sort of person she was. She knew something to Murray's discredit – that he got a girl in the family way years ago and then deserted her when she really needed help – and she persuaded him that she had in her possession a letter he'd written, a very heartless letter apparently, in order to try to make him do something she wanted. Something to do with the scene they played together, Meg, you'd understand about that better than I do. Anyway, the ironical part is that she didn't have any evidence, the lie she told brought about her own death.'

'All seems so trivial,' said Vera. Antony and Jenny exchanged an amused look. If either of them had ventured such an opinion, or Meg or Roger for that matter, they'd have been in for a lecture on the sanctity of family life. Even to Vera, a privileged person in his eyes, Sir Nicholas ventured to remonstrate.

'I don't think I should call it trivial, my dear.' But Vera had already gone on to another idea.

'Blackmail,' she said censoriously. 'Should think they'd take that into consideration when this man Murray comes up for trial.'

'Yes, I'm sure they will,' said Jenny eagerly. 'But was that all Andrew Murray told you .. just about the motive?'

'Not much that we didn't know. Well, guess, if you prefer it, Uncle Nick. He'd worn the extra dark glasses – that was an unexpected bonus out of Briggs's evidence, by the way – to make doubly sure that nobody noticed he was conversing with Mrs Buckley with his eyes tight shut. He had the stiletto concealed in his chair, obvious when you think of it. And the black cloth was really a sort of mitten, the kind that some people use to put coal on the fire. So that was that, but you still think I ought to have played for safety, Uncle Nick?'

'I'm surprised Geoffrey didn't warn you of the dangers of the game you were playing.' said Sir Nicholas bluntly.

'Oh, but he did. He said I'd no idea what Briggs would come out with, or whether Mr Cruickshank would identify anybody or nobody, or perhaps even the wrong person. But as it turned out

188

it was much more effective, don't you think? Briggs was so very obviously heart and soul with the prosecution, and that made his evidence about the black cloth far more compelling.'

'Think you're right,' said Vera nodding.

'I still maintain – ' Sir Nicholas began, but Roger interrupted him with a question of his own.

'What do you suppose Briggs is thinking now?'

Sir Nicholas sat up suddenly very straight. 'That brings me to a question I wanted to ask you, Antony. What did the Chief Superintendent ask you as you left the Court?'

'I was hoping you hadn't noticed that he waylaid me,' said Antony, temporising.

'What did he say?' his uncle repeated.

'Nothing much, Uncle Nick.' Maitland's reluctance was very marked. 'He just wanted to know how much I paid the bookseller for his evidence.'

That brought a general outcry, in which Sir Nicholas's, 'I knew it!' predominated.

'But, Uncle Nick, he'd have been thinking that anyway,' Antony protested. 'I mean, you're blaming me for calling him as a witness, but I can't see it matters whether it annoyed him or not. It won't have made the slightest difference in the long run to what he thinks about me.'

'As a matter of fact, I don't know how you dared,' said Meg.

'If you're thinking he'd have lied to spite me, you've got him all wrong,' Antony told her. 'Though I've an idea Uncle Nick doesn't agree with me about that.'

'He was on oath of course,' said Jenny.

'I don't know whether that makes any difference to him or not, but I think he'd always tell the truth as he saw it. Which means,' he added thoughtfully, 'that I've a better opinion of him than he has of me, but that can't be helped.'

It was obvious to Jenny, at any rate, that a good argument with his uncle was just what he needed that evening to take his mind from more unpleasant things. She proceeded to throw a little fuel on the fire. 'I can't think,' she said, 'how it is you have such an odd effect on every policeman you meet, Antony. Even Inspector Sykes – '

'Chief Inspector,' said Antony automatically. But then he looked at her, saw her expression of impossible innocence, and decided that the world wasn't such a bad place after all. Jenny knew him better than he knew himself, a fact that in anybody else he would have bitterly resented, and if this was her idea of cheering him up it was up to him to follow. 'Sykes never suspected me of anything worse than concealing evidence,' he said. 'And Conway dislikes me intensely, but I think he trusts me. Inspector Watkins on the other hand ... well, I don't really know what to say about Watkins. Sometimes I think he quite likes me. The funny thing is I've always got on pretty well with their subordinates.'

Sir Nicholas had sat back in his chair again and reached out his hand in a leisurely way to select a cigar. 'Perhaps because they haven't yet reached years of discretion,' he said dulcetly.

EPILOGUE

When they came to talk about it later, the Maitlands and the Farrells decided that there was still one unsolved mystery: had Victoria Buckley really been trying to poison her husband or not? After a few days, Leonard slipped quietly back into his role in the play, to everyone's satisfaction except that of his understudy, and Meg unashamedly brought her wiles to bear on him to persuade him to see his doctor. The tests took time, but it was eventually decided that he had developed an allergy to seafood. 'Though I don't think Leonard's altogether satisfied,' said Meg, reporting the following Sunday. 'He says, What about the bottled water, and you have to admit he's got a point there.'

'He probably ate sardines on toast for lunch and forgot all about it,' said Roger idly. But later on Antony admitted to Jenny that he still entertained some doubts about that.

Meanwhile, *Done in by Daggers* went from strength to strength. Inevitably, Roger grumbled that the damn play would run for ever, but only in the half-hearted way they had all become accustomed to. Jeremy Skelton had long since lost interest – except, perhaps, in the financial aspects of the enterprise – and was busy with yet another addition to his long list of novels; while all the signs were that Leonard Buckley's career would in no way suffer from his being deprived of Victoria's backing. Meg, in another report from the front line, maintained that his self-confidence was increasing, and that he and Ellie Dorman were now as thick as thieves. 'A happy ending after all, darlings,' she said, and if both Antony and Jenny had the private thought that the Michaelmas Term would see Andrew Murray on trial for murder, they kept it to themselves.